THE BABY NURSE

STACEY H. RUBIN

Copyright © 2025 Stacey H. Rubin

The right of Stacey H. Rubin to be identified as the Author of the Work has been asserted by them in accordance with the Copyright, Designs and Patents Act 1988.

First published in 2025 by Bloodhound Books.

Apart from any use permitted under UK copyright law, this publication may only be reproduced, stored, or transmitted, in any form, or by any means, with prior permission in writing of the publisher or, in the case of reprographic production, in accordance with the terms of licences issued by the Copyright Licensing Agency.
All characters in this publication are fictitious and any resemblance to real persons, living or dead, is purely coincidental.

www.bloodhoundbooks.com

Print ISBN: 978-1-917705-22-6

*This book is dedicated to NICU nurses.
Every day and every night you are a vigilant presence in the hospital. With skill and tenderness, you heal the sickest, smallest patients and you love the babies the world has forgotten. Your compassion is my inspiration.*

*Save one life and you're a hero,
save one hundred lives and you're a nurse.*

— Unknown

ACT ONE

Nurses are a unique kind.
They have this insatiable need to care for others,
which is both their greatest strength
and fatal flaw.

— Jean Watson, Nurse Theorist and Nursing Professor

CHAPTER ONE

The double doors part. I adjust my surgical mask and enter the Neonatal Intensive Care Unit at Lakeview Hospital with a tote bag on my shoulder. The doors thud behind me. I head for the sink where the digital clock above the scrub basin reads 06:10. Day shift begins at seven, and I have the place all to myself. In the background, a baby cries, an IV pump beeps and the phone at the nurses' station rings. Staff, occupied with end-of-shift tasks, are too busy to notice my arrival.

When day shift officially begins, the scrub station will crowd with nurses' naked forearms, jutting elbows and banter floating along with soap bubbles. I stow the tote bag from home under the sink, knee the lever, and activate the faucet. Water drums the stainless-steel basin. I gather my hair, damp from a predawn shower, into a ponytail, twisting the scrunchie twice to prevent any strands from escaping. After I scrub, I can't touch my hair.

My work schedule leaves no time for blow-drying or makeup. We still mask to protect the babies, despite the relaxed Covid precautions in the rest of the hospital, and the mask hides my freckles, otherwise, I'd find time for concealer. Most days my shoulder-length wash-and-wear curls are tied back or tucked under a hospital-issue bouffant cap. Strawberry blonde is my natural color, but in the hospital's fluorescent light, I look like a redhead. The dispenser deposits a glob of antibacterial soap onto my palm and I spread it over my hands and forearms, careful not to splatter my scrubs. While I can't be bothered with an elaborate cosmetic routine, I spare a few minutes to iron my uniform, taking care to steam a crease into my powder-blue scrubs pants and smooth the top. Wrinkles might give parents the impression that I'm careless, but a sharply creased set of scrubs sends a reassuring message. In the NICU, attention to detail is the difference between life and death. The first time I put on scrubs, adjusted the yellow drawstring around my waist, shrugged the V-neck top over my head, and surveyed myself in the locker-room mirror, I squared my shoulders and swore I gained an inch to my five-foot-four frame. The uniform transformed me from hesitant and shy to confident and purposeful. In other words, a nurse.

The cold gel gives me a full-body shiver, and the slippery suds cause my wedding ring to spin on my finger, the only jewelry permitted in the NICU. I massage the medicinal-smelling bubbles under my nails. Artificial nails harbor bacteria and are prohibited in the NICU. My natural nails are filed short —a leftover from my cello-playing days—giving the impression I'm a rule follower. I used to be. But I have a warning in my employee file, penned by Glenda-The-Terrible NICU nurse manager, proving I bucked convention. The accusation: "engaging in inappropriate patient-caregiver conduct." Harsh. It's not like I kidnapped the kid and took her home.

While I'm not proud of the reprimand, I can't stop caring either. Glenda-The-Terrible is not due for work for another hour, but she's known to make surprise appearances, hoping to catch a nurse checking Facebook instead of charting, or worse, drinking coffee outside the designated breakroom. So, I need to be quick. Rinsed and dry, I retrieve the tote from under the sink and cross the hall from the Acute NICU into the Special Care Nursery.

Unlike the brightly lit Acute Care Unit, Special Care has cycled light, to help adjust the babies' circadian rhythm in preparation for their transition home. Monitors glow above the cribs, a tireless galaxy of undulating lines and blips, recording infinite tiny heartbeats. Special Care babies have outgrown *isolettes*, the protective, plastic-walled boxes, commonly called incubators. Additionally, their lungs have healed, and they no longer need supplemental oxygen. The Special Care Nursery is a bridge between hospital and home. Nearing discharge, the emphasis in the Special Care Nursery is on feeding, from a bottle or breast. Parents are taught to take their infant's temperature with a digital thermometer, measure vitamins in a dropper, and the babies wear onesies brought from home.

The baby I seek is in the back. I pass rows of cribs without pausing to peek between the metal slats. The cribs aren't Pottery Barn cute like the one I ordered online with coordinated bumper pads and bedding. Nothing cozy about stainless steel and hospital-grade mattresses. I approach the last pod. An alarm beeps at a neighboring bedside and Nicki, the night nurse, silences the alarm. She asks me, "Here for Olivia?" Nicki disconnects a pump. "I'm running behind."

"I'll feed her."

Nicki waves her gloved hand in thanks and tends to a wailing baby. Technically, I'm no longer assigned to Olivia's care, a consequence of the reprimand. Nicki is aware of my past trouble with Glenda-The-Terrible but is understanding and won't report my visit. I enter Olivia's bedspace. Swaddled in a blue hospital blanket, she looks like an expertly wrapped five-and-a-half-pound gift. My heart flutters not only from seeing

Olivia, but from relief. We're alone. Hospital visiting hours don't begin for another two hours but driving in, the Jetta's headlamps slicing predawn dark, I couldn't shake the fear that someone or something would steal my time with Olivia.

I lower the crib's side rail. Olivia's cheeks are full, her chin a delicate point. Even in the low light, her slightly puckered lips are pink. I exhale, dismissing my next thought, Olivia is inching closer to discharge home with her parents. I brush a stray wisp of her ginger hair from her forehead, careful not to startle her. Preterm infants need sleep to foster growth, and despite my desire to hold Olivia, I don't wake her. Instead, I unpack my tote bag. Olivia's freshly laundered onesies smell of lavender fabric softener. The NICU clothes washer is broken, and Jamie, Olivia's mom, forgot to take the dirty laundry home. Despite the possibility that Glenda-The-Terrible might see me, I took the pile home with me when I left work last night. I stack her clothes on the shelf beside her mother's breast pump.

Olivia's pale lashes flutter and suddenly she's awake. I say, "Good morning, Olivia. It's Nurse Annabelle."

I've greeted many newborn patients during my two years as a NICU nurse, and I know it's silly, introducing myself to a baby who can't answer. But baby Olivia is special. The marvel of Olivia is that she began life ten weeks early: twig-limbed, gaunt-faced, and with a nearly bald scalp. In the past two months, I've watched her evolve. I was her nurse when she was in the Acute Care side of the NICU, before she could breathe on her own, before she even had a name. Baby names are a sensitive topic in the Neonatal Intensive Care Unit. Parents are encouraged to invest emotionally by naming their infant. Yet, parents might hesitate to have their hearts broken if their baby dies. Understandable. Naming too early—before a child is born—can bring bad luck, a Jewish superstition my mother passed along. "Wait," Mom had said, a finger to her lip, when we volleyed potential baby names. "Keep those baby names quiet."

I'd obeyed. Bad luck found me anyway.

Baby Olivia remained nameless for a month. Her parents, Jamie and Don, had been vacillating between two awful names: Summer or Stevie. Summer is seasonal and misses the mark for a winter baby. Stevie is a frizzy-haired ancient Fleetwood Mac rocker idolized by Don, the baby's dad. He even owned one of the band's original guitars.

Between the Covid visitor restrictions and a case of maternal postpartum depression, the parents were hardly around. I took care of her for a block of shifts, and worried that being perpetually referred to as "Baby Girl" would leave her feeling unwanted or unloved or both. Instead of "Baby Girl Dutton" I called her by a proper first name, something I had never done in my two years working in the NICU: Olivia. A top contender on the list we'd compiled for a daughter. The name stuck like Dermabond. Jamie Dutton checked in one afternoon at the security window, and the unit clerk greeted her with, "Hi, Olivia's mom."

Jamie came to the bedside and thanked me for ending the name debate, her face awash with relief. "Olivia suits her." Glenda-The-Terrible got wind of it. A nurse naming a patient had never been done. A nickname perhaps, but not an official birth certificate name. And I got in trouble for breaching the patient-nurse boundary. I imagine Glenda-The-Terrible, her forehead furrowing if she knew I was here with Olivia and that I spent last evening rinsing her clothes in organic fabric softener. Definitely falls into the overstepping professional boundaries category, but I don't regret a thing because Olivia is thriving. I promise myself the laundry is a one-and-done chore.

The bottle warmer at Olivia's bedside chimes. I tell Olivia, "Breakfast time."

Olivia blinks. Her sapphire eyes widen, and she yawns.

I peel away her swaddle. Except for a diaper, she's naked. I dress her in a pink long-sleeved shirt from the clean stash I brought. I hold Olivia on my lap, and through my mask, I detect the hospital soap that she was bathed with, she smells like a cough drop. Olivia sucks the warm bottle of expressed mother's milk. Nicki rounds the corner. "All done?" I pat Olivia's back and she responds with a soft burp. Nicki is a Disney enthusiast, the Minnie Mouse pinned to her scrubs jacket has a polka-dot dress and a broad smile. Nicki tells me, "I'll take over. You better change. You're wearing Olivia's meal."

I relinquish Olivia. Scrubs are stocked on the linen cart in three unisex sizes: small, medium, and large. Mix and match, tops on the first shelf, bottoms stacked on the second. Small pants still fit, thanks to the drawstring tie, even with the leftover bulge around my middle. Until my bra size shrinks, I upsize to a medium top. I take a pair. In the nurses' lounge I trade the set, scratchy like new denim, for the scrubs stored in my locker for an emergency like this one. I'll take the hospital set home and bring them up to standard. Thanks to the lavender laundry rinse, my locker smells indulgent, like a day spa, and one whiff calms my nerves. My stored scrubs retain their iron crease. I emerge from the locker room, my scrubs pants snap when I walk. Dressed like I am, how can I feel anything less than confident?

With all of us in uniform blue scrubs, it took me a month of working in the NICU before I recognized the subtle ways that nurses individualize. Nicki's impressive collection of seasonal Minnie Mouse pins includes red, white, and blue Minnie in July, orange and black for Halloween and Minnie under a Christmas tree in December. Coleen's gel manicures, technically forbidden, match her fluorescent-blue Dansko clogs. Robyn doesn't have particularly unique accessories, but she stands out as the only African American nurse in the NICU. Todd, well, he's a guy. In the emergency room, he wouldn't be unique, but women traditionally staff the NICU.

A few minutes later and I'm assigned to respond to the delivery room, along with Robyn. I'm happy not only because we're expecting the birth of twins but because I'll see Peter.

The attending neonatologist wears a long white lab coat over sea-green scrubs and Nike running shoes. Privately, we nurses renamed her "Dr. STAT" because nothing is accomplished fast enough for her liking. If the lab takes an extra fifteen minutes to spin a hematocrit, she files a complaint with the supervisor. Same for the delivery room. If the NICU is beckoned to stand by for a cesarean scheduled for ten in the morning, the obstetrician can expect a cringeworthy email if the baby isn't delivered by half-past the hour.

The delivery room doesn't keep Dr. STAT waiting. Robyn, Dr. STAT and I have time enough to glove. The purple gloves fit snug, a second skin, fingers to wrist, with a subtle bulge around my left ring finger for my wedding band. Robyn tells me to take the first twin and she'll take the second.

Refrigerated air circulates in the operating suite, a shock compared to the heated NICU, and it's an effort to suppress shivering. The newborn warmer is across the room, and I walk, careful to avoid touching the sterile equipment, which is everything draped with blue towels. The operating room is anything but silent, an empty suction canister on the wall has been turned on, and gurgles, an IV pump beeps and a pager chimes. The scrub nurse and the circulator count each shiny instrument on the blue-draped table.

The room is ready, but the patient has yet to arrive. Medications are drawn into syringes, liter IV bags are spiked and tubing primed, the wall-mounted monitor with dual vital sign tracings, for the mother and her unborn baby, blinks on standby. The operating room lamp hangs from the ceiling on an adjustable arm, a bulbous white moon above the empty operating table. Red numbers on the digital wall clock tick. An obstetrical emergency is measured in seconds, each one irreplaceable. Staff wait, an anxious vigil circling the empty table as if it were an overturned raft in a shark-infested ocean.

Suddenly, a stretcher crashes through the doors, steered by a nurse. The woman on the stretcher moans. The sheet over her pregnant belly is stained red and the musky odor of fresh blood weights the air. A pair of nurses lift and roll the patient from the gurney onto the rectangular operating table. My breath catches. The table is skinny and I'm afraid the woman will fall, but a nurse secures the woman with black safety straps.

The stained sheet is cast to the floor and nurses prepare the naked woman for the procedure. Razoring her pubic hair, bathing her torso with Betadine, the disinfectant paint turns her belly into an orange mountain. An anesthesia mask is placed over the woman's mouth, she is immediately silent in a drug-induced sleep. The nurse anesthetist closes the woman's eyes with adhesive tabs.

Peter enters. Handsome even in baggy blue operating room scrubs.

My heart skips.

Peter scans the room. His gaze settles on me and through his safety glasses his cobalt eyes brighten with recognition. I smile, and from behind my mask, silently wish him luck. His wet hands are steepled at his chest, signaling he's scrubbed. If he weren't a doctor, I've joked that he possesses the long, delicate fingers of a piano player. His wedding band, an exact match to mine, glints. A nurse passes him a sterile towel. He dries his hands and then discards it. He faces the anesthetized patient, but I can tell from the fit of his bouffant that he's gone a stretch without visiting the barber, his thick black curls, freed from the cap would cover the back of his neck. He dons a Tyvek gown, double gloves, and we connect again for a nanosecond.

Peter's decisive voice cuts across the room. "Time out."

Chatter ceases. Except for the hissing suction, the room is silent.

The circulating nurse reads from her patient data sheet. "Blood type: O positive. Allergy to penicillin. Twin pregnancy. Twenty-eight weeks gestation. Emergent C-section for reason of placenta previa." The mother's placenta is too low, blocking the birth canal, and is the cause for her bleeding. Natural delivery, especially for preterm twins is not only dangerous but impossible.

Peter, scalpel poised like a pencil in his gloved fingers, answers, "I concur." He glides the blade low on the woman's abdomen. The scrub nurse vacuums droplets of blood from the incision with a suction catheter. The obstetrical resident, a doctor in training, stands on a stool, across the table from Peter and cauterizes the bleeding vessels. The Bovie wand buzzes and emits a puff of smoke. I smell the burning through my mask, and I empathize with Peter. We don't barbeque in the summer because the smell of charred meat nauseates him.

The nurse announces, "Uterine." Amniotic water fountains. Staff shuffle around the table. The suction canister on the wall vibrates, coiled tubing stiffens and slurps the gushing fluid. Birth is imminent.

Dr. STAT stands at attention in front of the infant warmer.

My thumb is on the warmer's Apgar timer. Apgar numbers are an infant report card assigned at one and five minutes. Through a gap in the huddle of staff, I see a round head, the size of a large apple, covered in red goo, poke through the incision. A torso follows. I trigger the timer.

A small, perfectly formed baby is deposited onto the table. The world shrinks and time is counted in seconds. The infant's skin is ashen with cyanotic lips. I realize what's lacking. Sound. The birth is silent. The baby is supine, motionless, with floppy rag-doll arms, and has yet to draw breath.

My palms turn clammy inside my gloves.

A labor and delivery nurse asks, "Boy or girl?"

My throat constricts. But my fingers work automatically, placing EKG leads, two on the chest, a third on the abdomen. A heart rate skips across the monitor.

Dr. STAT inserts a suction catheter between the baby's lips, clears the mouth, and then each nostril. The Apgar timer buzzes. "One minute of life," DR. STAT announces. "Turn up the oxygen."

I twitch the dial, plug a stethoscope into my ears and listen for a heartbeat. Steady.

"Boy or girl?" the labor and delivery nurse repeats.

Dr. STAT covers the newborn's mouth and nose with a dome-shaped respiratory mask. The baby's chest lifts. I listen. The heart accelerates. A positive sign. "One hundred and fifteen beats a minute," I say.

"Boy or girl?"

The baby pinkens.

"Boy or..."

"Boy," I shout. "He's a boy."

My shoulders relax, and I exhale. "Welcome, Little One. I'm Annabelle, your nurse."

The second twin is a girl. Dr. STAT and Robyn tend to her.

If the Neonatal Intensive Care Unit were an orchestra, Dr. STAT is our maestro who conducts the nurses, doctors-in-training, practitioners, and respiratory therapists. There's no dress rehearsal in the NICU. Each shift is a sold-out performance but instead of concert black, I wear blue scrubs.

The twins are admitted to the NICU in neighboring isolettes. An isolette, a modernized incubator with piped-in moisture, heat and muted sound is designed to replicate a mother's uterus. A poor approximation if you ask me. Astronauts circle Mars in a hermetically sealed space station, but here on Earth science can't duplicate anything close to a woman's womb in which to grow a preterm infant.

Honor, the nurse practitioner, threads intravenous lines into the stump of the infant's umbilical cord. Honor started out as a nurse, like me. She went to graduate school, but unlike me, she completed her degree. The two spaghetti-thin catheters are literal lifelines and provide a continuous heart rate and blood pressure display on the monitor and infuse IV fluid to the baby who is too small to feed by mouth.

Alarms ding. With his isolette lid raised, my two-pound patient is vulnerable prey, assaulted by sound. The fluorescent ceiling lights permeate his thinly sealed eyelids, disrupting his sleep cycle. The diaphragm of Dr. STAT's stethoscope, the circumference of a quarter, rests over my patient's sternum.

"The baby needs to rest." I remind Dr. STAT of NICU protocol: premature and low birthweight babies can tolerate stimulation only in small increments. Hands-on assessments are limited to every three hours. Dr. STAT lifts the stethoscope, signifying she's finished her exam.

With the push of a button the isolette roof descends, a protective shell over the baby. Dr. STAT's pager blares. She silences it, presses her phone to her ear and true to her nickname, jogs from the pod, her unbuttoned lab coat a billowing white cape in her wake.

I have Robyn, my preceptor, to thank for teaching me how to be a NICU nurse. She insisted that I advocate. "Speak up," Robyn told me. "Yours is the only voice the baby has." Her words have double meaning. Our sickest patients, those requiring a ventilator, like my nameless patient, make no noise. The breathing tube obstructs their vocal cords and silences their cry. Robyn never doubts herself. A mom four times over, her last baby was a NICU patient that she fostered and adopted on his second birthday.

I have a million reasons to doubt myself. Not the least of which, despite our efforts, Peter and I are childless. A loss I don't permit myself to dwell on while at work. Besides lacking parenting skills, I've only been a NICU nurse for two years, a fledgling by critical care standards. Most of my shifts still sync with Robyn's schedule. If she has the day off or is busy and I'm faced with a challenging task, I ask myself: *What would Robyn do?*

The X-ray technician rolls the portable machine into the pod, colliding with the bedside cart. The machine grinds to a stop at my elbow. The alarm dings: low saturation. I titrate the oxygen higher. The shift is shaping up to be busy and it's only nine in the morning.

In the breakroom, I retrieve my phone from my locker. I stow it to prevent distraction. I can't deal with all the texts and phone calls during work. A dozen missed calls and five voicemails. Debt collectors. Bottom feeders, all of them. Enough to turn my hunger pangs to cramps. Delete. Delete. Delete.

I unzip my lunch bag. I missed my first meal break. It's almost dinnertime and my Greek yogurt is room temperature. My messages are all downers except for Peter's text. He sent me a moon and a threaded needle. He's staying late tonight to operate. Emojis, our go-to communication.

I reply with a sad face and a broken heart, but then I backspace and replace the cracked heart with the whole beating heart and push send. The broken heart might cause Peter to feel guilty about our night apart. Overnights are part of his obstetrical fellowship. Technically still in training, his hours begin before mine and if there is an emergency requiring surgery—which is always—he's at the hospital long after my nursing shift ends. I work my share of midnight shifts, but tonight, at least I can sort our mail without doing gymnastics to hide the incriminating envelopes. I rerouted my Visa bill, but mail stamped "OVERDUE" in red caps has been known to slip through. There simply isn't time to explain my Amazon shopping to Peter, not when he's laser-focused on obstetrics. During our rare evenings together, I'd rather we share takeout, not dissect my Visa balance.

I intend to tell him. But the timing is always wrong. Is there a right time?

I stir my yogurt, lick the spoon, and peruse my email.

A message from Dr. Edna Hayes, my graduate studies advisor at Drexel University. She's after my thesis statement, which like my credit card payment, is overdue.

The next email is an instant mood booster: *Amazon Picks for Annabelle*. What could it hurt to look? I might find the exact thing I'm missing. And shipping is always free.

CHAPTER TWO

Peter's overnight shift gives me the opportunity to visit baby Olivia after my shift ends. Her parents rarely stay past seven in the evening but despite the tiring hour-long commute, Jamie, Olivia's mom, makes the trip almost daily for these past two months. Leaving a baby behind in the NICU is trying for parents. According to Fernanda, the NICU social worker, Jamie blames herself for Olivia's prematurity and her guilt precipitated postpartum depression.

I cross the hallway and enter the Special Care Nursery. Static crackles from the overhead speakers. The unit clerk announces the end of visiting hours. The fluorescent lights dim. Another burst of static is followed by recorded lullabies. Olivia's crib is in the back of the unit. I see Jamie, her mom, lean into the crib and take pictures with her cell phone. I don't want to disrupt her visit, but before I can sneak away, Jamie waves for me to join them.

Jamie scrolls her phone, shows me the screen. "What do you think?"

The angle is off. Olivia is a beautiful baby, but Jamie's

picture accentuates the bald patch on Olivia's scalp. Wanting to encourage Jamie, I tell her, "You're a good photographer."

"Good news. Olivia is almost ready. She just drank a full bottle of milk. I can't believe she's big enough to come home." Jamie puts her phone down, leans over the crib rail, and pats Olivia's tummy. "Almost time for your big send-off."

A lump rises in my throat. Although not every patient admitted to the NICU goes home, most do. "Congratulations." Not only do I fail to sound happy but my surprise at the news must show.

Jamie parses her words, as if to avoid getting her hopes up, but it's impossible to miss the shift from her usual flat demeanor. "We're not leaving tonight—could be tomorrow or the day after —if she gains weight and doesn't have a spell."

A spell means a pause in a preterm baby's breathing. The heart rate and respiratory monitor are programmed to alarm if an episode lasts longer than a few seconds.

Jamie is animated. She gathers her blonde hair into a ponytail. "Anyhow, I started packing. Can't hurt to be optimistic." The shelf behind Olivia's crib is bare, cleared of children's books and baby clothes. Jamie's breast-pump supplies are missing from the drying rack beside the sink. Because of Jamie's dedication to pumping and her steadfast determination to contribute what she can to her daughter's medical care, her breast milk, Olivia has never received formula. A feat I admire. Hooking oneself to an electric pump for twenty minutes, eight times a day and sanitizing the equipment afterwards, if that isn't an act of love, what is?

A large plastic bag, labeled *patient belongings*, is stuffed with Olivia's pink clothes, labeled O.D. in indelible marker. Parents learn fast, if they fail to label items from home, the outfits become hopelessly lost when mixed with hospital laundry.

"By the way, look what I brought. Do you think it will work?" Jamie heaves an infant car seat from the floor. "I didn't buy a preterm one. Hopefully she'll reach six pounds."

Before travelling home, Olivia, like all recovering preterm infants, will need a trial of monitoring in her car seat. Occasionally a small baby can't tolerate sitting upright and reacts with interruptions in normal breathing.

The car seat proves it. After months in the NICU, Olivia's discharge is inevitable. A stoic nod is all I can manage. Jamie hoists the plastic bag onto her narrow shoulder. Her jeans are fashionably faded and ripped at the knees. She bestows a kiss on Olivia's pale forehead.

The moment strikes me as holy, and I bow my head, reminded of the only church service I'd attended while a student at Villanova. Awed by St. Thomas's towering spires, I'd jumped at my lab partner Mary's invitation to attend a Sunday Mass. Inside, sunlight filtered through the chapel's stained glass and dappled the pews. A silver thurible billowed incense. The space was sacred, beautiful, and to an outsider like me, awe-inspiring. Acutely out of place, I'd asked, "What should I do?"

Mary was on her knees, on a folding footrest in front of our pew. "Sit," Mary whispered. "Quit trying so hard. Don't do anything. That's why I come here. To relax. And give my worries away."

The prayer book read like a library book. Different from the siddur at Main Line Reform Synagogue, the temple where, in preparation for my Bat Mitzvah, I attended weekly services, and learned to read traditional Hebrew prayers. Thirty minutes later, Mary rose and tapped the footrest with her Ugg, stowing the kneeling bench under the pew in front of us.

From across the crib, Jamie is different, no longer hollow, she practically glows from within. I recognize that light: hope. Jamie says, "Is this what keeps you coming to work? Shift after shift. Moments like this? I bet this is why you do what you do—why you became a nurse."

I should be happy. Joy would be the appropriate emotion. Jamie is healing her depression so that she can mother Olivia. I trust that the pair will thrive at home, in their own space. If it were a different patient, any baby, except Olivia, I'd be thrilled to see them go home. But a stab of longing to keep Olivia in the hospital where I can be with her leaves me cold.

"Yes. This is why I became a nurse." I reinforce Jamie's assumption, except it's not exactly true. I was undecided about a career. Nursing was my father's idea. Dad had lung cancer, caused by breathing toxic air from burning Kuwaiti oil fields during twin tours in Saudi Arabia and Afghanistan. Before he passed, he'd told me, "You're destined to help people. Be a nurse. Care. For people... who..." His last words were grunts between coughing spasms, his final sentence left unfinished. I imagine his intended message might have been "Care for people who are alone. Like me." The army scarred more than Dad's lungs. As a result of experiences that he couldn't or wouldn't share, he needed to be alone. Dad was unreachable, a solo inhabitant on an emotional island, surrounded by a moat. Even Mom couldn't help. His army death benefit paid my tuition at Villanova University, the top-rated nursing school in Pennsylvania. Being Jewish, I hardly fit the mold of a Catholic Villanova student, but the crucifixes mounted on the classroom walls comforted me, a signal that my father watched me realize his final living wish for me to become a nurse.

In Dad's honor, I studied human anatomy, physiology, chemistry, and pharmacology. I memorized the Krebs cycle and the twelve paired cranial nerves. In my junior year, I was assigned a clinical rotation in Philadelphia Children's Hospital. I arrived ready to put all those facts I'd crammed into practice. I could hardly contain my excitement, my eagerness to cure and comfort patients. Sleepless, I spent hours starching and ironing my student-nurse whites the way Dad had pressed his army fatigues, a habit I continue to this day. I shadowed a nurse named Yvette. She smiled and asked, "Ready to work?"

I assured her I was.

She sent me to retrieve an IV pole with a trio of infusion pumps. "Follow me," she said, "bring the pumps." Yvette carried a green-and-pink Vera Bradley cosmetic bag under one arm and a red plastic pharmacy bag labeled *Handle with Caution. Chemotherapy* in her other hand.

A cart in front of the room was stocked with gowns, gloves, and masks.

Yvette said, "Gown up. Maggie is in reverse isolation."

I understood this meant the patient inside the room was vulnerable to infection.

Yvette masked, put on a yellow disposable gown, covered her thick brown hair with a cap, and slipped on gloves. I lagged outside the room a good five minutes, tying the gown and fitting the cap over my hair, opening and closing the drawers on the cart. This was before anyone had ever heard of Covid, well before donning PPE became like breathing.

I entered the patient's room, leading with the IV pole and the stack of infusion pumps. At the bedside Yvette introduced me to the patient. "Maggie, meet Annabelle."

Maggie was a child, but my immediate impression was that she was an old woman. Not only was she bald, but she did not have eyebrows or lashes. Maggie's smooth, pale scalp was the very definition of alopecia, a term I'd learned in school. I realized too late that I was staring.

Maggie's nose wrinkled and she said, "Nice to meet you, Student Nurse. I have cancer. The killing kind."

Yvette clucked her tongue.

"The student nurse should hear it like it is. No

sugarcoating..." Maggie coughed. Minutes passed before her hacking subsided.

Yvette prepped the Hickman port in Maggie's chest. Maggie licked her cracked lips and said, "Student Nurse, come closer. You don't want to miss this."

I stepped to the bedside, and Yvette explained the process of accessing Maggie's port. Yvette flushed it with normal saline, assuring patency, and explained the regimen of Benadryl and dexamethasone infusions that preceded the actual chemotherapy infusion as she programed the three pumps.

Up close, Maggie's unhealthy complexion fit the definition of a nursing vocabulary word: "sallow."

Maggie wasn't listening to Yvette's lesson, her attention absorbed by the Vera Bradley satchel Yvette set in Maggie's lap. Cellophane crinkled. Maggie sounded incredulous. "You remembered."

Yvette said, "Happy birthday. Let's make the most of today."

Surprised, I'd said, "It's your birthday? How old?"

Maggie said, "Half birthday, Student Nurse—twelve and a half."

Yvette asked, "Where's your hair? We've got work to do if we're going to turn you into a teenager."

Maggie coughed. The protracted spasm prevented her from speaking but she pointed to the nightstand. I opened the top drawer and found a platinum-blonde wig. Maggie handed me a comb and for the next hour I tamed the snarled hair.

Maggie put a cap on her bare scalp to secure the wig in place. I held a small makeup mirror and Maggie clipped red, pink, and yellow ribbons into the blonde wig. Yvette had stocked the Vera Bradley bag with new sample-size cosmetics. Maggie applied lip gloss, blush, and eyeliner but passed on the brow pencil. She handed me her phone. "Take my picture."

I did and passed the phone back.

Maggie scrolled the photos. The wonder in her barely audible voice was unmistakable. "I look beautiful... like a teenager." She fell asleep, glossed lips upturned in a triumphant, watermelon-red smile.

Her lunch tray arrived with a vanilla cupcake. Yvette gathered oncologists and nurses outside Maggie's room. Staff serenaded Maggie; a spirted rendition of "Happy Birthday" rang through the hallway. I sang, tears welling.

Maggie woke to hear the singing, but her cupcake and her lunch remained untouched.

The following morning, the door to Maggie's room was open, the isolation cart was missing. The bed stripped. Maggie's blonde wig was on the nightstand, the ribbons undone. I smoothed the hair, retied the ribbons. Yvette stood in the doorway.

"Where is..." My voice faltered.

"Maggie's heart stopped overnight."

When I regained my voice I said, "But chemotherapy. The treatment regimen—" The strands of Maggie's wig were soft between my fingers.

"Medicine can't cure every patient."

"The wig... the ribbons. Maggie's half birthday. You made her dying wish—"

"No. Her living wish," Yvette said. "Being a teenager, even for a few hours, was Maggie's last living wish."

At that moment I committed myself to nursing.

Maggie's life lesson isn't printed in a textbook or explained in a pharmacology lecture. She received treatment in a top-rated hospital and died anyway. But she taught me to honor each patient's life. I loosened a pink ribbon from Maggie's wig, pinned it to my clinical whites, and when I graduated from nursing school, I wore the ribbon on my robe, over my heart.

The car seat thumps on the floor and brings me to the

present. Jamie pushes the seat to the corner. I grasp the crib's cold side rails and stare at Olivia. She sleeps.

Jamie says, "I have Olivia's goodbye outfit at home. I have waited all these months to dress Olivia for her big send-off. Will you be here the next few days? I want you to see Olivia in her outfit when we finally go."

It's tradition for staff to send a discharged patient home with cheers and applause. Jamie has earned her victory. I say, "I won't miss it." Jamie looks so happy that I fear she will try to hug me.

Jamie says, "We have something for you. I'll give it to you now in case we don't have a chance to say goodbye." Her voice catches. She slips a square plastic box, big enough to hold a penny, into my hand.

The opaque box balances weightless on my palm. My vision blurs and I blink to stay tears. The box isn't empty but contains coiled threads, strands of Olivia's ginger hair, a shade lighter than my own. A leather cord is attached to the box.

Jamie's voice rises. "Do you—"

"I love—her—thank you."

Olivia whimpers in her sleep. Her eyes dart behind closed lids and her pale lashes flutter.

Jamie says, "Don't worry. I didn't cut Olivia's hair, I saved it from when her veins—"

"I remember." Olivia had needed an IV but the veins in her hands and feet were either already blown from prior sticks or too small for the IV catheter. Honor, the nurse practitioner, clipped and then shaved a precise square on Olivia's scalp, exposing a fat blue vein on the left side of her head. The IV had lasted a week, the exact amount of time that Olivia needed it. I'd collected Olivia's shaved hair in an envelope and had given it to Jamie.

Olivia's bald spot above her left ear is slowly refilling with new downy hair.

"I want you to keep a part of Olivia after we go. We have you to thank for naming her. And—" Jamie shifts the plastic bag to her opposite shoulder. She lifts a scrapbook from the rocking chair behind her. "I wrote about you in Olivia's baby book. Coleen told me that you read to Olivia. Of course, I can't remember everything else that you did for her. Thank you for staying after your shift and holding her when I couldn't—" Jamie cries softly. She lowers her mask; tears dampen her cheeks.

Without the mask I notice Jamie's delicate nose, her thin pink lips. Olivia resembles her mother.

"I wasn't myself after she was born. But I'm better now. The medication helps and I'm ready to be Olivia's mother. She is my first baby and I plan to give her my undivided attention. Growing up an only child can be a good thing, don't you agree?"

Technically, I'm an only child. But September through June, I shared my mother with twenty-five third graders. A popular teacher, parents jammed the Rose Lane Elementary School principal's voicemail—demanding their child have a spot in Mrs. Gold's class. Mom's twenty-five students became my ghost siblings, each vying for attention, a tug of war for Mom's affections that I inevitably lost. In the afternoon, Mom stayed at school long after the dismissal bell rang, tutoring, grading papers. I took the bus home from school, retrieved my house key, unlocked the door, and diligently practiced my cello music. Mom arrived home in time to cook dinner. "A teacher's work is never done," she'd say.

I tell Jamie, "Olivia is a lucky baby."

Jamie's thick scrapbook has block letters on the yellow cover announcing *BABY'S FIRST JOURNAL*. The snapshot inserted in the front pocket is out of focus. The naked preterm infant attached to a ventilator bears no likeness to Olivia. *Happy Birthday, January 15* is stickered in the picture's margin.

January fifteenth. A winter night two months in the past that initially drew me to Olivia. My own baby's due date. Peter had remained overnight at the hospital and performed Jamie's cesarean section. I was alone in our empty house, mourning what could have been, if only our baby had lived.

My breath catches. I'm unprepared for the swelling memory. Unable to push it away, there's no escaping and I succumb to the murky tide. I smell meconium. A bitter taste coats my tongue, blood mingled with sweat.

A joyless voice pierces the silence. "It's a girl."

There's weight on my chest. The voice tells me, "It's good for you to hold her." A round head rests between my breasts. The head, covered with matted hair, too wet to discern color or texture, curly or straight. Only that there is enough to clip with the seashell-shaped barrette I'd received at my shower.

A voice asks, "What's her name?"

"I don't know." If only she'd wake up and cry.

"Take as much time as you need."

"Her eyes?" I want her to have Peter's blue eyes. Mine are light brown. Peter says my eyes remind him of a caramel latte. "Wake up," I say.

Silence.

The baby in my arms slept. The cry I hear is mine.

Jamie grasps my wrist from across the crib. "I've upset you."

The memory melts. I'm grateful that Jamie's touch brought me back to the present but reluctant to be accused of overstepping yet another boundary by holding hands with a parent, particularly Olivia's mother.

"Thank you for the gift." I fist the locket. My knuckles blanch.

"I best go. Get ready for tomorrow in case it happens."

Jamie releases my wrist. "Goodnight, Olivia." Jamie pauses, eyes misty, for an awkward moment. Jamie holds BABY'S FIRST JOURNAL like a shield across her chest.

"Thank you. Again. For the gift." I put the locket in my scrubs pocket.

"You'll make a great mom. Someday."

Jamie's parting words are an unsheathed scalpel, the point opens a barely approximated wound. I struggle to speak but can't find the right words. I regret my silence and wish for something significant to tell her. But I don't know at this time that I will never see Jamie again.

I dim the light above Olivia's crib and acclimate to near darkness when a pair of fluorescent-blue Danskos round the corner. The sturdy clogs are a nursing wardrobe staple. I own a pair, and they're collecting dust in my closet; my feet are narrow and the first time I wore them, I tripped off the elevator. Robyn had laughed. "A year of shift work will expand those skinny feet."

In the meantime, my Converse are double knotted.

Coleen's blue clogs halt.

I ask, "You're on again?"

"Pulling an extra." Coleen's aqua-colored manicured nails disappear into a pair of latex gloves.

I rarely volunteer for overtime. According to the creditors pinging my phone, I should. "I'll weigh Olivia."

One less task for Coleen. Her clogs clunk to the crying baby in the next crib.

Olivia stirs, opens her eyes, and squawks in unison with her crib-mate. With exposure to natural light, her eye color will change, a process that will take months. For now, Olivia's eyes are pristine as the lake in the Adirondack Mountains where Peter and I spent our honeymoon. Our wedding was small, squeezed between the end of Peter's medical residency and the beginning of his obstetrical fellowship. We met here at Lakeview Hospital. I had been a student nurse sent to observe a vaginal delivery, but I entered the room to find Peter holding a dripping newborn in his hands. He'd said to me, "Nurse, a towel please?"

Being addressed as a nurse, not a student, thrilled me. My instructions were to observe, not participate in patient care, but I put on gloves and spread a white towel across the mother's abdomen.

With tenderness, Peter set the wet baby on the towel. I wiped the baby dry as it cried. I cried too, touched by Peter's gentleness and the mother's happiness. The labor-and-delivery nurse finished her task and introduced us. "Dr. Kaplan, Annabelle Gold is a student."

But the baby was loud, and Peter mistook my name for "Belle."

In the ensuing weeks I saw Peter in the hospital hallway, the elevator, and he bought me a coffee in the café, which I'd been excited about until we were interrupted by his pager. I drank my coffee, steam was curling from Peter's cup, but he didn't return. Disappointed, I disposed of his cold latte. At the end of my clinical rotation, I saw Peter again. I was walking in the corridor with a group of nursing students on our way to a conference and Peter stepped from an elevator. "Belle," he'd called out, "have a minute?"

Belle left me breathless. It still does. I told my classmates to go ahead without me.

"I hoped to see you... Are you free for lunch on Saturday?" He blushed and rubbed the back of his neck.

I realized he was nervous. Endearing. I didn't let him finish.

"Yes," I blurted, before a pager would short-circuit our conversation.

"Saturday. No interruptions." He stared at my hospital student ID. His blush deepened to fuchsia. "I'm sorry, your name... Annabelle. I thought—"

"Lunch. Yes," I'd said again. "But only if you call me Belle."

The following Saturday, Peter kept his promise. We had lunch and coffee and dinner and wine. There were no interruptions, and to this day he calls me Belle.

I undress Olivia, she smells like the hospital's eucalyptus diaper ointment. I tuck her under my arm, and she focuses on my face, the half that isn't covered by my surgical mask, which is a promising developmental sign. Part of the fun for parents is anticipating their newborn's eye color, a change that usually happens by their baby's first birthday. I bet Olivia keeps her mountain-lake blues.

My breasts tingle, a reflex from holding Olivia. The twinge recedes, and I marvel at the persistence of maternal hormones. With my free hand, I spread a disposable Chux over the scale, zero it, and set Olivia on the tray. She's naked except for the security band around her left ankle. The sensor is hospital protocol, dictated by administrators who imagine that a baby-snatcher lurks behind every laundry bin. The sensor will ring, triggering hospital-wide havoc if an infant is in the vicinity of an exit.

The scale displays Olivia's weight in red digital numbers: 2.720 kilos.

"Olivia, you're up thirty grams." But behind my mask, I'm not smiling. Six pounds means Olivia will be going home. I diaper her before she pees on the scale.

The secretary behind the nurses' station accidentally bumps the intercom dial. "Hush, Little Baby" floods the speakers at an obscene volume. But Olivia, accustomed to the constant thrum of the hospital, is unbothered by noise. I lower her into the crib, withdrawing my hand from the back of her head only after she's flat on the mattress. While she's desensitized to sound, sudden movement will activate her Moro or startle reflex.

I sit in the rocking chair, scroll my phone's story app, tap *Little Red Riding Hood,* and lean my forehead against the crib rails. The stainless steel is cold, and I read, whispering into the open space between the slats. Except I stray from the text. Olivia is the heroine who braves the forest, enters the cabin, and tames the hungry wolf.

Olivia's lashes flutter, feather-thick and translucent at the tips, like she's spent an afternoon at the beach. But Olivia's entire life has been indoors. Her only sun is the dome examination light that hovers above her crib.

A swipe of my Lakeview Hospital ID badge and the NICU's double doors *swoosh,* reconfiguring at my back with a thud. Except for an abandoned stretcher with a rumpled sheet, the corridor is vacant, it's nine at night and visiting hours ended an hour ago. Midway down the hall, an environmental service attendant's vacuum drones from the waiting room.

My phone vibrates. The text necessitates an unplanned visit outside the hospital before going home. I bypass the elevator. Without breaking stride, I message:

> Be there soon.

I walk to the end of the corridor and thumb the buzzer, hoping that Edwin can help. If he is working tonight, I know I can count on him. Behind the door, there's shuffling, the top door opens, like a drive-through pickup window. Edwin is happy to see me. His keen brown eyes are warm. I make my request.

"Let me see what I can do."

Feeding NICU patients requires a prescription and Edwin is a pharmacy tech. His workspace is as intimidating as a college chemistry lab, with a suspended hood over a black countertop and industrial freezers tucked beneath it. Canisters of chalky powders are stowed behind glass cabinets.

I ask, "How's the donor human milk supply by the way?"

Edwin punches a code on the freezer, the chrome door opens, plastic specimen containers of donated milk, rivaling my hoard, line the shelves. "Above par. Enough to feed the NICU patients for now."

"Let me know if you're low?"

"I know I can depend on you." Edwin gives a thumbs up and smiles. He passes a rectangular cardboard box through the pickup window. "It's heavy. Too near the expiration date for hospital use."

I accept the box with both hands. "It won't go to waste."

I duck into the stairwell, plod down the steps. Lakeview's glass atrium arches skyward. The night is an ebony blanket, beaded with silver and gold stars. The security guard ushers me through with a wave.

I load the box onto the Jetta's passenger seat and settle behind the wheel. Jamie's gift pokes my thigh. I retrieve it from my pocket and loop the leather cord around the rearview mirror. In the lamppost's light, Olivia's ginger hairs are saffron threads.

CHAPTER THREE

The Jetta stutters. Before the car quits, I floor the accelerator and reverse from the space. The Jetta is Mom's, or it was. Before retirement she commuted three miles, five days a week to Rose Lane Elementary where she taught third graders reading and math. When Mom died, I adopted the Jetta, but we haven't bonded. The odometer remains stuck at eighty thousand miles, as if mourning its original owner. The engine coughs. I turn up the radio, the Jetta's single device that never lets me down, Classical NPR. Bach, *Cello Suite No. 1* flows from the speaker.

Transportation woes. Peter and I live in the boondocks where the train doesn't run, and Uber is expensive. Peter's Subaru is reliable, but our schedules don't match so I can't depend on carpooling to the hospital. Not what you'd expect from a nurse married to a doctor.

As newlyweds we lived within our means. Peter's fellowship at Lakeview Hospital amounts to very little money. We were comfortable in our one-bedroom apartment, close to the hospital. My nurse's salary covered the rent and on occasion, Mom's rent, if her pension check was late. When our lease ended, Peter wanted to buy a house. He assured me we could make it work. "My fellowship comes with an expiration date. Dr. Cumberland all but promised me partnership in his practice."

"Of course Cumberland wants to hire you. His patients love you."

Peter was excited about our potential earning power. "You're on track to graduate from Drexel. With a masters, you can apply for an assistant nurse manager position and earn more money."

That was before Olivia's naming incident blemished my Lakeview Hospital personnel file. But I hated to dampen Peter's optimism and had bitten my lip, keeping the stagnant status of my graduate studies to myself.

Ever positive, Peter repeated the refrain. "We won't just be a professional couple but a family. We need a proper house."

We bought the house.

Our combined belongings had fit into a small U-Haul.

The family thing didn't happen.

Our new house, built on a three-acre lot in Woodline Manor, is surrounded by uncleared forest with a mile-long gravel driveway that contorts like a python. The neighbors? Pine, maple and oak. The contractor shared their plans to develop the surrounding lots. "You're buying into a future. Woodline Manor will have a playground, a market, and a Montessori preschool."

Our future is jinxed. Peter and I have no need for swing sets, jungle gyms, or exclusive nursery schools. After we moved into the house, my baby—ours—died. I came home from the hospital without her and discovered a terrible secret. When a dream dies, it doesn't go peacefully. It thrashes, writhes, and kicks up a turbulent wake.

I was discharged home to recuperate. Alone in the house, I discovered that the quiet was a misnomer. From the front porch of the house, I heard chainsaws chew lumber, tractors tread gravel, and hammers pummel nails.

Inside, I was introduced to our house's built-in quirks. Hinges creak like arthritic knees. The boiler moans. A toilet flushes, unsettling pipes in the basement's bowels. The staircase's third step is grumpy. At night, I swore I heard my baby cry. My infant daughter needed her mother.

"Listen," I said to Peter.

He squeezed my hand. "You need rest."

I answered my baby's hungry cry by expressing breast milk. I spread blankets in her crib and filled her dresser with onesies ordered on Amazon. The cries diminished to whimpers, an echo, and finally silence.

A month later, desperate to return to work, I laundered my scrubs. The evening before my NICU shift, I sprayed the scrubs with starch and prepared the iron, so that it spit steam. I massaged the blue scrubs until they were free of even the suggestion of a wrinkle, until they practically stood on their own. My patients still needed me.

But between shifts, when I'm not at the hospital, I'm home. Worse than quiet is emptiness, silence's evil first cousin. The house is vacuous, the arched entryways wide mouths. The closets, an empty room within each empty room, are insatiable.

Enter Amazon. I click *add to cart*. Boxes arrive, like putty plugging holes. Initially, I shopped with Peter in mind, choosing items in his favorite colors. Stocking the linen closet with midnight-blue bath towels and matching washcloths. That purchase segued to curtains. Not so simple. Dozens of windows necessitated rods, and hardware to mount the window treatments. Paper towels. Laundry soap pods. Rolls of toilet tissue. Boxes crowd the closets.

I focused my attention to the kitchen. Pots large enough to boil two pounds of pasta arrived. Followed by cases of *angel hair, cavatappi, fusilli, penne, rigatoni, spaghetti,* and *ziti* in boxes, arranged alphabetically in a cabinet above the cookware. I'd intended to surprise Peter with dinner. But I returned to the hospital before ever filling a pot, salting the water, and bringing it to boil.

Each online shopping spree ends with a vow that next time I follow the Amazon link, *Top picks for Annabelle,* I'll browse for fun. But I have yet to leave the site without a purchase or deleting any items from my virtual cart. Shopping to satisfy the empty house tipped me into uncharted territory: debt.

I detour, instead of driving home. I visit my best friend. Light shines behind Sheila's kitchen window. I avoid her cratered driveway and park along the curb. Night is kind to her house, concealing its shredded paint, the roof's missing shingles, and a lawn that surrendered to an invasion of dandelion weed. The house's nameplate, *Kitty Haven,* etched above the mail slot, is Sheila's life's work.

The box I'm carrying is heavy, but I pause at the threshold, fortifying my lungs with unspoiled air. The door is unlocked, a good thing because there's no doorbell. Sheila disconnected the ringer years ago after one of her residents, a thirteen-year-old Siamese, screeched in terror when the chime sounded, eventually requiring a sedative to be coaxed from behind the clothes dryer. The foyer's embrace is immediate—kitty litter and the musty scent of accumulated dander. A cat hisses. Amber-eyed and missing an ear, its black fur porcupines over a curved spine. I halt. "Sheila?"

Cat hair tumbleweeds the linoleum foyer. My throat tickles and I suppress a sneeze. I ignore Kitty Haven's "bare feet" rule, wear my Converse, and tread mindfully to avoid stepping on a furry resident, an ever-present possibility. The one-eared guard-cat meows, flicks its tail, and slinks around the corner. Box on my hip, I follow the cat into the kitchen. The one-eared cat leaps onto the second tier of a pet gymnasium in the center of the kitchen.

Water sloshes. Sheila bends over the sink, her black hair a braided rope that extends midway down her back, secured with a tie-dye bandana. She's taller than I am, but the unisex denim overalls she's wearing are long and the bottoms flop over her bare feet. Forearms submerged in water, red flannel shirtsleeves rolled to her elbows, Sheila lathers the cat in the sink to a white froth, and she aims a spray nozzle, rinsing the cat's back. The creature is surprisingly tolerant.

I say, "I thought cats hate water."

Dawn soap bubbles float above the sink. Sheila turns off the faucet and sets the sprayer in the sink. "Cats are a misunderstood species."

"Same as babies."

"Hand me a towel."

I plant the box on the counter beside a plastic laundry basket. "I brought what you need." A tabby jumps from a nest of towels in the basket, lands on the counter, and sniffs the box. I give Sheila a faded bath towel. I point to the box. "Infant formula. No mixing. Ready-to-feed."

Sheila lifts the cat from the sink, fluffing calico fur over skeletal ribs. The oven timer dings. "They're hungry. Bring the formula." Sheila burrito-wraps the cat in the towel and tucks it under her arm. A pair of emerald eyes watch me from the crook of Sheila's elbow.

I grab the formula and we enter the medical ward adjacent to the kitchen. The Maytag dryer hums on tumble-dry, a perpetual source of moist heat. Sheila deposits the skinny calico in a "cottage" and closes the door. "Cage" is a forbidden word at Kitty Haven.

I ask, "What's wrong with..."

"She arrived last night. Anemic from fleas."

The cat retreats to the back of the cottage and licks her front paws.

The room is a sauna. My forehead is damp and I'm thankful to be wearing short-sleeve hospital scrubs. A bench in the middle of the room serves as Sheila's exam table. The open tackle box, evidence that a resident required emergency attention, contains medical-grade instruments that she learned to use at the University of Pennsylvania Veterinary school: scissors, hemostats, tweezers, and suture thread.

If I had a cat, I'd trust Sheila, she would have made a great vet. But for reasons she won't discuss, she withdrew after her first year and never went back. She lifts a white sheet covering a rectangular Amazon box.

I say, "A litter. Quadruplets."

Sheila says, "Kindle is the correct term. Born not more than a couple of days ago."

I hear them, their mews like vibrating cello strings.

Sheila reaches into the box and lifts a kitten, a tennis ball covered in grey fur. "I couldn't very well turn them away. Without proper care, they'll die in hours." Sheila's voice is thick with emotion. Cradling the kitten, she says, "Warm your hands."

Rubbing my palms to generate heat, I sit on the carpet and accept the kitten ball with cupped hands. Sheila tells me, "She or he. Too early to discern gender. Your guess is as good as mine."

I'm breathless. The kitten is painstakingly fragile. It squirms and I fear dropping it between my fingers. "How do you feed—" Weightless, with sealed eyes, a tiny heart thrums against my thumb.

"Nurser bottles. Every two hours."

Sheila studies the label on the hospital formula that I brought. Frown lines punctuate her mouth. She reads the ingredients, swirls the two-ounce plastic bottle, unscrews the lid, and sniffs the NeoSure.

I tell her, "Human preemie formula."

"Not ideal, but it will do. I'm out of kitten formula."

Sheila dispenses the formula and passes me the nurser. The kitten hones to the scent, its pink tongue flicks a drop from the nipple. Satisfaction floods my heart to near bursting.

Sheila sits across from me and feeds the remaining three kittens simultaneously, a chocolate pair and one with fur as white as whole milk. A sheen of sweat dampens Sheila's forehead and I notice the hair around her temples is no longer jet black but streaked silver.

We're the same age, twenty-six. We've been friends since sixth grade, but Sheila shoulders way more responsibility. Kitty Haven, a no-kill shelter, operates on charitable donations, and is in the red. The house belonged to Sheila's father, who willed it to her. She has yet to refuse a cat and for that reason, the cottages remain occupied. Is angst over Kitty Haven's day-to-day operations aging my friend or is a new worry to blame for the etched lines at the corners of her eyes? I resist prying. Sheila is fiercely private, parsing details about herself, even with me, only when she's ready and then, in miniscule bits. She wasn't always like this with me. I've learned not to probe. Instead, I ask about the kittens.

"The Sunoco station attendant discovered the litter in a tire well, emptied a case of spark plugs from an Amazon box, packed the kittens, and delivered them here."

"Their mama?"

"Run over."

I swallow a swell of sorrow. The kittens are orphans. "Any prospects?"

Kitty Haven's online adoption application is six pages long, requires two references and a self-reflection essay. When the pandemic was in the early lockdown stages, Kitty Haven was inundated with adoption requests. Sheila deleted the bulk of the inquiries, predicting people would tire of their adopted-on-a-whim pets. Now with the pandemic in its end stage, she has a slew of unwanted cats.

"You interested? Fill out—"

I balk. "We've been friends forever. You know everything..." I falter. But that was before this house became Kitty Haven, before cottages crowded the living room. In middle school we spread sleeping bags across the floor, spent the night swapping secrets and eating Pepperidge Farm Milanos instead of doing our algebra homework. We're not kids anymore. I can't pinpoint when our friendship shifted. Perhaps growing up does that to friends, creates distance instead of closeness.

"Think it over. I'll give you a break with the adoption application. I'll be your reference." Sheila's giggle sends me back to those sleepovers. I wish I could think of something funny to say and make Sheila laugh again. I surrender the sleeping grey newborn to the Amazon box, where the kitten rolls into its orphaned littermates like another ball of yarn.

Sheila points to my top. "You spilled formula on your scrubs."

NeoSure has a distinctive medicinal odor, like concentrated vitamins. "I'm a NICU nurse. Infant formula is my perfume."

I giggle, hoping Sheila gets my joke. She smiles but doesn't laugh.

Compared to the humidity inside Sheila's house, the night is a frigid shower and I exhale, rinsing my lungs of cat dander, dust my hands of shed fur, and blot the formula stain on my scrubs top.

My phone vibrates. Peter's text, an emoji wearing a pajama cap and trailing *zzzzs*, is code for napping in the hospital call room. I respond with a smiling moon. The best

Peter can hope for, barring an obstetrical emergency, is a few hours of uninterrupted sleep before being jarred awake by a nurse with a question or the emergency room needing a consultation on a pregnant patient in triage. Peter never complains about lost sleep, powered by caffeine and passion for delivering babies.

A second ping. The Amazon Prime driver texts a picture. Neatly stacked boxes smile at our front door. I can't recall what I ordered. The text includes a survey:

> Annabelle, rate your delivery experience.

From the gamut of facial expressions, I submit the full smile. The delivery driver deserves an award for navigating our driveway in the dark.

The prospect of driving home, collecting the boxes, stowing them in a closet, and spending the night alone leaves me despondent. Tears gather. I settle into the Jetta and drive, not bothering to dry my face. Sheila's house with the light in the kitchen window fades in my rearview mirror. The charm containing Olivia's hair swings, a steady pulse.

The Jetta, as if on autopilot, travels to Radcliff Apartments, chugging past the condominiums dressed in cedar shingles to the rentals in the rear sorely in need of power washing. The Jetta glides into its former home, the carport corresponding to unit K2. Mom's arthritic hip entitled her to the coveted carport. I unfold the handicapped parking pass so that it's visible through the windshield. There's not a thing wrong with my mobility but I use her pass; next time, I promise I'll park in the visitor lot.

Peter doesn't know I've kept Mom's apartment. I've rehearsed a hundred confessions. Each imaginary scenario ends with Peter absorbing my admission and commenting clinically,

"You kept Genie's place? For months? How do we afford the rent?"

We don't. Yet I can't bring myself to end the lease, donate the contents and leave Radcliff once and for all. The apartment is a one-bedroom dinghy, floating on an ocean of memory. After Mom's death, I communed with the smell of freshly brewed coffee, lemon Pledge, and roasted chicken, pretending that Mom was temporarily away, not permanently gone. But after nine months Mom's scent evaporated, the shine of her belongings dulled.

I fish Mom's key from the cupholder and exit the Jetta. The walkway to the apartment is crumbled; the green weeds that had sprouted through the concrete during the summer are shriveled bits of straw. Despite the late hour, after midnight, my arrival arouses no suspicion, the tenants, old and tired, are asleep behind drawn window blinds.

The key slips into the lock, the bolt tumbles, and I enter. The door thuds shut, and I exhale my held breath. The living room smells un-Mom like, not stale like I'd dreaded, but like Febreze. I say, "Hi, Mom. It's me."

Silence reverberates like a tuning fork against my ear. The apartment is uninhabited. My heart, even after so much loss is not immune to a fresh tide of grief. I navigate the shadows, my movements economical, calculated to cause minimal disruption like a minnow gliding through a dark pond without rippling the surface. I skirt the coffee table, avoid knocking my shin against the loveseat, and make my way to the bedroom. The night-light that I'd purchased for Mom's trips to the bathroom shines from the wall socket.

Stripping my scrubs, I crawl into Mom's double bed and shiver between the cold sheets. But the chill is momentary, the bed warms and in the instant before sleep, I notice Mom's beloved ficus tree in the corner. The braided trunk, the branches pruned and the olive-green leaves glisten with dew from recent misting. Not by me. Plants aren't my thing.

Mail at the Radcliff is delivered to a central kiosk. The next morning, I retrieve Mom's mailbox key from a porcelain teacup on the Keurig. The Keurig, a gift from Peter, remains on the kitchen counter where space is a commodity, but the well was never filled and the box of Green Mountain pods, also a gift, is unopened. Mom considered Keurig "instant coffee," preferring the ritual of grinding, measuring, and plunging the French press. A dusting of pulverized coffee coats the grinder, enough that the galley kitchen smells like espresso beans.

The bank of mailboxes is unoccupied, and I'm grateful that there are no tenants to question why I'm collecting Genie Gold's mail. The attempt at a disguise, Mom's navy-blue peacoat and knitted cap, is unnecessary and I feel foolish. The superintendent is bound to find out that Mom died and that I've been squatting part-time in her apartment. The mail slot is crammed, besides five forwarded credit card bills addressed to me, Genie Gold, despite being dead, receives an electric and internet bill, an advertising circular, and a reminder to bring the Jetta to the service station for an oil change. But the envelope bearing a Pennsylvania State Board of Education stamp isn't there.

A pickup truck rumbles to a stop, the engine growls like a feral dog. I lock the box, shove the wadded mail under the peacoat, and wrap my arms across my middle. I recognize the truck's dented fender and peeling green paint as belonging to the Radcliff Maintenance crew. The driver opens a newspaper, his eyes dart from the newsprint to me. He folds the newspaper along the crease, rolls it, and touches the brim of his baseball cap. The innocuous salute sends me jogging back to the apartment.

Vacuum marks track the carpet, and the loveseat cushion is indented as if Mom momentarily vacated the spot and intends to return. Careful not to disturb her preferred cushion, I sit, dump the mail I'd collected on the coffee table, and tap a link on my phone. Janice phases into view. Her wrinkled forehead smooths when she sees me. Her white lab coat is buttoned to her neck. I notice an open file on her desk and regret my lateness, giving her reason to record a demerit in my chart. She's talking, and I connect to audio.

Janice says, "Annabelle. I worried you forgot our visit."

I can spare a few minutes without falling to pieces.

Janice fires a question. "Your mood?"

"Good..." I discreetly sort the mail. The envelope with the official Pennsylvania State stamp is hidden between a coupon for a free Dunkin' Donut and a flyer from A&P.

The gully on Janice's forehead reappears. "Have you journaled?"

"I bought a notebook." Even though that's not exactly true.

"Care to share an entry?"

"Maybe. Next time."

Janice jots a note. "Work. How are things with your nurse manager?"

I organize the mail, setting the official envelope aside, grateful that the pension office missed the memo: Genie Gold is dead and no longer needs her monthly check.

Janice says, "The hospital probation period—"

My cheeks burn with humiliation. Therapy with Janice is a hospital-mandated punishment for overstepping my professional boundary. Naming baby Olivia earned me six Zoom therapy sessions.

Janice's stare pierces the phone screen. "I'm worried that

you are taking our sessions too lightly. You have significant trauma around loss. A pregnancy, the hope for your own baby. Your mother—"

I lower my gaze to the envelope balanced on my knee. Mom's computer-generated name is visible through the envelope window. A trifecta of emotions knots my gut. Sadness for my own baby, the one I couldn't save. Regret over my pile of credit card bills. Guilt for omitting the truth to Peter about keeping Mom's apartment.

Janice waits expectantly on the phone screen, but the wad of emotions clogs my throat. I can't talk to a therapist or anyone about my feelings. Especially about the crime I'm committing. Cashing the pension check meant to sustain Mom in retirement is wrong. "This is the last time," I vow.

Janice leans forward. "What's that?"

"Nothing."

She speaks slowly, emphasizing each word. "No one gets through life without a few bruises. You have suffered your fair share and have the scars to prove it. I'm here to help."

I swallow the question: *What if I don't want help?*

"You owe it to yourself to heal your hurts." Janice softens. "Grief will catch up, Annabelle. Emotions are destined to overboil. It's a matter of time."

"I'm figuring things out..." My scalp tingles. "My battery—the phone is about to die."

Janice gets the final say. "I'll send a link to our next session." Before I disconnect, she says, "Don't forget to journal."

Overwhelmed by the urge to shop, I log on to Amazon. A coincidence? Maybe. But I can't resist a sale and Amazon has a special on spiral-bound journals. Not ordinary journals either, the pages are lined and sandwiched between yellow floral jackets.

CHAPTER FOUR

Evening shift starts at three in the afternoon and ends eleven at night. I jockey for a parking spot on the edge of the employee lot, reversing several times to maneuver the Jetta between a white BMW and a red Tesla. The locket containing Olivia's hair oscillates from its string on the rearview mirror.

I jog, joining the other nurses like a school of fish swimming upstream. Prior to the pandemic, Lakeview Hospital was architecturally symmetrical and organized according to patient acuity. The first four floors were day surgery and diagnostic procedures. Maternal-fetal medicine, including the NICU, occupy floors five and six. Adult intensive care was confined to floors seven and eight. A visitor could gauge their loved one's illness by how high the elevator rose. But Covid changed all that.

The ground-floor atrium's added security station is a proboscis protruding onto the circular driveway. The emergency department sprouted military-style tents, drab appendages to isolate contagious patients. But in the past few months, the parade of ambulances off-loading gurneys for triage thinned and days pass without an admission to the Covid care unit.

Despite receiving the best treatment available, Mom died of Covid, in a third-floor ICU that, pre-pandemic, was an outpatient surgical recovery area, where before Covid, a nurse hadn't opened a crash cart in years. I like to think that Mom felt my presence through the haze of her drug-induced coma. I sat at her bedside, my safety goggles steamed with tears until her heart slowed and the ventilator, unable to oxygenate her tired lungs, quit. That was nine months ago. But I avoid the third floor. It will always be synonymous with her death.

The entrance doors shimmy apart, and the grey cinderblock hospital engulfs the group of us. We reconfigure, single file, and are each issued a blue surgical loop mask. Robyn is three nurses in front. I adjust my mask and run to catch Robyn at the elevator. Inside, I elbow the button for the sixth floor. "How's little Robbie?" She named her youngest son after herself.

"Mischievous as ever. He was too quiet while I was getting ready for work, found him in the kitchen, spoon-feeding his stuffed bear an entire jar of peanut butter—what a mess." We exit the elevator and Robyn swipes her hospital ID against the badge reader. Shoulders touching, we enter the NICU. "I soaked the bear in the sink and told Thom to set the clothes dryer on delicate. Robbie won't go to bed without that bear."

We approach the bank of scrub sinks. Robyn holds up her palms. "Kids. Nothing but trouble but you love them anyway. You know?"

My shoulders slouch. I fiddle with the faucet and avoid Robyn's gaze.

Her voice is soft. "Forgive me. That was a thoughtless thing to say."

"It's all right. You didn't mean anything." Water drums the stainless-steel sink, making conversation impossible.

The charge nurse divvies the patients, assigning me the twin boy from yesterday. Robyn has the girl. I'm excited because the pair are a day stronger.

During shift changes the unit is closed to visitors, allowing staff to update each other without confidential information spilling between bedspaces. I lean against the counter in my patient's bedspace with a fresh sheet of paper, uncap a blue ballpoint pen, eager to hear what Todd has to say.

Todd says, "Up until lunch, smooth sailing—"

"Honeymoon over?" I ask. An uneventful first day is deceiving. Complications for a preterm infant are inevitable.

"Turned dusky and his blood pressure dove. Honor ordered a gas and hematocrit. Long story short—he needed blood. Next labs are due in twelve hours."

I draw a square on my paper and write *evening labs* as a reminder. I'll check the box when the labs are sent. "Anything else?"

"His name. Nathanial." Todd leaves.

I write NATHANIAL in capital letters at the top of my report paper. His mother believes in him, loves him enough to name him—a sign that she is willing to travel this months-long roller-coaster ride with him. I'm happy for Nathanial, yet caution tempers my joy. Nathanial is preterm and destined for setbacks and complications. The crib card attached to his isolette is still blank. I cap the ordinary pen and retrieve my calligraphy pen. I write *Nathanial* in my finest lettering.

I tap the foot pedal; the isolette descends, settling at my chest. As I lift the light-blocking drape from the isolette roof and peek inside, a glimpse of my patient is all I need to adjust my perspective. Nathanial has changed since our first meeting. His skin, exposed to air, has keratinized and is less spongey. Due to water loss Nathanial appears even smaller. The ventilator, an oscillator, hums like a jet before takeoff and its rigid tubing delivers air into Nathanial's lungs at a rapid clip, causing him to vibrate or "wiggle" like a sock on top of a dryer.

"Hello, Nathanial. Remember me? I'm Annabelle. We have work to do. Let's grow you into your name."

The unit clerk steers a wheelchair into the pod. The woman in the chair is ashen, dressed in a "johnny", the flimsy nightgown that opens in the back. A mother's first visit requires a gentle introduction. A positive initial meeting lays the foundation for a strong parent-child bond; a negative experience causes irreparable damage that can't be undone. "I'm Annabelle, your baby's nurse. Congratulations."

The woman clutches the wheelchair arms. Her eyes dart between bedspaces. She settles on a pair of twins wrapped in flannel blankets. The pair have outgrown supplemental oxygen and they breathe unassisted. Except for the feeding tubes in their nostrils, they could be mistaken for small newborns, but they have spent months here. When space is available across the hall, they will be transferred from critical care to the Special Care Nursery.

"Let's get you closer." I lift the cloth cover. "Here he is."

The hairless being inside the isolette bears no likeness to the chubby babies in diaper commercials. Even a prenatal ultrasound picture can look cute, but when plucked from a cushioned womb, that same infant bears no resemblance to the black-and-white photo.

I ask, "Can you see his hands? Ten perfect fingers." His fingernails are tiny dots, each no bigger than the head of a pin. His arms and legs twitch.

The woman stares through the plastic walls.

"There's tape across his mouth."

"The tape keeps the breathing tube in place."

"What did you say your name is?"

"Annabelle. I'm the only nurse with red hair. This will get easier." I want to promise her everything will work out. But I can't, there are no guarantees in the NICU.

"It's time for me to pump."

I retrieve a yellow Symphony breast pump from the neighboring pod, plug it in, and arrange a privacy screen. The double electric motor begins to cycle. "Twenty minutes," I say.

A twinge of empathy courses through my breasts.

I've heard some nurses admit to being relieved when a baby is formula, not breastfed. True, it's easier in the short term. But colostrum has protective antibodies, designed to fight infection. In nursing school, I saw living breast milk. One of the professors had a six-month-old and brought her expressed breast milk to class. The professor mounted a drop on a slide and inserted it under a microscope. Peering through the lenses, I hadn't expected anything, but the milk quivered with activity. Cells skittered across the slide. In contrast, the store-bought formula under a second microscope sat motionless on the glass slide.

"Here." Nathanial's mom holds a one-milliliter syringe containing viscous yellow fluid.

"Great... job." I saturate a cotton swab with the colostrum, and we swab the colostrum around Nathanial's lips, careful not to disturb his breathing tube. The mom whispers, "I love you, Nathanial."

Is this what keeps you coming to work? Shift after shift. Moments like this? I bet this is why you do what you do—why you became a nurse. Jamie's question rushes back.

Elated, I want to shout my answer, *Yes. Yes. Yes.* I love being a nurse. I wouldn't do anything else and there is nowhere I'd rather be than in the NICU, where bonding happens in small increments. Outside of Lakeview Hospital my life is a series of failures and missteps: a collection of unopened Amazon boxes, a pile of unpaid credit card bills, and an unwritten master's thesis. But in the NICU I am a nurse, my every action infused with certainty.

The unit secretary makes an announcement over the speakers. "Come congratulate our new NICU graduate. Staff are invited to the entrance for a goodbye send-off."

My stomach drops. Olivia. She's leaving. But I can't leave Nathanial without a nurse. I don't need to ask Robyn to watch Nathanial. Our eyes meet, she leans over Nathanial's isolette and mouths, "Go."

Eyes stinging with unshed tears, I make my way to the entrance. How do I bid sweet Olivia goodbye? Staff crowd the corridor in front of the doors. I can't see Jamie holding Olivia, or her new dress. There's laughter, applause. I stand in the back and clap, but my damp palms make no sound. The double doors swing apart. Nurses wave and shout, "We'll miss you, Theo."

My heart skips. It's not Olivia. The doors close. Staff return to their assigned duties. Weightless with relief, I jog to my patient. Robyn slips her gloved hands from Nathanial's isolette. I sanitize with Purell and tell her, "I'll take over."

"It wasn't her, was it?"

I shake my head.

Instead of my half-hour dinner break, I wolf a Clif Bar while sprinting to the bathroom. Sitting to pee is luxurious and an opportunity to listen to a phone message. Dr. Edna Hayes, my thesis advisor, sounds like she bit a lemon. "Ms. Kaplan, regarding your thesis topic." I picture Dr. Hayes's face pucker. "The lit review is past due. Schedule a conference. I trust you're familiar with my office hours." For whatever reason Dr. Hayes maintains faith that I'm master's material but we're on different wavelengths. I enrolled in Drexel University's graduate program with hope of furthering my knowledge and my career. So far, the research articles from the library are esoteric. I flush, wash my hands, pocket the phone, and race-walk to the bedside. Shifts like this turn nursing into an endurance sport.

Evening shift ends at eleven and before leaving, I scan the charge nurse's clipboard for news about Olivia's discharge. According to the census sheet Olivia Dutton is slated for discharge tomorrow. Tonight, my last opportunity to see her. I cross the hall to the Special Care Nursery, propelled by a palpable urgency. I find Olivia is awake in her crib. "Hello, night owl," I say.

I Purell again, lower the side rail, and reach into the crib. Before I lift her, she does the most amazing thing. Monumental, really.

Olivia smiles.

At me.

Her pink lips blossom. Her chin dimples. The light behind her lake-blue eyes assures me that her smile is meant for me. And only me.

My heart tumbles.

Olivia is happy to see me. Olivia loves me. Everything that happened later can be traced back to that single smile. When Olivia needed me, betraying her trust was impossible.

I lift her from the crib and hold her against my chest. I don't realize I'm crying until I lay my cheek against Olivia's head and her hair is wet with my tears. I reach for a tissue.

Someone passes the box to me. Peter steps into the pod.

I accept the tissue and ask, "How long have you been standing there?"

Peter's lips are a tight line. A moment passes and he says, "My shift is over. Let's ride home together. I'll drive."

I put Olivia in her crib. Her lashes flutter with sleep. I lean down to kiss Olivia's forehead.

"Belle." Peter's voice is husky.

I freeze. My lips millimeters from Olivia's forehead. I'm

horrified for broaching nursing professionalism and nearly kissing a patient. Except, this is baby Olivia. Not a random patient. I stand and secure the crib rail without startling her. I swallow. The pebble of emotion in my throat descends, sits in my stomach, heavy as a boulder.

CHAPTER FIVE

Peter takes my hand and without speaking, we leave the Special Care Nursery. In the elevator he releases my hand and leans against the rear wall and lowers his mask. In the elevator's anemic light, Peter's eyes are bloodshot, he needs a shave, and his expression beneath the stubble is grave. His white lab coat with *Dr. Kaplan, Chief Fellow, Obstetrics* embroidered on the front pocket is unbuttoned, and a black pager is clipped to his green scrubs pants. Lakeview Hospital upholds the white coat tradition. Short jackets are for medical students, interns, and residents. The hem of Peter's coat reaches mid-thigh, signaling a position of authority in the medical pecking order.

I'm ashamed of what Peter witnessed. Overstepping, no—violating yet another patient-caregiver boundary. "Baby Olivia is being discharged. I'll never—"

The elevator doors whoosh. Peter clasps my hand, and we exit the elevator. The lobby is empty except for the security guard who waves and says, "Storm coming in. Be careful."

Outside, the March night causes a full-body shiver. I inhale. The air is ripe with the promise of rain but cold enough for snow. Our shoulders bump.

Peter says, "I'm in the first row."

The moon is a yellow disc. I feel exposed beneath its lidless eye, like a patient awakening from anesthetized sleep to find herself naked under the operating room examination light.

Peter's palm is smooth and warm.

The heaviness in my core lightens. My mood lifts. I imagine Peter working that same magic on his patients, dissipating an apprehensive woman's anxiety with mere words. *Yes, labor is scary. But trust the normal process.* I match Peter's stride and let myself be led.

Peter's Subaru wagon is parked under a red sign: *Reserved. Dr. Webster Cumberland, Chief of Obstetrics.* Cumberland permits Peter to take the space when the old doctor's gunmetal-grey Mercedes isn't there. Which lately is multiple times a week. Somehow the Subaru rises to the privileged parking, its powder-blue paint appears less faded, the missing hubcap hardly noticeable. Peter never locks his car. Activating the door locks is a sign of distrust, as if he doubts his coworkers and his patients' intentions. Peter holds the passenger door for me, tossing the March issue of *American Journal of Obstetrics and Gynecology* from the front seat onto the heap of periodicals on the back.

I settle into the seat. The car smells like old coffee, paper, and leather. Peter snaps his safety belt and waits for me to do the same. The Subaru idles. Heat flows from the dashboard vents. We exit the lot. Lakeview Hospital recedes in the side-view mirror. Through the windshield, the night is a dark blur punctured by the blink of an occasional traffic light. I notice we miss the freeway on-ramp.

Peter breaks our meditative silence. "Back roads. We need to talk."

I don't answer. The anxious pebble in my throat returns, occluding my voice box.

"It's time," Peter says, "for us to consider alternate pathways. To parenthood."

My hands fist in my lap. A hiss escapes my throat.

"Belle." Peter grips the steering wheel. "A gestational carrier is a perfectly reasonable option."

"No." I can't—won't permit a woman to nest my baby in her womb, stealing every wiggle and somersault from me. "No," I say again. My jaw clamps. I have my reasons but can't articulate them to Peter. I'll never trust a woman to willingly give up our newborn, not after she's grown our embryo into a fetus, and births our baby.

Rain dribbles the windshield. Peter stares through the rain-dappled glass but doesn't activate the wipers. He says, "Dr. Cumberland literally began the surrogacy program at Lakeview Hospital." Peter admires his mentor, Dr. Cumberland. They met while Peter was a resident and Cumberland had been thrilled when Peter chose to specialize in obstetrics. There is no use debating anything Cumberland told Peter.

"Gestational carriers are bound by contract to relinquish the infant. If you're worried about the money—Cumberland will give us a steep discount."

"Love isn't a contract." I'm crying. "Love is a force of nature."

"Cumberland has a candidate in mind."

"It's no wonder Cumberland wants to help..."

"Webster would do anything—"

Words erupt through my tears. "He feels guilty—for what he did to me." My feelings about Dr. Cumberland, suppressed to spare Peter, who loves his mentor like a father, flow like molten lava from a volcano. My hot anger is impossible to cap.

"Cumberland? What—"

I open the window. Sleet pellets my cheeks, cooling my

burning tears. "Because of Cumberland, I can't have a baby of our own. It's his fault that I'm the way I am. Infertile."

Peter brakes sharply.

The safety harness tightens across my abdomen, presses my incision site, the pin-and-needle sensation of regenerating nerves—a reminder of the babies I'll never conceive.

Peter's voice is pained. "There was no other way, Belle... You'd lost consciousness—on the verge of irreversible hypovolemic shock." Peter pauses. "I was there. I promise you that a hysterectomy was the only solution..." He reaches for my hand.

My fingers unfurl and intertwine with his.

Peter repeats, "There was no other way. Trust me. You lost too much blood to remember. Webster did what needed to be done."

I shift in my seat. I remember more than Peter realizes. My memory is hazy and fragmented, but not absent. The bleeding occurred hours after I gave birth, during the night's darkest hours. I'd been transferred to a private room on the postpartum floor, and because my baby was stillborn, the room was on the opposite end of the hall, nowhere near the newborn nursery.

Yet I heard crying. An enchanting chorus. I imagined if my daughter had been in the mix, I'd have recognized her solo pitch. I ignored the sticky, warm gush between my thighs, saturating my peri-pad and the bedsheets and focused instead on other mothers' babies.

I'm a nurse, trained to assess postpartum lochia. What was happening to me was beyond normal bleeding. My rapid, thready pulse warned of a life-threatening postpartum hemorrhage. Instead of summoning help, I let the call bell at my bedside drop to the floor. I regret my inaction. It brought me frighteningly near death. I paid with my uterus. Infertility, a lifelong penance. By the time a nurse entered my room, activated the code button, and saved my life, the babies in the newborn nursery were silent.

Peter activates the high beams, and the Subaru's headlamps slice the dark. We're approaching Woodline Manor. Gravel pings the car's underside. We swerve past surveyors' stakes and lots cordoned with yellow tape.

The windshield fogs. I close my window and rub my face dry. Sleet taps the roof. I wait for Peter to deploy the windshield wipers. He doesn't. Peter exhales, a jagged sound. He says, "If there is anyone to blame—blame me. Not Cumberland. I told him to do whatever was needed to stop your hemorrhage."

A hulking mass blocks the road. "Watch out!" I scream.

"I see it." Peter releases my hand. The Subaru skids, tires screech, and the four-wheel drive engages. Peter navigates a bulldozer, parked on the street, its bucket raised like a trumpeting elephant. Peter's shoulders are hunched, and he grips the steering wheel with white knuckles. I imagine that's how he'll appear when he's old, like Webster Cumberland, driving through a hurricane or a blizzard on his way to the hospital to deliver a baby.

"Our daughter was beautiful, Belle." His voice is thick with emotion. "She looked like you—but you are everything to me and I couldn't risk—you. I told Webster to do the hysterectomy."

My heart gallops. The rush of adrenaline recedes. My pulse decelerates. I'm weak with relief after our near disaster with the bulldozer. I cover Peter's hand with mine. His skin is icy, and his fingers, bare and slender, wrap the steering wheel. He's not wearing gloves. A surgeon's hands are their livelihood and Peter takes particular care, a habit he adopted in medical school. I want to ask about his missing gloves. Instead, I say simply, "Thank you."

He doesn't release the steering wheel. We reach our street, deep in the Woodline Manor development. The headlamps illuminate the mouth of our driveway, and the Subaru ascends the hill. Automatic lights spiked in the lawn pop awake. The garage yawns, and we enter our house through a connecting door, bypassing the Amazon packages stacked on the front porch.

I sit in the foyer and untie my Converse. Peter is on the staircase. The third step creaks twice. A few seconds later I hear the fan in the hall bathroom. My husband loves a hot shower, so I have a good twenty minutes. Shoelaces dragging, I open the front door and collect three Amazon boxes, lifting each individual box, testing its weight. Nothing heavy. The contents shift in the third box. I'm curious about what's inside but right now, stowing them is the priority. I promise myself that I'll explain everything to Peter later: the shopping, the Visa bills, Mom's apartment.

The foyer coat closet is full, there's winter boots, coats, and an Amazon box of wool gloves in every color. I make a mental note to leave a pair or two out for Peter. I lug the latest delivery through the hallway and into the room earmarked as a future office. No furniture, except a built-in bookcase, and without ceiling lights, it's dark. I feel along the wall for a knob. The closet opens, and I slide one box, two, but the third initiates a landslide. I duck. There's a metallic clank as ski poles tumble. I freeze. Not ski poles but curtain rods. A final package lands. Hardware to mount the rods.

I right the fallen rods, rearrange the boxes, and give the door a firm shove. The contents shift and I hear a box bump, but the door stays closed. I leave the study. What this house really needs? Lamps.

Abandoning my Converse sneakers in the foyer, I climb the

stairs barefoot, stealthily skipping the third step. I enter the spare room and close the door. The night-light—a yellow moon with a leaping cow—provides all the light I need. I sit in the rocking chair, prop my feet on the ottoman, position the flanges, attach the tubing, dial the pump. I could do this in my sleep. My breasts respond to the rhythmic tug. Alabaster drops coat the collection bottles and then my nipples spray.

In the bathroom I dial the water hot, the mirror above the vanity fogs. I strip my scrubs, roll them, and toss the ball into the laundry basket, shampoo twice. Lavender-smelling bubbles tornado the drain. I climb into bed, my hair wet.

I dive into sleep where I'm hostage to restless dreams. The night is a spider, spinning a silk web and I'm enveloped by sticky threads, drawn into a pulsating core where escape is impossible. The mattress dips. The dark is absolute and I'm uncertain if I've opened my eyes.

Peter is beside me. Instead of falling unconscious like an exhausted surgeon, he gathers me in his arms. We kiss. His damp skin smells like Ivory soap. Clearly, he's not at all concerned about losing precious sleep.

"Belle? You awake?" Peter is wearing green scrubs the next morning. He sets a travel mug of steaming coffee on the night table.

I dress in a clean set of scrubs, grateful for the extra sleep after working evenings and switching to day shift. Peter is outside, warming the Subaru and waiting in the driveway. Before leaving, I open the closet where I'd stored last night's delivery. I can't resist opening one. Journals. The purchase would earn Janice's approval. The floral jackets are attractive, and I slip one into my bag and hurry outside.

The car is toasty, and smells like coffee. Peter refilled our travel mugs. The radio is tuned to the weather station, detailing the rainstorm. The Subaru's fog lamps pry through the murk. Wipers swipe the windshield. Overnight, freezing rain iced the highway, causing numerous car crashes. A tractor trailer overturned on the interstate. Peter says, "We're taking back roads, there's a major pileup in the highway. How's the coffee?"

I lift my mug from the holder and take a sip. "Tastes like Starbucks."

"Made it myself," Peter says. "Keurig. I searched the cabinet for a stray pod and stumbled upon a lifetime supply. I picked Verona for you." He lifts his travel mug from the holder. "Green Mountain hazelnut. Thanks for buying a variety."

I sit taller. "You're welcome." Riding with Peter is a bonus.

Olivia is scheduled for discharge, and I'd promised Jamie when she gave me the locket that I'd celebrate Olivia's send-off. But I have mixed feelings. My eyes well at the thought of Olivia, dressed in a fancy outfit for her NICU discharge.

Peter says, "I'm on call tonight. Your car—"

"The Jetta is in the employee lot. I'll be fine."

Lakeview Hospital appears to squat, as if shouldering a heavy burden, the upper stories draped in fog. Peter and I walk across the wet sidewalk, heads bent. Inside the hospital we take the elevator. On the fifth floor, the doors open, and we lower our masks for a quick kiss. Peter exits and I push the button for the sixth floor.

Robyn and I are assigned to the twins, Nathanial and Natalie.

I'm immersed in caring for my twin and it's noon before I realize that I hadn't heard Olivia's send-off announcement, scheduled for this morning. My heart sinks. Had I missed it? But maybe a clean, unsentimental break is for the best. I force

Olivia from my mind and focus on Nathanial. He's requiring more oxygen.

Robyn goes to the breakroom to check her phone and eat lunch. I "babysit" Natalie. She is active, waving her reedy arms and kicking her legs. She swats her breathing tube, scrunches her face in a silent cry. I whisper to her, "You won't need that tube for long. I can't wait to hear your beautiful voice."

Robyn returns, ten minutes early from her break. I tell her, "Hey. I got this. Take your time."

But her eyes are red, her winged eyeliner smeared. Her tone somber. "Annabelle."

My breath hitches.

For a split-second Mom pops to mind. And I remember that she's already gone. Whatever has upset Robyn ripples through the NICU. Nurses cluster, whispering, there's a harsh gasp.

My mouth is dry. "Peter."

Robyn says, "He's fine."

I close my eyes and imagine my husband dressed in green scrubs, happily guiding an ultrasound wand over an enormous abdomen.

A ventilator sounds. I am about to answer the alarm, but Robyn takes my hand between her palms. I'm wearing gloves and I feel her naked, cold skin. Robyn says, "There was a crash. A tractor trailer overturned and the car behind it flipped. Dead at the scene... It's so unfair. Poor baby. Lost both parents."

An oxygen desaturation monitor dings.

"Who? What poor baby?"

"Olivia." Robyn drops my hand and wipes her tears with a cloth diaper. "Jamie and Don. Their car flipped on the freeway. They never made it to pick up Olivia."

My knees lock. Sound recedes. I see Jamie floating above an overturned car, Olivia's special send-off outfit clutched in her ghost-white hands.

Nathanial's heart-rate alarm emits a dreadful shriek.

Robyn says, "Press the code alarm."

The alarm, a repetitive whoop, is a magnet, attracting nurses, the respiratory therapist, Honor and Dr. STAT. Nathanial is pallid. His heartbeat, an ominous, too-widely-spaced tracing on the monitor screen.

"Bradycardia," I say. I prepare a suction catheter. Robyn dials the oxygen to one hundred percent.

Honor extracts Nathanial's endotracheal tube from his mouth and says, "The tube is plugged. Prepare for reintubation."

The respiratory therapist fits a mask over Nathanial's mouth and nose.

Dr. STAT says, "Begin chest compressions."

I wrap my hands around Nathanial's chest, position both thumbs on his sternum and compress. He weighs two pounds, with delicate ribs that can easily snap. I coordinate my compressions with the respiratory therapist's ventilations. "One and two and three and breathe…"

Blood bubbles between Nathanial's lips.

"Pulmonary hemorrhage," Dr. STAT says, "prepare epinephrine."

Blood fountains from his pinpoint nostrils. My gloves are stained. Not breaking cadence, "One and two and three and breathe…"

Dr. STAT says, "Stop compressions."

My hands encircle Nathanial, thumbs over his sternum. I wait.

Dr. STAT listens, her stethoscope over the baby's heart. "Continue chest compressions."

"One and two and three and breathe…"

Dr. STAT says, "Anyone know the parents?"

Robyn answers, "We do."

Dr. STAT tells Robyn, "Get them. Now. While their baby is still alive."

The isolette sides are unlatched, the lid lifted, the heating coils deactivated and cold. The monitor screen is blank, a black slate. Nathanial is supine on a Chux. A marbled pattern creeps across his skin, a function of pooled, uncirculated blood. My thumbprint, a discolored indent on his sternum. I press his eyelids shut. Donning fresh gloves, I fill a plastic basin with tepid water, dampen a cotton sponge and wipe his face. I rinse the sponge in the basin and the water turns pink.

The privacy curtain around the isolette parts. "Let me," Robyn says. Her eyes red-rimmed and puffy, she steps between the curtains with a NICU memory box tucked under her arm. The box contains items, tangible proof to help a family remember their deceased baby. Setting the box on the counter, she tells me, "It's too soon. After what you went through." She puts on gloves. "Let me finish his bath."

I can't meet her gaze without crying. Staring at the basin of pink bathwater I say, "I'm his nurse. This is what I do." The importance of the bath and the memory box, a memento for Nathanial's parents and later for his twin sister, is a responsibility that I don't take lightly.

"You're my friend." Robyn wrings the cotton sponge. "We do this together. Or not at all."

Through my tearstained mask I say, "Thank you."

We finish bathing Nathanial and wrap him in a blanket and take his picture. Imprint his palms and feet with ink, creating a reminder for his parents, of their son's small, but perfect fingers and toes . He doesn't have hair, but if he did, I'd clip a strand and deposit it in an envelope. In calligraphy I record the date and time of his birth on his crib card, underneath I record his death. When the ink dries, I hand it to Robyn. She arranges the items in the box and secures the lid with blue satin ribbon.

I have a box at home, tied with pink, instead of blue, ribbon.

From the neighboring bedspace, Natalie grieves her brother. Her cry is stifled by her endotracheal tube but her ventilator squawks and her monitor alarms protest. Finally exhausted, she sleeps, and the room is quiet.

After my shift, at the scrub sink, I hear the night-shift nurses. "So unfair... A freak accident. Channel Six had a reporter on the scene. With pictures. Twisted car parts littered the highway. A shoe... might have been Jamie's sneaker."

My throat tightens. I walk past, wanting to plug my ears.

I need to find Olivia. To hold her and explain that her parents love her. I run past the NICU scrub sinks, cross the hall and into the Special Care Nursery. Olivia's spot is in the back, but her crib is shoved against the wall, the bare mattress sprayed with disinfectant. On the floor, under the rocking chair, I see a pink onesie.

The housekeeper exits the pod, dragging a soiled linen bag.

"Where is she?" I ask the housekeeper. I rescue the onesie; I recognize it as Olivia's.

"Who?" The housekeeper loads the bag onto his cart.

Behind me, I hear Glenda-The-Terrible nurse manager's voice. "Ms. Kaplan. Your shift ended at seven this evening."

I face Glenda. Her lab coat buttoned to her neck. I fold Olivia's shirt into my scrubs pocket. I ask, "Where is she?"

Glenda's black-framed glasses dangle around her neck on a beaded chain. She puts the glasses on, glances at her clipboard. "Losing one's parents at a young age is a tragedy."

I blink to stay tears.

"We're over census. Understaffed. The infant in question

no longer requires intensive care. The hospital has resources better suited to her needs."

"Where?" My voice cracks.

"I advise you, Ms. Kaplan, go home. Baby Dutton is well tended in the boarder nursery." Glenda does an about-face.

"The boarder nursery." My hands fist at my sides. Seething, I ask, "How could you send her there?"

Glenda's black heels ricochet down the hall like pistol fire.

CHAPTER SIX

Postpartum quiet hours begin after dinner and continue until six in the morning. Intended to promote rest, overhead fluorescent lights are dimmed, and track lights along the floor illuminate the hallway, but I doubt the new moms are asleep. Behind the closed doors babies wail and, in the background, televisions murmur. The carpet mutes my footfall.

Walking does little to cool my rage over Olivia's transfer to the boarder nursery. Jamie would be heartbroken if she knew that Olivia had been banished from the NICU, her home since birth. Nerves steeled, I open the door. The boarder nursery is lit by a fluorescent bulb in the ceiling, the glow fades by gradation, leaving the fifteen bassinets lining the three walls in near darkness. A shelving unit bolted to the back wall stores disposable diapers, formula bottles, boxed latex gloves and Purell dispensers.

Separate from the newborn nursery, where babies are cared for immediately following birth, the boarder nursery is a temporary space for infants who require care but don't qualify for intensive care in the NICU. Babies born to heroin-addicted mothers suffer withdrawal and often spend days or weeks in the boarder nursery until they can be weaned from medication. Treating, monitoring, and caring for addicted neonates requires staff and space. Resources that the hospital doesn't have.

Cecil, the patient care assistant, and a night-shift regular, is focused on changing a messy diaper. I'm accustomed to the sound of crying babies, not the shrill pitch of opioid withdrawal. Cecil deposits a rancid diaper in a lidded trash receptacle, snaps off his gloves and greets me. "Annabelle. Visiting from the NICU?"

I'm relieved that Cecil remembers me. "I'm here to see my patient, Olivia Dutton."

"Last in the third row. In the old-fashioned wooden number—we're low on supplies. Glenda raided the storage depot to find a bassinet." Cecil points. "Careful. The wheels are wonky." He returns to his duties and tends to the next infant in line.

Olivia is on her back, staring at the ceiling, cheeks dewy with recent tears.

I say, "Hi, baby Olivia," and gather her in my arms. Her crystal eyes are wet gems. I wrap her in a blanket and sit in a stiff-backed chair. There are no rocking chairs.

I tell Olivia about the accident. "Your parents love you. But accidents—they're part of life. That's why Mom and Dad can't take you home."

Olivia's brow wrinkles.

"Your mom and dad can't be here, but they're watching." Tears stream my cheeks, collect on my chin and drip onto Olivia's blanket. "You did nothing wrong." Olivia's feeding schedule is printed on memo paper and taped to her bassinet. Olivia's next bottle is due at 9pm, not for another thirty minutes, but judging from her tear-stained face, she's hungry. I tell Cecil I'll feed Olivia. He's happy for my help. I retrieve a bottle of Jamie's pumped breast milk. I'll need to ask Edwin how much of Jamie's milk remains in storage, she'd intended to provide breast milk for a year and Olivia has never had formula.

Olivia finishes the bottle and her eyes become drowsy. I lay her across my lap and pat her back. "I know that you miss your mom. I'm a lot older than you and I miss my mom every day." Olivia burps, and a warm blob soaks my scrubs pants.

An uncomfortable notion bubbles from my subconscious. Olivia is no longer attached to a monitor. Cecil, preoccupied with his high-need patients, pays her little mind. Her alarm anklet? I could disarm it from the computer. All I need is a car seat. Amazon delivers. My arms tingle with goosebumps. The very idea, stealing Olivia.

"No," I say.

Olivia jolts. I sit her up, pat her back again, eliciting a second burp and a milk dribble.

I put Olivia in her crib and sit in the chair. I rub my forehead, erasing my crazy fantasy. An outlandish notion. I'll page Fernanda tomorrow; the hospital social worker will find a solution for Olivia.

Olivia sleeps. I check my phone. Peter texts two emojis; a hospital and a sharp knife. He's operating. I want to tell him everything that's happened. My patient, Nathanial, died and most of all, I want to tell Peter about Jamie and Don. Parents that never took their daughter home from the hospital.

Sort of like us.

I answer Peter with a pink beating heart.

A door slams. Startled, my neck stiff from a night spent slouched in a chair, I straighten. The nursery is quiet. It's morning and I never went home. The babies, Olivia included, sleep.

Fernanda, the social worker, dressed in a navy-blue skirt and matching jacket, speaks to a man I've never seen before, but his black suit, narrow red necktie, and polished loafers peg him for a hospital administrator. The temperature in the boarder nursery room is uncomfortably warm.

The administrator says, "Insurance won't pay for intensive care. What options does the hospital have, given the situation?"

Fernanda says, "Ideally? Placement with a family member."

They're talking about Olivia. I strain to hear their conversation.

The administrator catches a whiff of soiled diapers, replaces his mask, and pinches the bridge of his nose. "Any prospects?"

"A maternal sister."

Jamie had a sister? News to me. She never mentioned her.

The administrator pales, unknots his red tie, and tugs his collar.

Fernanda says, "Good Samaritans keep phoning, asking after the baby's welfare. *The Inquirer* ran a piece, 'Orphan after Birth.' The local television news coverage of the highway crash is a tearjerker." Fernanda approaches Olivia's bassinet. The social worker's eyes brighten with surprise.

I imagine how I must look after a night in a chair, without a shower, my hair in a lopsided ponytail, wearing wrinkled, spit-up stained scrubs.

Administrator Man inches toward the door.

Fernanda says, "I'm meeting the maternal aunt in an hour. We have a court date to grant emergency guardianship."

"Keep me posted." The administrator opens the door and leaves.

Fernanda stands at Olivia's bassinet.

I force the question past the lump in my throat. "The aunt didn't know. Did she?"

"About Jamie and Don's accident? I told her late last night. Quite a shock."

"I mean about Olivia?"

"No. She wasn't aware that she's an aunt."

Fernanda checks her phone. "These things have a way of working out for the best." She leaves.

Worry for Olivia knots my stomach. This isn't what Jamie would want, leaving Olivia in the care of a family member who is a stranger. I need to speak to Fernanda in private. I stand, intending to find her office.

Olivia is awake. Her blue eyes track to my face. She coos, asking me to hold her.

"I won't leave. You're safe," I promise her. Despite my worry, I keep my voice light and lift Olivia from the bassinet. She swats a loose strand of my strawberry-blonde hair. I hold Olivia to my chest, her heart thrums with mine. My hair drapes her head, a protective tent. I sway. In cadence with a private symphony, a concert playing only for the two of us.

I'm off from work today and instead of going home, I remain with Olivia. She needs me more than ever. After a brief lunch break and an unsuccessful attempt to find Peter, who is occupied, I return to find the boarder nursery in an uproar. The shrill cries rattle my nerves.

I hear Olivia. Distinct and separate from the fray. She's in her bassinet, arms waving. A stranger struggles to wrap her with a blanket.

Fernanda sanitizes her hands. She directs the woman I've never seen before to abandon the blanket and sit in the chair, the same straight-backed chair that I'd sat in overnight. Fernanda, in her gentle social-worker voice, says to Olivia, "Quiet down. Meet your Aunt Darlene."

The stranger is Olivia's only living relative.

Fernanda attempts to roll the bassinet close to Aunt Darlene's chair.

"Watch out," I say from the doorway. But too late. The wonky wheel on Olivia's bassinet sticks and the off-track bassinet drawer opens, knocking Aunt Darlene's knee.

Olivia wails.

Aunt Darlene says, "Damn."

Fernanda apologizes.

Olivia is suddenly silent.

Fernanda says, "No harm done. Perhaps you'd like to practice feeding your niece?" Fernanda puts on latex gloves, lifts Olivia, and deposits her in Aunt Darlene's lap.

My feet feel cast in cement. Can this burly stranger be Jamie's, obviously older, sister? They look nothing alike. Unlike delicate Jamie, Aunt Darlene is stocky, thick-waisted, with beefy hands. Jamie was blonde but Darlene's chin-length hair, the color of raked autumn leaves, is imprecisely parted and falls over her eyes.

Aunt Darlene says, "What do I feed the baby with?"

Fernanda grabs a ready-to-feed formula bottle from the shelf. "Formula."

"No." I force my legs to move. "Olivia takes mother's milk."

Lower lip quivering, Olivia tracks to my voice.

Fernanda sets the formula on the counter. Fists on her hips, her brow knits. "Well... that complicates..."

I retrieve Jamie's breast milk from the fridge and tell Fernanda, "Warming a bottle takes a minute."

Fernanda utilizes the time to instruct Aunt Darlene. The social worker flips through documents on her clipboard, pauses and aims her pen at the spots requiring a signature. Aunt Darlene squints like she forgot her glasses.

Fernanda tells Aunt Darlene, "The State is behind—three weeks until your first foster-care check. The Administration for

Children and Families will be in touch, but not tomorrow, they're swamped. Expect a minimum of three days before a case worker reaches out. But you have the essentials. Olivia has a new car seat, and she passed her car-seat trial with flying colors. So, no worries about driving her home."

Aunt Darlene signs the document. Doubt seeds my gut.

Fernanda passes a business card to Aunt Darlene. She shoves the card into the pocket of the red apron tied around her waist.

"Olivia is all yours, but if you need anything, you have my number."

I get the feeling that Fernanda hopes Aunt Darlene will lose her phone number.

Fernanda taps her clipboard. "Everything is in order."

I bite my lower lip to keep from shouting, *No. Everything is very much out of order.*

"Annabelle?" Fernanda taps her pen against the clipboard. "The bottle?"

I force an answer. "Right here. Olivia's bottle. Jamie's milk is ready."

Darlene faces me and asks, "Are you my niece's baby nurse?"

Fernanda answers, "Annabelle Kaplan is a NICU nurse."

I'm close enough to smell Aunt Darlene through my mask. Cooking oil and fried food. Aunt Darlene takes the bottle with both hands and Olivia tumbles from Aunt Darlene's lap. "I got her." Except she hasn't.

I have her.

Darlene fists a blue-and-white hospital blanket.

I press Olivia to me. Her heart flutters against my chest. Her scalp smells sour: she's missed a shampoo. I pat her and tell her, "You're safe." But it's all I can do not to choke on the lie.

Aunt Darlene says, "Give her here. We need to get on our

way." Aunt Darlene is all business. She rolls her white button-down shirtsleeves to her elbows exposing a tattoo. A black ink cherub, slinging a bow. She repeats, "Give her here."

Because I have no choice, I give Olivia to Aunt Darlene. The red tattooed arrowhead is aimed directly at Olivia.

My arms ache from emptiness. A sensation I recognize. I had that identical whole-body hollowness the night my baby died. The boarder nursery door opens. The suit-wearing hospital administrator enters. "Where's the new auntie? Congratulations," he says.

I leave before the door swings shut. My empty arms swing at my sides, matching my brisk stride. The hurt in my heart dissipates, replaced by an undeniable call to action.

CHAPTER SEVEN

In the hospital lobby a security guard inspects Aunt Darlene's paperwork. The guard verifies Olivia's name band, checks her ankle, the security sensor has been removed. Moments later, Aunt Darlene exits the hospital with Olivia strapped in her car seat. Aunt Darlene carries a hospital bag with diapers, wipes, and a portable cooler packed with Jamie's breast milk. In her opposite hand she clutches Olivia's car-seat handle. It's baby Olivia's first time outside, I'd give anything to gauge her reaction. But I lag a safe distance behind, imagining Olivia's eyes wide with wonder at the expanse of sky. Except the world is dull, grey, and damp with drizzle.

I expect Aunt Darlene to walk to the visitor lot but, surprise, she's finagled a spot in employee parking. She unlocks a blue Nissan, a row from my Jetta.

Head bowed, I linger at a black Toyota RAV4, pretending to search for my keys. Aunt Darlene snaps Olivia's car seat in the back seat and tosses the plastic diaper bag and cooler beside Olivia. Aunt Darlene's cell phone rings. She answers it, shuts the rear door, and gets into the driver seat. I can't hear her conversation. The Nissan reverses and exits the lot.

The Jetta starts first try and I'm directly behind Aunt Darlene's Nissan, close enough to read the bumper sticker: *I brake at The Rusty Sub Tavern*. Other than the bumper sticker, Aunt Darlene's Nissan is nondescript. Not fresh-from-the dealership, but newer than my, or rather Mom's, Jetta.

I don't have a plan. My next shift isn't until tomorrow. My sole agenda is to make certain that Olivia is safe. If that requires an afternoon weaving in and out of traffic, one car length behind the blue Nissan, so be it. At this time, I can't predict that the sequence of events will alter my life, risk Peter's career, and change Olivia's future. Later, my motivation will be dissected down to incremental seconds. My state of mind will be called into question. *"Was your judgement impaired by sleep deprivation?"*

I'll be grilled. "Did Ms. Cobb's driving concern you?" Aunt Darlene is a decent driver. She stops for red lights. The fact that I manage to follow proves she obeys posted speed limits.

I attest that my only concern is and always has been for Olivia's safety. I wipe my sweaty palms on my scrubs and secure a grip on the steering wheel. A glimpse of Olivia is all I desire. If she is safe and happy, then I will backtrack. I promise. I'll go home. After twenty minutes, the Nissan slows, the rear blinker signals right, the car cuts sharply into a one-way alley. I hesitate. What if Aunt Darlene noticed me tailing, lures me onto a side street with plans to confront me? My heart lurches. I maneuver the right turn and brake, facing a red *Wrong Way* sign. I've lost sight of the Nissan.

But the blue Nissan idles on a gravel lot behind The Rusty Sub Tavern, in a space marked with a hand-painted sign, *Employee Parking*. The Tavern's entrance faces the street. The rear lot is vacant except for an old model minivan, a dumpster, and a plastic recycling bin overflowing with crushed beer cans.

I release the breath I've held. Before I can absorb the fact that Aunt Darlene has taken her sister's sweet baby to a bar, the pub's screen door opens. A man wearing a white cook's uniform stands in the doorway and tosses a plastic garbage bag into the dumpster. The bag thuds on landing.

The Nissan's engine stills, the driver side window lowers, and Aunt Darlene waves. The cook returns the greeting. Aunt Darlene gets out, leans against her car and they converse. The man pulls a pack of cigarettes from his pocket and offers one. Aunt Darlene shakes her head.

I lean forward, chest braced against the steering wheel, unable to hear anything except my hammering heart. I watch, afraid to blink, waiting for Aunt Darlene to take Olivia from her car seat and carry her into The Rusty Sub Tavern. When she does, I'll grab my phone, take a picture, and tell her—what? That I was driving by—and happened to notice—but Aunt Darlene doesn't take Olivia into The Rusty Sub Tavern.

Aunt Darlene shuts the car door.

Something smacks my forehead. The locket that Jamie gave me containing Olivia's hair hangs on a cord from the rearview mirror. I take it and hold the locket in my palm, bring it to my lips and I promise Jamie, "I won't let Olivia out of my sight. I'm here for as long as she needs me." I slip the leather cord over my head and the locket dangles over my sternum.

The NICU is miles away but I'm a nurse. Protecting Olivia is my job. I guard Olivia in the blue Nissan with the same vigilance that I had monitored her heart rate and temperature in the NICU. I can't drive away, not until I'm certain that she is safe.

Gravel crunches. Aunt Darlene follows the cook. The screen door claps, and the pair disappear inside The Rusty Sub Tavern.

Olivia is alone.

The risks to Olivia are numerous. She might be sleeping

now, but when she wakes, she'll be frightened. Excessive crying will leave her breathless and apneic. If she vomits, a result of motion sickness from her first car ride, she might aspirate. Exposure to extreme heat or cold is deadly to a fragile infant. Most unnerving of all? I imagine a stranger roaming the alley, stealing Olivia from Aunt Darlene's car.

Heart hammering, I spring from the Jetta. I cross the one-way alley, scrubs pants swishing, a spray of gravel beneath my Converse. I run to the blue Nissan as if it's an isolette and I am responding to an alarm in the NICU. I call to Olivia, "I'm here."

I hear Olivia cry, muffled inside the car. I recognize the unique timbre of her wail. She's afraid.

"Olivia," I yell. "I'm here." A pebble lodges in my Converse and stabs my instep. Limping, I reach the Nissan. Olivia is in her car seat, flushed and tearstained.

I tap the glass and say, "Don't cry." Olivia's eyes widen with shock. She's never seen me mask-less. A heartbeat later her mouth opens in a hard shriek. But what she does next empowers me, erases any doubt over my immediate actions. Olivia lifts her arms in my direction, her fists open, fingers splay, asking me to hold her.

The car is unlocked. The key is in the ignition, on a Rusty Sub Tavern keychain that doubles as a bottle opener. Relief that I've found Olivia turns to anger at Aunt Darlene. I tell Olivia, "You're safe." Fingers trembling from adrenaline, I release the car-seat harness, freeing Olivia. She clings to me, hands fisting my hair, her head burrowed under my chin. I sway to soothe her, hug her close. She smells like perspiration. And my lips brush the crown of her head, an accident.

But on purpose, I press my lips to each of her cheeks, taste her salty tears. Alone in the parking lot, with no one to stop me, I kiss Olivia's nose, her delicate chin and finally her forehead.

Olivia whimpers, trembles, and settles.

I formulate a plan.

First: calm Olivia. Second: secure Olivia in her car seat. Third: wait in the Nissan for Aunt Darlene to return.

That's not what I do. Blame the weather.

The sky is woolly, blotting any hope of sunshine. A damp wind swirls through the parking lot, rattling the crushed cans in the recycling bin. The spit of drizzle transitions to rain. Olivia blinks, droplets gather on her pale lashes.

She's never experienced rain. "Water from the sky," I tell her.

There's no sign of Aunt Darlene. The door to The Rusty Sub Tavern is shut. I duck into the Nissan to avoid the rain but there's not much space. I attempt to return Olivia to the safety seat. Except she won't go. She protests, yanks a strand of my hair in her fist.

"Ouch," I yelp.

Olivia starts, gasps, and cries louder.

"I'm sorry, baby Olivia," I say. My voice is shaky, not comforting. I'm cold—the rain, blowing sideways, soaks the half of my body outside the Nissan. How long can I wait in the rain for Aunt Darlene? I try again to coax Olivia into her car seat. She arches her back.

My three-part plan, so simple a moment ago, flops.

I consider confronting Aunt Darlene. But entering The Rusty Sub Tavern with Olivia in my arms? I'll be mistaken for a kidnapper. For the same reason, I dismiss summoning the police. I consider phoning The Rusty Sub Tavern, asking to speak to—Aunt Darlene.

I pat my scrubs top pocket for my phone. The pocket is empty. My phone is missing, left in the Jetta in my hurry to rescue Olivia. Holding Olivia on my lap, I sit on the narrow edge of the back seat with the door ajar. Olivia is inconsolable. I scootch to the middle, dislodge the car-seat base, close the door, and stretch my legs. No more wind. But without fresh air, I smell the car. Aunt Darlene's Nissan smells like stale beer. Under my Converse, there's an aluminum can. Pabst Blue Ribbon. Empty. Drinking while driving is a crime.

Olivia is quiet. Her head on my chest, comforted, I imagine by my thumping heart. What I see next causes tachycardia. A second can, Bud Light, empty, and dented, lodged under the front seat. Had Aunt Darlene been drinking beer after picking her niece up from the hospital?

Olivia is calm, her breath steady. She releases my hair. But in her fist is the locket Jamie gifted me. I stroke Olivia's silky ginger hair, nearly strawberry, like my hair. I know what I must do. I clutch Olivia tight. Again, because I can, I kiss her crown. "I promise to keep you safe. We'll teach Aunt Darlene a lesson."

The hospital diaper bag and the cooler containing Jamie's breast milk fit into the car seat. I exit the Nissan with Olivia pressed against my chest and her car seat containing her belongings slung over my free arm. I close the Nissan door, walk across the lot, and cross the one-way alley to the Jetta.

Olivia clings to me, wide-eyed, but she doesn't cry. Fitting the car seat with its base into the Jetta's back seat isn't easy. Imagine what Aunt Darlene must think if she can see me? Is she watching? But Aunt Darlene doesn't deserve Olivia. At least not until Aunt Darlene learns to cherish her sister's baby. I had planned to return Olivia to Aunt Darlene on the condition that she's sober. Except that's not how my plan played out.

I say to Olivia, "Your mommy's heart would break if she knew. Aunt Darlene should never have left you alone. I'm going to figure things out. Please, sit in your seat."

Olivia softens into the car seat. Her fingers release the locket around my neck. I prop Olivia's head with a folded receiving blanket. Her eyes, puffy from crying, close. She's instantly asleep.

Suddenly, I'm tired. I'd napped, not slept, in the boarder nursery's hard-backed chair. My head throbs, my thoughts muddle. I sit in the driver's seat and turn the ignition. The Jetta engine whines. Rain drums the roof, douses the windshield, and the wipers swoosh. I lean against the steering wheel, fixated on the Nissan, eyes stinging from exhaustion. I remove the locket from my neck and suspend the cord from the rearview mirror. Condensation fogs the windshield.

I rehearse what I will say to Aunt Darlene when she emerges from The Rusty Sub Tavern. My anger diffuses. Self-doubt tarnishes my polished self-righteousness. Had I overreacted and judged Aunt Darlene too harshly? Maybe there's a rational explanation for the beer cans, and for leaving Olivia in the car.

My phone is in the cupholder. There's one person who will understand my need to protect Olivia. One friend who won't judge but listen. Talking to my best friend is exactly what I need. I thumb my autodial. "Sheila?"

The screen is black, the battery dead. I find the charger in the glove box. It stopped working, even after I'd wrapped the frayed cord in white medical tape. I try anyway. But it's useless. For all my online shopping, why didn't I purchase something useful: a spare charger?

Behind me, Olivia stirs, whimpers and starts awake. Maybe it's the unfamiliar environment but she's not happy. I reach over the seat, touch her cheek. She's warm. "You're safe," I tell her.

But Olivia is worked up, her sobs interspersed by hiccups.

I face forward. The locket knocks my forehead. I know what to do. Drive. Until Olivia is calm. If Aunt Darlene emerges, all the better. She abandoned her niece in a parking lot, without bothering to check on her. Let Aunt Darlene think she lost Olivia, maybe then she'll realize her mistake and value her. *Loss brings out the best or the worst in people.* Isn't that what Mom said? Let's find out what Aunt Darlene is all about.

Rain puddles the Rusty Sub lot. I drive slowly in case the screen door opens. I want to judge Aunt Darlene's reaction to discovering her blue Nissan empty.

Olivia howls.

I circle the Tavern and turn onto the alley. "What do I do now?" I say out loud.

No one answers. *Wrong Way,* the sign reads.

This time I don't park.

Olivia is suddenly quiet, save for a hiccup. Foot on the accelerator, I drive. At the end of the wrong-way alley, I angle the rearview mirror so I can see Olivia's ginger crown in her seat. I hear her suck her thumb.

The Rusty Sub Tavern fades from sight. About ten minutes pass, we've gone a few miles on Lancaster Avenue, a Philadelphia police car speeds in a fit of whirling red light. Bile rises from my stomach. Tears prickle my eyes. Aunt Darlene reported Olivia missing.

I'm a kidnapper.

I tap-tap-tap the brake, five-miles-below the speed limit. The police cruiser flashes red and blue on the side of the road, stopped behind a white sedan. The officer in black rain gear issues a ticket.

I tune the radio to a local station, bite my lip, anticipating an "Amber Alert". But the reporter drones about the rainstorm, nothing as newsworthy as a stolen baby. The wipers whisk the windshield. I drive. "Slow but not too slow," I tell Olivia, "or we'll arouse suspicion." But we don't see any black-and-white police sedans, no red-and-blue spinning lights. I'm possessed with fear. Not a global fear, like being arrested by a policeperson but a subtle personal realization, remarkable because it is completely novel: I've never chauffeured a baby.

The responsibility for Olivia's safety is a heavy weight that I square my shoulders to carry. I meld with traffic, obey posted speed limits. I'm an ordinary woman. A nurse. A mom with a child in the back seat.

I practice saying, "Olivia is mine."

Louder, with conviction I shout, "She's my baby."

I'm almost convinced.

ACT TWO

Every nurse was drawn to nursing because of a desire to care, to serve, or to help.

— Christina Feist-Heilmeier, RN

CHAPTER EIGHT

Olivia is hungry. It's seven in the evening, an hour past her usual bottle, and she won't let me forget it. Her cry drowns the swishing wipers. In the rearview mirror all I see is her ginger-haired crown and a pair of miniature fists punching air.

A car horn blasts. Tires squeal. I veered over the double-yellow line.

I'm startled back on course. Normally I'd wave an apology to the offended driver, but the last thing I want is to attract attention. The angry driver dashes past. Condensation fogs the windows, but I avoid activating the Jetta's defrost function, preferring to keep both of us concealed. I'm five miles under the posted speed limit. And I drive without a destination.

I toggle between radio stations for local news. Fifteen minutes elapse and no Amber Alert. Aunt Darlene must have notified the police—unless she hasn't noticed Olivia, the baby entrusted in her care, is missing?

"Let's try music," I tell Olivia.

I tune to NPR Classical, a violin concerto by Johann Strauss. "You can learn violin," I tell Olivia.

Olivia's cry escalates to an ear-splitting decibel.

"The Suzuki method trains two-year-olds, along with a parent. Fun. Right?"

NPR features a violin pizzicato or string plucking which, accompanied by Olivia's screech, rubs my nerves raw. I turn the radio off. Rain patters. Wipers whoosh. I trace a circle with a tissue on the windshield and activate the defrost.

"Red means stop," I tell Olivia. I brake.

Olivia burps. And is suddenly quiet.

A warning light on the dashboard flashes yellow. The fuel needle hovers perilously on "E." I need gas. Why hadn't I paid attention to the gas gauge? Somehow, I've associated the fuel gauge with the Jetta's stubborn odometer, stuck on eighty thousand miles. But I can't risk stopping. Service stations have surveillance cameras and how would I explain the video? Me, in my hospital scrubs, at a gas station, with Olivia, a missing baby, in the back seat.

The traffic light turns green.

"What do I do? Where do I go?"

Even if I knew how far I could drive on the reserve tank, tracking distance is impossible. An empty tank limits my options. Miscalculate a mile and I'll be stranded roadside with Olivia. We'll attract the police and a nosy rubbernecker's cellphone video will be broadcast on the news.

Olivia sneezes.

Peter will know what to do. He never runs out of gas. Because he fills the Subaru's tank weekly. Call Peter. Desperate for his voice, I grab my phone, hoping for a miracle that the battery eked power from the limp cord. But nothing. No charge. The battery is spent, like the Jetta's gas tank. I disconnect the phone and toss the cord under the seat.

I'm on my own.

Driving to Lakeview Hospital is too far. Besides, the hospital betrayed baby Olivia. Glenda-The-Terrible moved

Olivia from her familiar NICU crib to the boarder nursery. Fernanda, the social worker, doesn't know the truth about Aunt Darlene—not like I do. Lakeview Hospital's administrator was too eager to give Olivia to Aunt Darlene who doesn't love her and abandoned her in a car behind The Rusty Sub Tavern.

I imagine Glenda's frown, terrible enough to melt her surgical mask, when she finds out I took—rescued—Olivia from Aunt Darlene's Nissan.

The car behind me honks. The traffic light is green. The locket containing Olivia's hair twirls from the rearview mirror. I untwist the leather cord. From inside the opaque box, Olivia's ginger strands glow, an iridescent compass. Olivia, my *true north*.

The car at my bumper honks three times.

I signal left, sit tall behind the wheel, toe the accelerator, and wave to the impatient driver. "Green means GO," I tell Olivia.

There's a sucking sound from the back seat. Olivia has found her thumb, a temporary reprieve. My thoughts gel. "Don't worry," I tell her, "I have a plan. You'll like it. Dinner is included."

Self-doubt recedes by gradation. My ribcage relaxes, permitting an inhale and a complete exhale. I loosen my grip on the steering wheel and flex my fingers. My wedding ring glints. Peter. I'll explain all of this to him—but not just yet.

I enter Radcliff Apartments and the dashboard fuel icon transitions from yellow to red. The Jetta digests its final sip of gas, and the engine emits a death rattle. I maneuver toward Mom's handicap space, which I need like never before. Except a green pickup truck with a dented fender hogs the spot that belonged to Mom and by default to me. The truck is the official Radcliff Apartment maintenance vehicle. What if Mom had returned from the market? The image of her struggling to carry her reusable grocery bag, limping across the parking lot infuriates me. Then I remember. Mom is dead.

Olivia cries, no longer placated by her thumb. I regret judging mothers I've seen in the stores, stoppering their crying infant with a pacifier, not recommended by Lakeview Hospital's lactation consultant for breastfed babies like Olivia. Except a pacifier would come in handy, to enter Mom's apartment unnoticed, I need Olivia quiet. I wonder if there's a pacifier tucked inside Aunt Darlene's diaper bag. My stomach cramps. Aunt Darlene. She's probably frantic. I should have left an anonymous note inside her Nissan reassuring her that Olivia is safe.

The Philadelphia police force must be combing the neighborhood around The Rusty Sub Tavern. Or worse, maybe Aunt Darlene saw me and is seeking revenge, the arrow tattoo quivering on her muscled forearm.

There's no option except visitor parking, and I coax the Jetta to an open spot and the engine quits. I sling the diaper bag and the breast-milk cooler on my forearm and with the apartment key between my fingers, unsnap Olivia's safety harness. Her blonde eyelashes, dark with tears, send my heart tumbling in my chest. I say to her, "I didn't forget. Feeding you is top priority, as soon as we get inside."

I carry Olivia and leave the car seat in the Jetta. With only dusk for cover, we cross the lot. Olivia is not too tired or hungry to survey her surroundings. Her head lifts from my shoulder, her lashes flutter against my cheek. Olivia absorbs the evening breeze, the smell of recent rain on the pavement. Her curiosity is a positive developmental sign. I say, "Look, Olivia, a green truck." I crinkle my nose at the odor of exhaust fumes.

The key fits, jiggles, but the lock doesn't turn. The lamplight is weak, and I verify, K2, Mom's, not a neighbor's apartment. I see it then, tacked to the frame: *Notice of Eviction* embossed with a circular notary seal, the superintendent's signature on the citation's final line. My recent payment, Mom's pension check, didn't cover what I owe. The rent remains in arrears.

The lock has been changed, the key between my fingers useless. Olivia reaches for the key, a choking hazard, and I pocket it. Mom's apartment, my safe harbor, inaccessible. The last of my energy along with my hope for a peaceful night with baby Olivia, drains. I lean against the door, my arm numb from clutching Olivia. She cries for a bottle. I too want to cry. I would give anything to have Mom here tonight, in her apartment. She'd understand why I had to take Olivia. With Mom gone, there is no one who'll listen, no one to help. Hot tears prick my eyes.

Behind the door, I hear a thud. Someone is inside Mom's apartment.

I say, "Open up." I knock.

Footfalls.

"Let me in. This is my apartment." I knock again, louder, not caring if I bother the neighbors.

The deadbolt slips. The door opens. A tall man wearing coveralls stands in the doorway. His baseball cap shades his face, but his smile is huge. His voice booms, "Genie, it can't be."

His smile disappears. "Can't be. Of course. But no hurt in hoping for miracles." He steps back.

I enter. Avoiding the red metal toolbox and scattered tools on the carpet. There's a can of Febreze and a folded newspaper on the coffee table. On closer inspection the custodian's name is embroidered in faded thread on his coveralls. *Marcus*.

He touches the bill of his painter's cap in greeting. "Pardon me. The resemblance—now I know how Genie Gold looked when she was a young woman." Marcus's shoulders droop.

"I'm Annabelle." I flick the wall switch. The corner floor lamp floods the room with white light.

"The baby nurse at Lakeview Hospital. Your mother bragged about you saving tiny lives. Babies the world forgot…" He studies Olivia. "Hello, Little One."

Olivia is hysterical, fists waving, mouth gaping, demanding to be fed.

Marcus steps close enough that I smell turpentine.

The diaper bag and the cooler slip from my shoulder and land beside the toolbox.

The custodian holds out his hands, his fingernails stained with black grease. "Marcus, at your service. Help is what I do." Marcus grabs the cooler and the diaper bag and sets the bags on the coffee table. The glass gleams, polished streak-free.

I should thank Marcus. But the simple words stick in my mouth.

Marcus kneels and collects his scattered tools; a screwdriver, hammer, the wooden handle wrapped with black electrical tape. Nails and fasteners cover the bottom of the box like loose change. Conspicuous, a doorknob. Marcus changed the lock.

Exhausted, I sit on the loveseat. The glass-topped coffee table mirrors my reflection. The woman in the table is knotty-haired, her face dotted with freckles. Olivia stops crying and fixates on Marcus and his toolbox.

Marcus polishes a needle-nose plyer with a handkerchief, replaces the tool, pockets the cloth. He snaps his toolbox shut, the metallic clang like a gunshot. "Scared you, did I?"

I blink back tears. I want to ask about the lock.

Marcus stands, lifts his toolbox, and I think he will leave, and hopefully let me stay with Olivia in the apartment for the night. Instead, Marcus settles onto the upholstered chair. A giant on dolls' house furniture. He picks at the chair's mint-green piping with his thumb, crosses his ankles, and his work boots have soles as smooth as bald tires. There is a nickel-sized hole on the left sole revealing his blue wool sock.

He's thin, but too muscular to be called lanky. He's older than I am, but younger than Dr. Cumberland. Marcus studies Olivia with intensity. He says, "How many months did you say your little one is?"

I don't answer. And I avoid his gaze.

Marcus's voice is low as if he's talking to himself. "For all Genie's bragging about her daughter being a baby nurse, she never mentioned you were expecting." His smile is sad. "Secrets. No matter how close we think we are to someone, there's always something more to learn."

Curiosity ripples through me. The custodian knew Mom?

"Friends—" Marcus adds quickly, noticing the look on my face. "Not that I—" There's a pink undertone to his brown cheeks. "Genie would have loved being called Grandma."

"Bubbie, she wanted to be a Bubbie," I say quietly. Yiddish for grandmother.

"Genie loved this place. I'd stop by in the morning on the way back from filling the gas cans, bring her a coffee, even though she has one of those fancy machines—Genie acted surprised, asking 'for me?'" His eyes are faraway, like he's watching a favorite television rerun. "Oh, and Genie could cook. Everything homemade. Her cookies? Perfect triangles."

"Hamantaschen." Mom never mentioned Marcus. But she baked for him. They must have been close.

"We'd drink coffee. Talk about whatever news hit the front page of the morning paper. But then with Covid our routine changed. I still brought her coffee, left it at her door. She liked that. Most mornings she had a brown bag waiting for me. But then she got sick. I had no idea how she got it—the virus. Happened fast. Since reading her obituary in *The Inquirer*, I waited for her family to empty the unit. But months passed and no one new moved in. So, I took the liberty of popping in every few days. Vacuum. Prune that ficus of hers. Mist it like she did. I figured whoever was paying the rent would eventually collect her belongings."

No wonder the tree stays perpetually green, the soil never dry. And this explains the vacuum tracks across the carpet, and the faucet that stopped dripping. It dawns on me then. I wasn't the only one using Mom's apartment as a reprieve from the world, taking comfort in Mom's memories. "I would keep paying —but I'm out of cash." I retrieve the useless key from my scrubs pocket and set it on the coffee table. I pat Olivia's back. She resumes her hungry cry.

Marcus's brown eyes focus on Olivia, his voice forgiving. "Ah. I get it. The lock? Not my idea. Blame the Super. But least I can do is get you boxes and help pack."

"I, we're not here to pack—not tonight."

"Leave the superintendent to me."

I exhale and take a chance. "Just for tonight, if it won't be too much trouble."

"Nothing is too much trouble to fix." Marcus stands, collects his toolbox and the newspaper from the coffee table, tucks it under his arm, and adds, "I dare say Genie would be angry with me if she knew that I locked her daughter and grandbaby outside."

I manage to thank Marcus, but the words feel trite.

The door closes. Olivia and I, at last, are safe. Olivia guzzles ninety milliliters, three ounces of Jamie's breast milk. There's no crib in the apartment. I improvise, pushing Mom's double bed against the wall and remove the pillows. Olivia hasn't learned to roll yet, but the potential for a baby to fall is an ever-present danger.

I kiss Olivia's forehead. She's on her back. I settle beside her, listening, Olivia's breath a steady tide. Her eyelids flutter, a sign of deep sleep. I whisper into Olivia's ear, "Jamie, if you're here, inside your daughter's dreams, know that I'm doing the best that I can to keep Olivia safe. I won't disappoint you."

Tears rain, warm and purifying.

"Goodnight, Jamie," I say. "Goodnight, Olivia." I kiss Olivia a second and third time.

A baby can never be loved too much.

CHAPTER NINE

Olivia stretches, arms starfished as if the mattress were a mile-wide beach. I smooth a spray of fine ginger hair from her forehead. My phone, fully charged overnight, erupts on the nightstand. I cringe, silence the ringer, but I need not worry about disturbing Olivia; accustomed to the NICU's beeping medication pumps, and whistling alarms, she sleeps unperturbed.

Peter's text, a series of emojis: a hospital, a doctor's bag, and the final emoji, a baby, sets me on edge. He can't know, can he? I contemplate how to respond but the phone ring-vibrates. I answer, "Hello?"

Peter blurts, "I want to tell you myself, before you hear the news from one of the junior residents—hold on." Peter deals with an interruption.

"Belle?"

"I'm here." Beside me, Olivia's lips pucker.

Peter gushes, "Cumberland is getting up in years. His back spasmed after delivering a breech last night."

Uncertain how best to respond, I muster a sympathetic, "Oh no."

"Hold on a second," I hear Peter say, "I'll be there. I'm talking to my wife."

My heart expands with love for my husband. I want nothing but to share Olivia with him. "Peter? I have news."

Then a shiver crawls down my spine. Peter loves me today, but he won't when he learns what I did yesterday.

"I called to tell you—I'm in charge. Practically running Cumberland's practice." A hospital-wide page makes it difficult to hear. But Peter's voice rises with excitement. He is jubilant. "Our time is near. Webster is too proud to admit it, but he needs to retire. His patients have been with him for a generation," Peter says. "Now it's up to me to deliver the next generation."

The gist is clear. I don't know Dr. Cumberland's exact age, but geriatric describes him nicely. Peter is shouldering the practice, temporarily. If all goes smoothly, Peter is assured a position with Cumberland as a full—not junior—partner. I imagine Peter as a little boy, decades before we met, being served a double ice-cream cone, and then being offered rainbow sprinkles on top.

Nothing stands in the way of my husband's career. Except for me. My overdue Visa bill, unpaid rent on Mom's apartment, my unwritten master's thesis.

Olivia hiccups.

And the baby that I kidnapped.

I choke on regret. I took Olivia from Aunt Darlene's car without considering the consequences to Peter and the harm harboring baby Olivia will do to his career. Married to a kidnapper, his reputation will be destroyed. I hear Peter walk; his scrubs swoosh and his bootie-covered tennis shoes pad the hospital corridor. "Three months left of fellowship. My research is going well. How soon until you defend your thesis?"

Olivia wakes with a sharp cry.

"Sounds like the nursery," Peter says. "You're on nights, right? Catch you this evening at the hospital."

I pat Olivia's tummy. Fully awake, her untroubled gaze is as blue as a June sky.

"Belle, I can't do this without you." Peter's pager erupts in a burst of staccato beeps. The call drops. But what Peter said resonates. It reminds me. Work. Tonight.

Olivia sucks her lower lip. I prepare Jamie's breast milk, thaw, and warm a bottle the old-fashioned way. No fancy electric, automated, hospital bottle warmers. Propping the bottle in an ordinary basin of hot tap water suffices. I guestimate the temperature, a single drop on my wrist is all I spare. Jamie's milk is too precious to waste. I tell Olivia, "Breakfast time. But first a new diaper."

Olivia's smile is all pink gums.

She nuzzles my chest, rooting. An infant nursing reflex. Milk wets my bra. I never fed my baby, but the leaking proves I'm more than Olivia's babysitter. We have a physical connection. Olivia trusts me.

I open the floral-covered journal, although not for the purpose that my Zoom therapist, Janice, intended. I never got around to recording my feelings. The lined pages are blank. However, the journal is exactly what I need to do the math. Olivia remains on her NICU-prescribed feeding schedule, consuming ninety milliliters, every three hours, eight times in twenty-four hours. I multiply. That's 720 milliliters or twenty-four ounces. Naturally, that's the minimum. Olivia will likely want to drink more.

I make an inventory of Jamie's pumped breast milk. The bottles are labeled in Jamie's block lettering with the date and time she'd produced the milk. Twenty ounces remain. Six feeds. Olivia and I are on borrowed time. I record the inventory in the journal, underneath the multiplication and a reminder not to waste a precious drop. "Breast milk dwindling. Olivia has never had formula."

I steward the bottles from the cooler to the freezer, a frosty cloud escaping. I shut the freezer. Goosebumps prickle my arms. The limited supply feels like a message from Jamie. She hadn't known her milk would feed Olivia after her own death. *You can't keep Olivia forever, any more than I could.*

I brainstorm solutions:

>*Olivia's Feeding Problem.*
>*1. Purchase Infant Formula at Target (camera in store a downside).*
>*2. Order Formula on Amazon (delivery at home traceable, a negative).*
>*3. Feed Olivia—*

A chill travels down my spine. I don't dare write it. *No*, I tell myself. *No.*

>*3. Check with Edwin (Best option, I work tonight).*

I circle that plan.

I outline a care plan for Olivia, using Mom's collection of calligraphy pens, headings for feeding, diaper changes, naps, baths, and enrichment activities like reading and music.

On the next page:

>*Plan to Return Olivia.*

My hand cramps. Anticipating our separation hurts. A full-body ache like having the flu. Returning Olivia will open the hole behind my heart. I know that unique agony. A pain not taught in nursing school and certainly it's not indexed in an anatomy textbook. The space is uniquely maternal, it's where mothers grieve loss.

I close the notebook. Olivia is on my lap and swats the pen.

I tell her, "We'll exercise your fine motor skills and one day you'll be ready to hold a pen." My cursive is surprisingly legible —for a nurse—thanks to Mom. Each June, Mom bid her students farewell and the army sent Dad to a distant duty station, so I enjoyed Mom's undivided attention. One summer she taught me calligraphy art. The process proved painstaking, I'm left-handed and prone to smearing wet ink across the paper with my hand. But I persisted. When school began in the fall, Mom surprised me with my own set of pens, an art form I'd hoped to pass on to my own child. I ask Olivia, "Are you destined to be left- or right-handed?"

I move the coffee table against the loveseat, spread a blanket over the carpet. I put Olivia on her back and bicycle her legs. She's focused on vocalizing, amused by her own giddy squeals.

What if a neighbor in the next unit reports hearing an unfamiliar noise? I'd lowered the window blinds, but depriving Olivia of natural sunlight is not ideal. Olivia's chin quivers, warning her mood is shifting. I lift her onto my lap before she cries, and I change her wet diaper. Along with breast milk, diapers from Aunt Darlene's hospital bag are in short supply. Rationing diapers, wipes, mother's milk, while confined to a sunless apartment is not the ideal life Olivia deserves.

I reposition Olivia, prone this time. She face-plants, unfamiliar with tummy-time. Lacking upper body strength and coordination is common for preemies. I turn her cheek to the side, flex her arms, unfist her fingers, and coax her palms beneath her shoulders. Olivia wails, ending our exercise session. I jot in my journal:

Add bright-colored object to reach for.

Olivia needs stimulating toys. I rifle through Mom's kitchen drawer, find a set of plastic measuring spoons, and jingle them. Olivia's eyes widen with curiosity. She reaches for the ring, and the tablespoon and teaspoon clink. Olivia smiles.

I note the measuring spoons in the journal, in the toy column. I record Olivia's wet and stool diapers. Encapsulated in Mom's apartment, our day escapes. I snack on the food in the cabinet. Feed Olivia. We nap, play and too soon, I need to change into the scrubs I'd laundered in Mom's stacked washer-dryer.

There's a thump at the door. I clutch Olivia.

The knocking persists.

Olivia cries.

"Shush," I tell her. My heart pounds.

"Open up," a baritone voice from behind the door says.

Olivia hiccups.

"Hush," I say. What if an overnight Amber Alert blanketed the news and the police are searching the apartment complex for Olivia? Now it's too late. My opportunity to surrender without consequence expired hours ago.

Olivia spits up. Half an ounce of irreplicable breast milk soaks my T-shirt. I crouch in front of the windowsill, part the blinds. The parking lot is empty. Except for a green pickup truck, parked in Mom's carport.

The doorknob turns. A man says, "I know you're in here."

The door opens and Marcus enters Mom's apartment. He

has a newspaper under his arm, and a brown paper bag in his opposite hand. "There's a pretty picture, the pair of you. If only Genie was here to see you. She'd plaster her fridge with snapshots."

The door is open. Marcus is alone. He hasn't reported me to the police.

Marcus shuts the door and sets the bag on the edge of the coffee table. "A gift. For you. Looks like you need it."

The brown bag is the kind Mom packed my lunch in when she sent me to elementary school. I smell coffee. But I don't let go of Olivia. She whimpers.

Marcus holds out his hands. Stock-still, a giant with a folded newspaper under his armpit. Hands outstretched. His fingernails washed but his palms are stained with newsprint. "Pass Little One here."

I back away, knock into the coffee table.

Olivia's whimper is now a wail. Arms flailing, legs kicking.

I realize I'm holding Olivia's middle too tight. I collapse onto the loveseat and sink into the worn cushion. I loosen my grip and Olivia regains her calm. I gasp.

Marcus drops his arms, hooks his thumbs in the waistband of his coveralls. "Genie took her coffee with creamer and extra sugar. I was at the gas station. Felt right to bring you the same."

Marcus has Mom's coffee right. Proof they spent time together. Yet she'd never mentioned coffee dates with Marcus. Not once. But I never asked. Why hadn't it occurred to me that Mom made acquaintances, friends who helped her pass the time? Somehow, I imagined her waiting patiently for me to phone and chat between my NICU shifts. Growing up the daughter of a schoolteacher, September through June, barring a true emergency, I kept life's dramas to myself. After Mom retired, and I became an adult, our relationship remained in a time warp. Mom cooked; I ate. Our conversations, as if by mutual agreement, never strayed beyond pleasant, into emotionally significant territory. The realization stings.

Marcus adjusts his cap. "If you don't mind me saying? It's not my business, but you look like you need coffee. Or something stronger."

I open the brown bag, lift the large Styrofoam cup, and take a sip. It's still hot. A few swallows later, my head clears. I thank Marcus.

He nods approvingly, not budging, back against the door. I wonder, fleetingly, if he's barricading me and Olivia here. Maybe he tattled to the superintendent that I'd bummed a night in the apartment. Maybe Marcus has connections at the police station and is waiting for a squad car to arrive and arrest me. I dismiss the paranoid thoughts and ask instead about Mom. "You and my mom met how?"

"At the recycling bin. Genie brought a stack of newspapers, neatly tied, except I'd just emptied the bin in my truck. I still remember the first words she said to me, "Hate to make more work, would it be a bother if I carried these to your truck?"

Marcus's smile brightens his eyes. "Most residents have copies of the *Main Line Times*. Genie had *The Jewish Exponent*. I asked her for a copy. She said, 'You read the paper? Which one?' I told her, 'All of them. Before I haul them to the transfer station.'"

I say, "Mom hated T.V., didn't own one."

Marcus says, "She and I agreed. Best way to get information is to read the paper. I get mine free. All delivered to various tenants. The next day, I dropped off a newspaper, unwrinkled and unread of course, to Genie. We talked for an hour. Never met someone more caring."

His smile melts by gradation until the memory dissipates and the light behind his eyes dims. Marcus unfolds his newspaper, holds it in front of his face and I imagine him studying the print. I lean into the loveseat, hoist Olivia onto my shoulder, and pat her back. She burps softly. I watch Marcus behind his newspaper, sprigs of wiry grey hair visible, poking from the brim of his painter's cap. He turns the page.

The silence unnerves me.

I'd checked my phone. There were no emergency Amber Alert notifications, but what if Marcus comes across a story about Olivia? With as casual a voice as possible I ask, "*The Inquirer* print anything worth reading?"

"Not today. No tragic accidents. Nothing worth crying over."

No missing baby.

"All the news is good. Norwegian cruise ships sailing from Miami." Marcus lowers the newspaper. His voice is light. "Ever want to escape?"

I answer, "Where to?" Silently, I ponder where I might hide with Olivia, and how to get word to Peter so that he can join us. The three of us, a family. I imagine an isolated place, someplace where people value privacy, and mind their own business. The Midwest perhaps? We can buy a farmhouse surrounded by yellow cornfields. And I'll shop in an old-fashioned country store that sells milk in glass bottles. Even a rural town needs a doctor. Peter could open his own clinic and deliver babies the natural way, like a country midwife.

Marcus says, "Jamaica. Blue Mountains. Now that is something... a blue mountain. Learned all about Jamaica from *The Sunday Times*—a full-color travel feature. Good coffee too, in Jamaica. Not that I'm a traveler. Been in an airplane once. But I've yet to fly out of the country. I got my passport, and one of those fancy leather carry cases too. Now, I'm no swimmer, but on a cruise, you get plenty of ocean air without dipping a toe in the water. Almost had Miss Genie convinced to cruise." Marcus clears his throat. "Separate cabins of course."

"Mom. On a cruise?" This is a lot to digest. I'm in Mom's apartment, cradling a baby, sharing coffee with a man I hadn't met before last night. A stranger who knew Mom better than I had. I want to change the topic.

I say dully, "Mom got seasick."

Marcus folds the newspaper. "You don't say." The look on his face is disappointment and something I can't discern. Embarrassment maybe.

I regret my words. Spoiling Marcus's make-believe trip with Mom. I imagine what it would be like to never travel, or visit a faraway beach, lounge in gentle waves. When was our last vacation?

Marcus steps in front of the window, parts the venetian blind with his thumb. A stray band of light, like an accusatory finger, pokes through the aperture and points at my feet. Marcus says, "Your mom kept her windows open. Loved sunlight and in the summer, a refreshing breeze."

He's right about Mom loving sunshine but I don't respond. Marcus's boots compress the carpet, and he stands close enough that I smell the coffee on his breath. He aims his phone. "Got you. She's one photogenic baby. And lucky to have a baby nurse." He snaps a picture. "Proof. A perfect pair or I'm a fool."

My cheeks burn but it's too late to protest. I don't ask Marcus to delete Olivia's picture. Besides not wanting to hurt his feelings, something about Marcus—I can't name it exactly, maybe his voice soothes me—makes me feel less alone. With Marcus in the apartment, it's as if part of Mom is here too, sharing Olivia with me.

Marcus toes the carpet with his boot, tamping the edge. He stands in the doorway and says, "The Super is bound to nose around."

"We will be on our way." The room is suddenly chilly, and I hug Olivia closer. "Thank you for letting us stay."

"Where did you say you and Little One are going?"

I study a worn spot on the carpet. My mouth is tacky, and I sip the coffee, no longer hot but lukewarm. I feel Marcus's gaze. But when I look at him, it's Olivia, not me, he watches.

Marcus's voice is a gentle whisper. "Might seem like I got everything in order. Steady job, and a room here at Radcliff. But the way something looks on the outside is deceiving."

I avoid eye contact. But I'm curious.

"I walked the wrong side of a one-way street. One misstep. Years ago. It gave me a nose for trouble. Can smell it coming from a mile away."

I squirm. What type of trouble was Marcus in? Did Mom know his secrets?

He says, "Loss brings out the worst in some and the best in others. That's what Genie told me." Marcus's phone buzzes. He takes it from his pocket. "Toilet overflowed. Unit A."

"You should go. Really. Go. We're fine. We'll be gone by the time the super gets here."

Marcus adjusts his cap and says, "See you around, Baby Nurse." He leaves.

Because my attendance record at the hospital is stellar, calling out sick tonight is guaranteed to raise eyebrows. Not the kind of attention I need while sheltering Olivia. Working tonight has an added advantage, the opportunity to talk with Fernanda. My plan is to page her before she leaves the hospital for the night. A few casual questions and I'll assess her willingness to find a new home for Olivia. I rehearse my conversation opener, *Have you been in touch with Aunt Darlene?* Maybe I'll even tell her the truth that Aunt Darlene is not cut out to raise a baby.

I'll inform Fernanda, arming her with incriminating information about Aunt Darlene's poor judgement: drinks beer while driving, and left her niece unattended behind The Rusty

Sub Tavern. Fernanda will be forced to rehome Olivia with a suitable caregiver. But I lack evidence. My phone had died, preventing me from photographing the smashed beer cans in Aunt Darlene's Nissan.

I complete my preparations. The cooler with Olivia's remaining bottle, and the plastic bag containing Olivia's dwindling diaper pack are at the door. No time for me to shampoo, a low ponytail is the best I can manage while tending Olivia. Clean, but wrinkled, scrubs will have to suffice. I pull the laundered scrubs from the dryer and change in front Mom's stackable machine. My admiration for Robyn doubles. Not only does she arrive to work on time, hair impeccably braided, winged eyeliner flawlessly applied, her four energetic kids at home are happy.

It's time to leave Mom's apartment and I'm nervous, my pulse too rapid, like I ran up a flight of stairs. I part the blinds with my thumb. There's not much to see late in the day. No police. No official-looking van from child protection services canvasing the apartment complex. Besides the Jetta, there's the green pickup truck with the dented fender.

I snap the blinds shut.

Olivia grabs a few strands of my hair. We reach the Jetta and Olivia yanks as I bend to buckle her car seat. Prying her fingers to free my hair is no easy task. At last Olivia settles. I pat my scrubs pocket, find the car key, and turn the ignition.

The Jetta is inert. The engine cold. The gas tank? Empty. I slap the steering wheel. "What am I going to do?" The locket that Jamie gave me hangs from the rearview mirror. A shadow falls across the windshield.

Through the driver side window, a deep voice says, "Trouble?" Marcus stands, thumbs tucked in his coveralls.

I open the door. "I don't want to be a bother." If Marcus was Mom's friend, that's reason enough to hope he'll help one more time. Marcus says, "Stay where you are." He walks across the asphalt to his green truck. Rummages through the bay, tosses a stack of newspapers tied with twine, rearranges the toolbox, and grasps a red gas can with a black nozzle. He lifts the can, gives me a thumbs up. Marcus returns with the fuel can. "Pop the tank." There's a guzzling sound and Marcus empties the can into the Jetta. He taps the windshield.

The ignition catches. The low fuel warning light transitions from red to yellow. I rev the accelerator. I lean from the window and try but fail to properly thank Marcus. He let me stay in the apartment, possibly risking his job by angering the superintendent. Marcus bought me coffee with money from his own pocket and gassed the Jetta. "I'm grateful for—" I cringe. My words sound inadequate.

But Marcus's friendly smile is gone. His jaw is set, and his tone is harsh. "You got yourself some trouble."

"I don't know what you mean." Except I do.

"Two and a half gallons won't get you far. You're young, but old enough to learn, you can't outrun trouble." He drums the Jetta roof with his fingers. "Genie is gone, but I feel her near. She'd tell you herself if she could." His jaw muscles twitch. "Running won't fix your trouble. That's the tricky thing about trouble. The harder you run, the sooner you end up where you started." Marcus sets the empty gas can on the asphalt.

The Jetta lurches. I press the accelerator with the ball of my foot. I glance in the rearview mirror. Marcus stands, thumbs in his coveralls, a shrinking statue. Even after the Jetta exits Radcliff, I feel Marcus watching.

CHAPTER TEN

"Where'd you get that baby?" Sheila stands in the doorway of Kitty Haven. The tabby in her arms hisses.

"Put the cat down, will you?" My wrist is pins-and-needles numb from balancing the car seat with Olivia in it. Lulled to sleep by the drive, I'm loath to wake her. I shift the carrier to the opposite arm, dropping the cooler and the diaper bag on the doorstep. "Do you mind? I could use—"

"Come in." Sheila strokes the tabby's head. "But my newest resident here doesn't like strangers. He needs time to adjust."

I retrieve the dropped bags and follow Sheila into the kitchen. She's added a third tier, a scratching post, to the playscape in the center of the kitchen. The tiny hairs on the back of my neck prickle, like I'm being watched. A pair of emerald eyes spy from the perch.

Olivia sneezes, startling herself from sleep. I rock the car seat, hoping to placate her.

Sheila deposits the hissing tabby into a cottage. The creature retreats to the back of the cottage, I notice its front paws are bandaged in white gauze.

Olivia stirs, her bottom lip trembles.

"That cat. Can it get out?"

Sheila secures the latch. "Nope." She stares at Olivia, frowns, and points to Olivia's head. "What's wrong with the baby?"

I'm confused. "Not a thing."

The tiny lines at the corners of Sheila's eyes wrinkle, she studies Olivia with concern as if she were a kitten in need of first aid.

I realize Sheila has noticed the bald square above Olivia's left ear. I hesitate. The less Sheila knows the better. She'll be protected, and uninvolved in what I've done. I settle on a grain of truth. "Her scalp was shaved when she needed an IV for some medicine. She's better now."

Sheila leans on the kitchen counter. She's not smiling.

"Baby hair is slow growing, like kitten fur." I want to tell the entire truth. Sheila is my best friend. But would she offer to help or hesitate to be involved? Lying by omission to Sheila, the person I once shared life's every detail with, has over the years become a habit. I change the subject and ask about the quadruplet kittens. "How many did you adopt out?"

"None," Sheila says. "You can put her down."

Multicolored fur dusts the floor and I don't want Olivia covered in it. A Peapod home delivery sack crowds the kitchen counter. I tend to Sheila's groceries. The carton of half-and-half is room temperature. "How long has this been out?"

"Nurse Annabelle, quit worrying. The creamer is for an underweight resident who prefers it warm."

I set Olivia's car seat on the kitchen counter. Twin Siamese, white-whiskered with ice-blue eyes, leap from the gymnasium and circle Olivia. I shoo the pair. Being stalked by semi-domesticated cats isn't how I imagined introducing Olivia to animals.

Sheila puts a gingham apron over her denim overalls. *Cat*

Lady is embroidered on the front. For no particular reason, I have a visceral dislike for the apron. Sheila fills the sink and scrubs bowls small enough to fit inside the American Girl dolls' house that we played with as girls. Steam billows from the sink. Sheila rinses each bowl and stacks them on a dish towel spread across the counter. The hot water turns Sheila's skin pink, accentuating a fresh claw-mark on her forearm.

The pair of Siamese spring from the counter, land at Sheila's feet, and bat her apron strings, which hang untied. Sheila twists the faucet and dries her hands on her apron. "The baby looks like you."

My heart swells. I study Olivia. Her ginger hair, pale skin. "Maybe she'll have my freckles," I joke. Except I'm half-serious.

Sheila covers the Kitty Haven serving dishes with a towel. "You going to tell me about the baby?" A pot on the stove boils. Sheila drops a raw chicken breast into the roiling water and covers the pot with a lid.

"Since when do you eat meat?"

"Not me—an allergic resident."

Sheila wipes her hands a second time on her apron. She stares at Olivia, asleep in her car seat. "So, the baby. You brought her here because?"

"I need a favor. Tonight. I won't be gone long. And she will sleep."

"Your shift ends, when?"

"Before midnight. Diapers and wipes are in the bag. She loves to be held."

"What do I feed her?"

"Her milk is in the cooler. Warm her bottle first. I'll keep my phone with me. Text me for anything."

"She's as cute as a kitten. I promise to do my best."

I'm grateful that Sheila doesn't prod. Not like when we

were girls and we shared every detail, all of life's woes with each other.

I kiss Olivia's forehead and linger to inhale her scent; the hospital smell is gone. I say, "I love you." Three simple words. For months the emotion stayed pent-up in my heart, suppressed by patient-nurse boundaries. This is our first separation since being together outside the NICU, and the words escape unfettered by hospital rules. "I love you. I'll be back to get you. Promise." I swallow burning tears.

Sheila opens the door.

Head down, I exit Kitty Haven.

Sheila stands in the doorway, hands tucked in the pocket of her *Cat Lady* apron. She says, "He doesn't know, does he?"

"Not yet."

Unable to shake the feeling I'm being pursued, I check the rearview mirror. The locket swings, a pendulum counting my borrowed time with Olivia. Without her I might as well have lost an appendage. And in a sense, I have. I'm twitchy, unsettled, and that dark, uncharted space behind my heart aches.

I'm late but I need gas. I can't tempt fate, risk burning through Marcus's emergency gallons. I pull into the Citgo self-service. The surveillance camera above the pump pivots its red beady eye. I avoid staring at the camera, insert my credit card. *Please, please, please...* Accepted. I exhale.

The Jetta guzzles fourteen gallons, extinguishing the dashboard's "low fuel" warning. I decline a receipt and leave the station. The fuel needle lifts from E to F, but I'm still uneasy. Behind me the base of Olivia's car seat is secured in the rear seat. How could I be so careless, to drive with the base still in the car, evidence that Olivia was with me?

I hear a siren. Panicked, I press the accelerator. The Jetta hiccups. An ambulance races, lights whirling and horn blaring, headed for Lakeview Hospital. The sirens don't quit. Police, a fleet of squad cars, streak past in a blur.

My heart rate skyrockets. My knuckles are pearl-white knobs, gripping the steering wheel. I edge to the curb, not breathing, willing myself to shrink from view. But the police pay me no heed, uninterested in the evidence, Olivia's car seat base, that I harbor in the Jetta.

Tachycardia is becoming my new normal.

I park in the employee lot. Sirens blare. Not in the distance but ear-splittingly near. My pulse swooshes behind my eardrums. Walking, my knees lock and my gait is stiff. Police sedans, lights twirling red-blue-red-blue, semicircle the emergency room.

I stop. Unable to breathe. "Excuse me." A nurse hurries past.

A security guard, baton in hand, stands at the hospital entrance. He barks, "No visitors. I.D. Employees only." A Philadelphia Police van blocks the valet parking entrance.

They're looking—for me.

My employee I.D. with my picture is clipped to my scrubs top, I tuck it inside my pocket for now, undo my ponytail so that my hair obscures my face. I wish for a cap to cover my strawberry-blonde hair. I pivot—and collide with a nurse.

I want to apologize but my tongue is glued to the roof of my mouth. It is Robyn. I fall into her.

She says, "Great timing for a lockdown. Shift change? Give me a break. At least we'll be late together."

A news van and a film crew stake a spot on the perimeter of the police activity. A reporter, press badge displayed on her blazer, runs her story. "The victim, a nineteen-year-old male, is in critical condition—treated by Lakeview Hospital's emergency trauma team... details just in, his condition is upgraded from critical to serious. Stay tuned, the gunman remains at large..."

Robyn adjusts her lanyard so that her employee I.D. is visible. She loops her arm with mine, propelling me forward. She says, "I tell my boys, violence solves nothing—"

The security officer repeats his mantra, "Employees only. No visitors. No exceptions. Employees..."

Robyn says, "Wouldn't take all the money in the world to work in the E.R."

"Badge," the security officer barks. "Lockdown protocol."

My fingers shake but I swivel my I.D. tag. The lockdown, a hospital-wide security response, is implemented after a gunshot victim is brought into the emergency room. Police cars ring Lakeview Hospital. Security officers monitor all exits and entrances. Visitors are barred. In the event of gang activity, a violent altercation can escalate and endanger staff. The heightened security remains in effect until there is no threat of retribution for the shooting or the perpetrator is caught.

I'm rattled. But the lockdown isn't about me. Or Olivia. Or what I've done. I need to quell my panic, stick to my plan, and speak with Fernanda on Olivia's behalf. Additionally, I need to visit Edwin in the milk room.

The security officer waves Robyn and then me through with barely a glance at our picture I.D. Inside the atrium I gladly accept a disposable mask, hook it around my ears to conceal half my face. I brace for Robyn to say something about Olivia's kidnapping. *Can you believe it? Baby Olivia was snatched from her aunt's parked car...*

But Robyn doesn't seem to know about Olivia. She launches into a tale about one of her four sons. I can't follow the details but Robyn's oldest is having issues in school. She says, "It's not attention deficit, I had him tested. He's bored. Needs to be challenged—I told Thom, if the public school can't accommodate him, we're switching to private..."

The urge to pee is overwhelming.

Robyn shifts gears mid-sentence. "Baby, you're diaphoretic."

I wipe cold sweat from my forehead with a tissue, ball the tissue in my fist. Telling Robyn would be a relief. An unburdening. Robyn would understand. She bonded with Robbie when he was a patient in our NICU and adopted him. But I can't risk involving her.

Robyn stares at me, her dark-brown eyes warm with genuine concern, her voice gentle. "We should talk."

I drop my gaze. My Converse are scuffed, the laces sloppily knotted, my scrubs pants wrinkled. The elevator doors slide apart. I bolt ahead of Robyn and race to the bathroom.

At the start of the shift, I'm assigned to Natalie, the surviving twin. Before I begin caring for her, I log into a NICU computer and send Fernanda a nonspecific message that the NICU requires a social worker. I'm on edge, waiting for her response.

Natalie's mom is skeptical. Behind her mask, I can tell she's frowning. "Take her out of the box?" She doesn't believe what I tell her. This is understandable because she's grieving Nathanial, the twin she lost.

But I persist. Holding her surviving infant, so soon after a loss, might be a healing experience. "Skin-to-skin contact helps Natalie grow," I explain.

"She's too little." Natalie's mom shakes her head. "What about the tubes and wires?"

"I'm here. Robyn will help."

Natalie has transitioned to a conventional ventilator with corrugated, flexible tubing, making it possible to move her from the isolette onto her mother's chest. My concern is that the window for Natalie to bond with her mother is narrow. Research proves that skin-to-skin or kangaroo care fosters the mother-infant bond. Additional benefits for a preterm infant are improved thermoregulation and growth. I close the privacy curtain and Natalie's mom unbuttons her shirt.

For a nurse, skin-to-skin holding is labor intensive. The isolette lid lifts, I gather monitor leads, double-check that the umbilical IV line is secure and do the same for the breathing tube.

Robyn parts the curtain, grabs gloves, and says, "I'll help. I've got the ventilator." My phone vibrates. My scrubs pocket, where I tucked my phone, glows.

Robyn's eyes dart to the lit phone in my pocket.

I lift Natalie; she fills my cupped, gloved palms. Her brow furrows. I tell Natalie, "Your first hold with Mommy is a milestone."

Together, Robyn and I transition Natalie between her mother's breasts. I cover the pair with a blanket. Robyn dims the lights. A few blips on the monitor and Natalie settles.

Her mother says, "I'm leaking."

"A positive sign," I tell her. Yet another advantage of kangaroo care, increased oxytocin, the hormone linked to lactation. I position a small mirror so Natalie's mother can view her daughter's face.

My phone vibrates, a flurry of insistent buzzes. It sounds like I'm hiding a hornet's nest in my scrubs pocket. The messages must be from Sheila about Olivia. I can't read her messages, not in front of Robyn. She's watching the lightning storm in my scrubs pocket. Covering my pocket with my palm does little to mute the buzz or dim the screen.

Robyn can't be fooled. She says again, "We should talk. Later?"

I fiddle with Natalie's monitor waiting for Robyn to leave the pod.

Robyn parts the curtain and before she exits, whispers, "Whatever it is, I'll understand."

I believe her.

My phone emits a final trill and falls silent. Dread washes through me. Whoever called, and it must be Sheila, left a message.

Natalie's mother gasps. She says, "Her eyes. They're open."

It's dinnertime, an hour into my shift and I say, "Stomach cramps." Before now, I have never lied to get off from work. I tell the charge nurse that I must leave. Robyn takes over Natalie's care. Robyn hugs me and says, "Go." Her ebony eyes mist. "Let's talk later. But whatever it is, be safe."

I tap my locker shut, leaving behind a box of chocolate-chip Clif Bars with five bars remaining, a spare set of ironed scrubs, and a brand-new hair scrunchie. I don't know that this is my final shift in the NICU.

My phone pings with a renewed barrage of texts, all from Sheila.

> She's crying. Won't stop.

Sheila's final text is an all-caps scream.

> COME BACK.

I approach the NICU exit. The phone to my ear, listening to voicemail. I can't understand Sheila's garbled barrage because Olivia is crying in the background. My heart thumps with panic. Is she sick or hurt? Did one of Sheila's feral cats attack Olivia?

The unit secretary announces, "On-call social worker is at the desk."

One glance is all I need. The pre-pubescent-looking guy in a pink Oxford shirt, faded denim, wearing a JanSport backpack is not Fernanda, but an intern, assigned to troubleshoot overnight issues. He stands at the desk, chats with the unit secretary, and passes her a business card. My problem with Olivia and Aunt Darlene is far outside his newbie skillset.

The double doors swing shut. Alone in the corridor, I walk, then break into a jog. Sheila doesn't answer. I text:

> I'm coming.

Unread. No response.

I have one stop. Risky but vital for Olivia. I tap the formula-room door. The top door parts. Edwin's friendly expression turns grim. "Whoa. What's wrong?"

"Between us?"

Edwin lowers his mask. "Between friends."

"Jamie Dutton. Is there any of her pumped breast milk left in your storage freezer?"

The ramifications of my request sink in. One, two, three seconds tick. I know Edwin is on my side because he doesn't ask a single question. "Let me check." He retreats into the milk lab, lifts the lid of an industrial freezer, disappearing in a frosty cloud. The lid slams.

Edwin returns to the door, rubs his palms. "The last bottles were delivered to the boarder nursery, yesterday. The baby is no longer on the hospital census."

My disappointment and desperation must show.

Edwin says, "Is something wrong? Can I help?"

"No one can know that I asked about Jamie's milk—"

"We'll keep this between us." Edwin shuts the milk-room door.

I wonder if I'll have any friends when this is over. I whisper to the closed door, "What am I going to do?"

A strong stomach is a prerequisite for a nursing career, but Kitty Haven smells worse than usual, vomit and diarrhea compete with cat litter. I retch.

Sheila is in the kitchen, wringing a wet mop. She's barefoot and her denim overalls are soaked, knees to floppy hem. Steam rises from the sink. Olivia sits in her car seat, which is on the floor, not the counter where I'd left her. Brow furrowed, eyes shut, sucking furiously on her fist, Olivia is naked, except for a diaper. No onesie, no blanket. Twin Siamese lick her toes.

I step into the kitchen, slip on the wet linoleum and land on my butt.

Sheila says, "Watch out, she barfed."

Olivia starts, spits her fist from her mouth and cries. I scoot to the car seat, lift her onto my lap, she smells un-Olivia-like, like emesis. Or as Sheila says, barf.

Sheila scoops the twin Siamese, one under each arm, and leans her hip against the counter. The cats' pink tongues lash her chin.

A cursory examination assures me that Olivia is healthy. She's happy to see me and gives me a weak smile. Her stomach is soft, not firm. Her skin pink and warm, not hot. Olivia tracks Sheila's movements. If Sheila found Olivia difficult, I get the sense that the feeling is mutual. Olivia's diaper is backwards. Disposable diaper tabs are designed to be secured from the rear, not the front. But I'm grateful. There's no permeant harm done. I right Olivia's diaper.

Sheila deposits the twin Siamese on the cat gymnasium. She wipes the sink with a wad of paper towels. Her back to me, she says, "I did my best with the baby." Sheila stuffs the paper towels and an empty half-and-half carton into a green plastic trash bag and cinches the neck.

"You fed her the bottle? The one from the cooler?"

"Unfortunately..." Sheila faces me.

I stiffen. And meet Sheila's icy gaze.

She leans against the counter. "The baby cried when you left. Never stopped... I couldn't heat the bottle fast enough." Sheila twists the *Cat Lady* apron ties in her fists. The apron has a new brown stain in the middle. "The baby milk spilled and attracted my residents. All of them. The residents lapped the spilled milk."

Olivia's last bottle, Jamie's breast milk, gone. I shift Olivia from my lap, her head rests on my shoulder. "She's hungry. That's why she cried."

Sheila says, "I know. So, I did feed her."

My stomach drops. "What exactly did you feed her?"

"Half and half."

"Creamer?"

"She was hungry." Sheila's voice is shrill. "I didn't know she'd barf all over the floor and poop through her diaper."

"I trusted you to recognize the difference between my baby and one of your strays," I yell.

Sheila wipes her eyes with her apron hem. "You've changed." Her voice is defeated. The last time Sheila cried was with me in the hospital. Peter called her after I lost the baby. Sheila came and sat not in a chair, but beside me in the too-narrow bed, combed the knots from my hair. Our silent tears for my stillborn daughter were conversation enough.

I don't respond to her accusation, but she's right. I have changed. I have Olivia to think about.

Sheila says, "You think I'm too dumb to guess that the baby is from the hospital. But you should have trusted me enough to tell me. The truth."

My hands tremble. I position Olivia in her car seat. "You can go back to worrying over your precious cats. I'm sorry to have interrupted whatever illicit medical procedure you were doing in the back room. You're not even a licensed vet."

"Because of you, I could lose Kitty Haven. I saw the label on the milk bottle. She's the orphan baby from the newspaper story. The baby whose parents died in a crash."

I stand. Reeling with a rush of hot anger.

"You're not her mama, Annabelle. And other people will guess it too. The police will find you. They'll know you came here and that I helped—"

"Except you didn't help. You poisoned my baby with soured milk." I instantly regret my words. But it's too late. The words strike.

Sheila sobs. "I thought you were my friend."

I sling the car seat over my arm and leave Kitty Haven.

Olivia's seat snaps into the Jetta, the engine catches and Olivia stays asleep. The light in Kitty Haven's kitchen goes dark. But I see Sheila's silhouette. A cat in her arms.

CHAPTER ELEVEN

The vacant garage is disappointing. I want Peter to meet Olivia, but I remember Cumberland's back injury and that Peter is busy at the hospital. Ironic, Peter bringing babies into the world while I'm ushering Olivia into our house. I lift Olivia, wrapped in a blanket, from her car seat, drop my phone in the diaper bag, and hoist the bag over my shoulder. Instead of entering through the connecting door, I exit the garage, and walk the cobblestone path leading to the front door. A proper homecoming.

The automatic porch light transforms Olivia's ginger hair into a fiery halo. There's mail. A long white envelope protrudes from the mailbox. I pinch the envelope between my thumb and forefinger, drop it into the diaper bag, and thanks to my experience with debt collectors, intuit bad vibes.

But nothing will ruin this occasion. I unlock the door, step over the threshold, and for the first time, I enter my house with a baby in my arms. "Happy homecoming," I say to Olivia. I stand in the foyer and manage to kick off my Converse without putting Olivia down. To the left, the living room is an empty, unfurnished square. The kitchen on the right with an immaculate, mile-long stone counter, the house, sterile as an operating room, rallies with an echo.

Propelled by a fierce desire to make the house homey, I flick every wall switch and turn up the thermostat. The hibernating house stirs awake. I climb, the third step groans twice, as if Olivia's extra six pounds are a burden. At the nursery door, I pause, remembering the hours I spent while pregnant, worrying —no, agonizing—comparing paint samples before settling on Perfect Peach for the walls. The nursery was the only room I'd managed to decorate. I'd hung curtains over the nursery window, stood on tiptoe to fluff the ruffle.

I envisioned not a room but a universe with a circular yellow carpet at the middle, the crib, dresser, changing table, and rocking chair in orbit. I planned to extend my maternity leave, and reduce my hospital shifts, with the intention of showering my baby with undivided attention. Never wanting my baby to doubt that she, not my patients, occupied center stage. When I was young, Mom's students needed her, even on weekends, a "just us" trip to the grocery store inevitably became an impromptu conference when a school parent recognized Mom and parked her cart adjacent to ours. "What a lucky surprise," the pupil's mom would gush. "Might I ask a question?" Mom would nod, introduce me to the mother and her student. There was never any mistaking the envy in the student's eyes. Shivering beside bags of frozen peas, they wished Mrs. Gold wasn't their teacher but their mom.

Peter associates the nursery with our lost daughter. He covered the crib with a white sheet and locked the door for a spell. The only curtains in the house that I'd successfully mounted stayed drawn. In the aftermath of losing our daughter, my skin prickled when I walked by as if a breath of refrigerated air slipped from under the door. I might have avoided the nursery except that I'd spiked a fever, a common side effect of postpartum breast engorgement.

The cure for milk fever is milk expression and the electric breast pump was assembled beside the rocking chair. The lactation consultant at Lakeview Hospital advises moms in the NICU to keep a pumping log. "Every three hours, record what you produce." Not me. There were no rules. I pumped when I thought I heard my baby cry. I sat on the rocking chair in the room with the empty crib, hooked to the humming pump, and drops, yellow as the nursery carpet, lined the collection bottle. A day later, white cream. My breasts rained white tears for the baby girl I couldn't hold, cuddle, or feed.

Discarding my daughter's milk had been impossible. Doing so was akin to erasing her existence and denying my love for her. Pumping snow-white milk affirmed her birth and proved that she was very much loved. Bottles stocked the freezer, and I donated a portion to Lakeview Hospital's mothers' milk bank, forging a friendship with Edwin. Knowing that my milk healed sick infants was a comfort.

After returning to work in the NICU, the thunderstorm of milk diminished, but I still pump and save milk in the freezer. Peter doesn't know. He eats his meals at the hospital, and busy as he is, cooking or shopping to stock the kitchen hasn't been on his radar. If he knew about the breast milk, he'd worry that I'm not moving on.

There's a clank followed by a rumble from the basement. "That's the heater," I say to Olivia. She sleeps in my arms. I shake the dust cover from the crib, and lower Olivia onto the mattress. I tour the room barefoot, pleased by the bouncy carpet beneath my feet, a perfect cushion for Olivia's knees when she's ready to crawl.

I separate the curtains. The nursery overlooks the front

lawn. The night, chocolate-pudding dark, the moon a white marshmallow.

Olivia cries.

I say, "I'm here."

Olivia's azure eyes brighten with joy.

I lift her and we cross the room and stand in front of the window. On the road below, a pair of lights, yellow as cat's eyes, sear the night. Gravel crunches beneath tires. I strain to see through the dark but can't discern the vehicle's model. It slows, pauses at the mouth of the serpentine driveway. I feel exposed, silhouetted between the curtains with Olivia.

I tap the glass, an effort to swat the intruder, and I close the curtains. They sway from the rods before settling. A moment passes, heart thrumming, I peek again. Nothing but dark. I tell myself I imagined the intruder.

Olivia cries like she means it. It doesn't require a nurse's degree to know that she's hungry.

Jewish women don't traditionally have baby showers. I'd been seven months along when Robyn asked if she could host a Sunday brunch in my honor. I agreed and saw no harm in gathering with my NICU colleagues. Mom had already died but walking into Robyn's living room, decorated with pink and yellow balloons, I sensed Mom's displeasure. Robyn's youngest son Robbie popped a pink balloon with a fork. The sound shook my bones, and I imagined Mom, deathly pale, her hands clasped in worry, whisper Yiddish from her grave. *Baby shower? A kinehora.* The evil eye, a precursor to bad luck.

Thanks to the shower, the nursery closet is stocked with Avent and Dr. Brown's bottles, Pampers, Huggies, eco-friendly unbleached Seventh Generation, size newborn through toddler, kimono-style onesies with ties and onesies that snap. Everything. Except infant formula. I assumed that when I became a mother, I'd breastfeed.

The solution to the problem how to feed Olivia now that Jamie's breast milk is gone? There is only a single option now. I thaw a two-ounce sample of my frozen breast milk in a hot-water bath and dispense the liquid into a bottle. Seated in the rocking chair, Olivia propped on a Boppy, a donut-shaped pillow, I offer the bottle.

She sucks noisily, her swallows interspersed by puffs of breath through that delicate nose of hers. Her lips maintain a seal around the bottle nipple, and I pry the drained bottle free. Olivia likes my milk. I'm elated. I kiss her downy hair. Her head bobs toward the two wet circles on my shirt. Feeding Olivia caused me to leak fresh milk. I stopped lining my bra with breast pads weeks ago.

Still hungry, Olivia nuzzles my shirt, a rooting reflex. She cries. Thawing a second bottle requires a trip downstairs to the kitchen. I've never nursed a baby, but assisted and counseled NICU mothers. Lifting my shirt, unhooking my bra, and attaching Olivia's wide-open mouth to my nipple is foreign yet familiar. Not entirely comfortable but not painful either. Nursing, not mine but another mother's baby, would have been unimaginable had it not been out of urgent need, Olivia's hunger.

Olivia swallows. A warm hormonal bath unknots my shoulders. I study Olivia's every characteristic. Her pink eyelids. The dimple on her chin, I swear it's there and then it vanishes. Olivia's eyes close and her lips loosen. Her arms flop at her sides. Her soft, round abdomen lifts with her tide of breath.

Seconds, minutes, hours, collapse. I'd hold her forever, but I force myself to stand and set her in her crib before sleep steals my strength. The night-light in the corner glows, a moon with a leaping cow. I cross the hall and roll into bed, unconscious before I can pull down the comforter.

I wake, startled by a beautiful noise. A baby cries. Not

conjured this time, a function of grief, but fleshy and warm, with a kitten-quick heartbeat. There's a baby in my house. My baby.

Dawn ushers morning, melds with noon. Time's sharp edges, so vital when working in the NICU, are no longer absolute, but smooth. I surrender to diaper changes, a bath, a book, mobile watching, thawed breast-milk bottles, and tummy time on the neoprene mat. I rehearsed this score, *Motherhood*, in my mind, and consider myself finely tuned. On stage, Olivia conducts, I intuit. Music emerges, a melody for the pair of us. Measure by measure, I record the high notes, low notes, the dynamics. Journal pages fill with my left-handed calligraphy.

Unknowingly, I write my future defense. The yellow notebook will later be seized, submitted in court as evidence. The judge will read, ponder, and render me guilty or innocent.

Olivia naps in her crib. I'm tempted to sleep but am jarred by an irregular tap on the windowpane. Rain streaks the glass, gushes through the gutters. A car engine backfires. I run downstairs, stand in the doorway, but there's no car, just a shiny puddle on the driveway. Who had parked there long enough to leak engine oil?

I step barefoot onto the rain-slicken porch. The air smells ripe from accumulated layers of unraked, decomposing foliage. I'm dressed in yoga pants and a T-shirt. I shiver, more from unease than cold, unable to shake the notion that I'm being watched. There are no obvious footprints left by an intruder. But something is amiss. I enter the house and the tiny hairs on the back of my neck prickle. I feel Child Protective Services, a Pennsylvania State Trooper, and Aunt Darlene watching with binoculars. I lock the door.

Olivia shrieks. I charge the stairs. Olivia is in her crib. She's rolled, a first, and woke on her stomach.

It's late afternoon. Although I'm suspended in time, cocooned in a world governed by Olivia, I welcome the waning light. Evening shrouds the house. The rocking chair is a raft, floating over dangerous waters. The tide sends us closer to shore. And I hug Olivia, keeping her safe. Mouth open, Olivia roots. I pull her to my breast. We nurse.

A question, posed by Marcus, pops to mind: *Ever want to escape?*

There aren't many viable options for a woman with a baby. Olivia and I can't simply evaporate into thin air. The anonymity of a ship, Marcus's cruise to Jamacia, seems like a perfect solution. Any option is preferable to returning Olivia to Aunt Darlene. I'll figure out a solution. But soon Peter will arrive. What will I tell him so that he'll understand that suddenly, we're a family? What will I say?

The front door opens. "Belle? I'm home." The front door shuts. "Late workday for the construction crew. I passed a pickup truck at the end of our street."

My feet plant. The rocking chair stills. I switch Olivia to the opposite breast before she cries.

"What's with your phone?" I hear Peter in the foyer. His voice fades as he makes his way to the kitchen. "I texted... You're not going to believe the day I've had. I looked for you last night, even bought you a latte in the café."

I left my phone in the diaper bag. My spine stiffens against the chair's back. How many messages have I ignored? The diaper bag is at my feet, and I fish for the phone and find the unopened piece of mail. I set the envelope on the Boppy. I grasp my phone. My throat is suddenly tight. I answer Peter with a panicked voice. "Sorry about the latte. But tell me about your shift."

"Webster's patient... pregnant with twins, went into labor —" A heavy object hits the counter. There's a pop. "Refused my advice for a cesarean... something about her birth plan with Cumberland to deliver naturally."

Olivia suckles with vigor.

I scroll my texts. Three from Robyn.

Call me.

Nothing from Sheila, no apology over the Kitty Haven mishap. An unsettling wave of regret rolls through me. What I said must have really hurt Sheila. I text:

Sorry. Still friends?

On second thoughts, why should I apologize when Sheila doesn't know the difference between an infant and a kitten? I delete the text. Peter's text is a champagne emoji. Not sure why but I'm about to find out. Finally, a phone message from Glenda-The-Terrible. She needs a doctor's note explaining my missed NICU shift. I was supposed to work. The details are hazy, but I left work early, feigning cramps. I don't respond and delete the message.

I drop the phone in the diaper bag. The envelope from the mailbox balances on the Boppy.

There's a foreign sensation in both breasts, pins and needles. My milk lets down, a first. I never experienced that pure hormonal surge from pumping. My worries recede and I'm suddenly exuberant. I hug Olivia close and press my lips to her forehead. She smells like the bath I gave her. Apple shampoo.

The third step groans. Peter's voice is louder. "Cumberland, his back in spasm, came to the hospital to oversee the twins' labor and coached me through... I delivered both. Twin A was vertex, easy. But the B twin flipped after the first baby delivered. Breech—"

I ask, "You sectioned the second twin?" The white envelope is long, business, not letter-sized. I hadn't noticed when I grabbed it from the mailbox, but it's obvious now, there's no address on the envelope. No return address either. No postage. The unmarked mail was hand-delivered. I peel the tab. The paper inside has a longhand message, penned in red Sharpie. I fold the letter into the envelope and tuck it under the rocking chair seat pillow. I'll read it later.

Peter says, "Nope. Webster is one of the few obstetricians skilled in breech presentation. It's a lost art." Peter is upstairs, his voice drifts as he walks into our bedroom. "You'll never believe... She nursed in the delivery room."

I adjust the Boppy pillow, position Olivia cross-cradle on my lap.

"Belle?"

My heart skips. "We're in here."

"Webster wants to have dinner. To talk. My, our future... Naturally, I told him I had to ask you for your NICU schedule..." Peter stops at the nursery threshold, hugging an uncorked champagne bottle in the crook of his elbow and a pair of flutes in his opposite hand. "What are you doing in here?" He sets the champagne and the flutes in the doorway, dressed in baggy, perspiration-stained scrubs, his black curls flattened, his forehead creased from the surgical cap he wore. He rubs the back of his neck, massaging his birthmark, a nervous tick that I thought he'd quit. Self-conscious about the red stain at the nape of his neck, Peter keeps his hair long to conceal it. We'd dated for months before he revealed the salmon-pigmented, heart-shaped patch. And then only as a teaching point. My nursing textbook was open to the dermatology chapter. He'd said, "A nevus flammeus. The real thing sure beats a photograph."

There's no sunlight in the hospital, and Peter is naturally fair, but I watch color leech from his face. He leans against the doorframe, his lips part, but before he speaks, his jaw clamps. Confronted with the unexpected, his childless wife *nursing a baby,* Peter's training kicks in. His silence is not without effort, his throat works, swallowing sharp questions.

Peter scans the room with detached calm, collecting, cataloging data. Multicolored blocks, plastic play rings in primary colors scattered across a neoprene tummy-time mat. The shelf under the changing table, stocked with Pampers, Burt's Bees Baby lotion, and a basin of sudsy bath water I've yet to empty. *The Very Hungry Caterpillar, A Color of His Own,* and Mom's copy of *Feminist Fairy Tales* open on top of the bookcase.

A mobile with black-and-white stars spins on the crib rail, the mattress dressed in a pink sheet. Peter's impassive gaze falters, his eyes widen with recognition; the Raggedy Andy doll in the crib, he'd had the classic Andy doll as a boy and ordered one while I was pregnant. But for obvious reasons, the doll sat in its box. I freed it from the package and Olivia was instantly attracted to the doll's red yarn hair.

Olivia releases my nipple with an audible pop.

Peter's gaze flicks over Olivia and lingers on the wet circular stain, leaked breast milk, on my T-shirt. Thoughts churn and Peter's eyes seem to transition from calm cobalt to stormy grey. Finally, he speaks. "Belle, you're nursing a baby."

"Her name is Olivia." I pat her upper back.

Olivia burps.

Peter pours. "I could use a drink." Champagne fizzes. The crystal flutes, along with a case of Dom Pérignon were a wedding gift from Dr. and Mrs. Cumberland. Peter sits in the doorway, sips, and then empties his glass in one swallow. "I'm going to shower. Clear my head. Then you'll tell me about the baby." He walks into the nursery, leans over the rocking chair, and kisses my lips. He smells like a sweaty hospital shift but tastes like fine champagne. "Belle, you look beautiful with a baby."

What he does next makes my heart burst. He presses his lips to Olivia's crown.

Peter walks to the door, looks over his shoulder and says to me, "After a shower, we'll talk, and when we do, you'll tell me. Everything."

Olivia watches, her eyes shine with little-girl light.

He leaves us in the nursery. A minute later the fan in the bathroom whirrs.

I put Olivia in her crib, and she follows the mobile's orbit, kicking her legs against the mattress with excitement. Olivia quiets, yawns and her eyes become heavy and close. My heart thrums with love, to near breaking, for baby Olivia. Taking her was right. I yearn to share Olivia with Peter, the person I cherish. The three of us could be the family, even for one night, that we dreamed of when we married.

The family fantasy evaporates. Involving Peter will implicate him in what I have done. I'm a kidnapper and my guilt will contaminate Peter's reputation. I can't tell him the details about Olivia, though I know he would understand, and he'll want to help. But I can't let him irreparably damage his career at Lakeview Hospital. Even Dr. Cumberland, old as he is, reads the headlines, and will rescind his job offer. Pregnant women will flee Lakeview Hospital, lest their newborn is abducted from a nursery bassinet.

The white, unaddressed envelope is on the rocking chair. I unseal the tab, freeing a single sheet of thick glossy paper. I press it smooth and recognize the image, a snapshot of a stethoscope auscultating a watermelon-sized belly, the familiar logo from a periodical. The March copy of *American Journal of*

Obstetrics and Gynecology. Addressed to Dr. Peter Kaplan, our home address label is on the cover, circled in red Sharpie. I read, dry lips silently mouthing the eerie message scrawled across the page. Months of living on the edge of bankruptcy, overdue Visa bills, and dodging debt collectors is nothing compared to the terse threat penned across the pregnant woman's abdomen.

> ~~BABY NURSE~~ BABY-NAPPER.
> MEET ME AT THE RUSTY SUB TAVERN AND RETURN WHAT YOU STOLE.
> TOMORROW BY 8 IN THE MORNING. DON'T BE LATE.

There is no signature.

I fold the note into the envelope, reseal it and hide it under the rocking chair's seat cushion. I underestimated her. Aunt Darlene knows that I took Olivia, and she wants Olivia back by 8am. How she tracked us down—the periodical—evidently stolen from Peter's unlocked Subaru—I don't know. What I do know is that keeping Olivia is a crime. I have less than twelve hours to do what's right. Until then, Peter is in Aunt Darlene's crosshairs. Home is no longer safe.

Olivia coos in her crib.

Water thunders from the bathroom. Peter showers. I have a good twenty minutes to prepare. Undoing my many wrongs is no longer possible. The best I can hope for is to shield Peter.

The only way to save Peter and the career he loves is to leave him.

CHAPTER TWELVE

I gather supplies, repack Aunt Darlene's plastic hospital bag with diapers, a clean onesie for Olivia, and a flannel blanket. I'm wearing black leggings and an oversized Villanova T-shirt, the light blue logo, faded to off-white. I'll live in these clothes for longer than I imagine. With Olivia in my arms, I tiptoe downstairs, hold the banister, and skip the creaky third step.

I imagine Peter fresh from the shower, wrapped in a midnight-blue towel. His black hair slick. He'll walk room to room, calling me, perplexed when I don't answer. When he realizes I'm gone, he'll rub the birthmark on the nape of his neck. Peter will worry. I owe him an explanation. But for now, a note is the best I can offer. In the kitchen, I rip a page from the journal I keep for Olivia, my hand surprisingly steady. With a calligraphy pen, I write to my husband.

Dear Peter,

Olivia and I need to leave. You are safer without knowing any details (I'll explain later).

Keep the door locked.

Trust me.
Love, Belle

I leave the note and my phone on the counter, beside the Keurig. My phone would be useful except that Peter will text me a string of sweet emojis, convincing me to come home. And the temptation to respond, to run back, will be too great. I must do this alone. Now. When all this is over, I hope that my note will have been enough, and that Peter will still love me.

Olivia tugs a clump of my strawberry-blonde hair. She giggles but her tone is different, the sound infused with wonder. I tell her, "You made a new sound." I make a mental note to record "giggle" in her journal.

The tiles in the foyer are cold. I'm barefoot. The urgency to flee is real and there's no time to search my closet. My Converse work shoes are in front of the coat closet where I left them, the laces in a loose knot. They will do.

Upstairs, the bathroom fan whirrs, but the shower is off.

I close the front door. The garage grumbles. I make quick work of harnessing Olivia in her seat but convincing her to release her grip on my hair requires negotiation. I offer her the measuring spoons from Mom's apartment.

Behind the wheel, I hold my breath, coax the ignition. The Jetta hesitates. My stomach drops. The engine catches and I pump the accelerator, reverse from the garage and down the twisty driveway. At the bottom, I pause, exhale, and steal a glance at our house. The light in the nursery glows from the second story like a July firefly.

I buckle my safety belt and leave Peter to discover himself alone in the empty house. The Jetta bounces over the unpaved road, gravel pings the underside. There are no streetlamps in Woodline Manor and driving without headlamps, I feel like a bank robber in a getaway car. The locket that Jamie gave me hangs on its cord from the rearview mirror. I steer left-handed, grasp the locket in my right palm, and repeat my vow to Jamie. "You trusted me once to name her. Don't lose faith. I don't know how yet, but I'll keep Olivia safe."

I drive, not daring to use the head beams. Out of habit I brake at the *STOP* sign, there's no approaching vehicles but I hesitate. Where can Olivia and I pass the hours until daybreak? Kitty Haven automatically comes to mind, but I hurt Sheila and even if I apologize, arriving unannounced a second time with Olivia, and expecting Sheila to help is wrong.

Mom's apartment. If only I'd kept up the rent. Marcus has a key to the new lock and if I could find him, he might permit us a second night. And risk being fired. "No," I say. Keeping Olivia safe is my task. Not Sheila's or Peter's or Marcus's. Headlights blink in the distance. I wait, my pulse accelerates. But the car is gone, and I wonder if I imagined the headlamps' yellow glow.

I settle on the only available solution. One that depends on no one except me. I accelerate through the *STOP* sign and veer from the gravel road onto a dirt road. I flick the lights, and the Jetta rattles over the unpaved path. Olivia remains quiet, oblivious to the jostling. I'm afraid of getting us stranded and thanks to the broken odometer, I have no way to tell how far we've driven. The Jetta chugs forward for what I estimate to be a hearty mile and the unpaved path meets a natural end, or someone's beginning; the site of a future home, cordoned by survey stakes. I park.

The engine idles. I lower the window, stick my hand into the dark and flex my fingers as if grasping for an edge of a dark blanket. The absence of light is complete, I can't see so much as a glint of my wedding ring. Even the moon is dressed in doughy clouds. The upturned earth from the construction site smells of decomposing leaves and wet bark. I withdraw my hand into the warm car, close the window and shut down the ignition. Silence seeps through the vents, enveloping the car in a sable cocoon.

A cry punctures the stillness. "Olivia." I crawl onto the back seat and hold her.

I can't see Olivia, but she finds her way and feeds, then, sated, her head is beneath my chin. She burps softly and her breath becomes a cadence of steady puffs. Her scalp smells crisp, like green apples. I melt into the Jetta's back seat, and marvel at the miracle, the comfort that is skin-to-skin. The capacity to warm one another.

I bring Olivia's hand to my lips, kiss each finger and finally, her delicate palm. She closes her fingers. I'm a NICU nurse and recognize the innate reflex, yet I interpret the gesture as purposeful instead of primal; my kiss might remain indefinitely within her grasp, a cherished reminder of my love.

I relish each moment with Olivia, aware that night must give way to morning. And with morning, the unavoidable task of confronting Aunt Darlene. But years later, I'll treasure these stolen moments. I sleep.

I'm at orchestra rehearsal. My cello stands on its single leg, *en pointe,* between my knees. I'm all nerves. I haven't tuned the strings and my bow needs rosin. A strip of EKG paper serves as sheet music, pinned to the black music stand. The chaotic squiggle, ventricular fibrillation, is a life-threatening arrythmia. I raise my bow to warn the conductor of the impending emergency. But the maestro ignores me. It's Dr. STAT. She cues the woodwinds.

Robyn purses her lips and kisses her flute. Sleek, shiny, the surgical steel instrument shrills 'ding-ding-ding.' Chimes cry. Dr. STAT signals me with a nod. The most significant note is mine. Spine straight, I position my bow. Instead of a tenor moan, my cello sounds a cardiac-arrest alarm. 'Whoop-whoop.'

I notice what's so unusual about the orchestra. The

musicians are NICU nurses. Coleen taps her Dansko clogs, I see Todd's conspicuous yellow Crocs, and Nicki's Disney pin, Minnie Mouse behind a piano. The nurses are outfitted in surgical scrubs, not tuxedo black. Instead of a concert hall, the stage is an operating room, lit overhead by a surgical lamp.

There's a single spectator, hidden behind an ether curtain. It's Peter. He shouts, "Bravo. Encore." But the orchestra disbands. I'm alone with my cello in the refrigerated surgical suite, shivering under the spotlight.

Olivia wakes with a wide yawn. Sunlight dapples the windshield. A deer forages at the clearing, oblivious to the Jetta. I watch, expecting a companion or a spotted fawn to emerge from the forest. I tend to Olivia and when I look up, the deer is gone.

The bit of sleep clarified the decision made in haste. Leaving home last night with Olivia was the only way to protect Peter. On instinct I reach for my phone to send a reassuring text; an infant and heart emoji. But I left my phone behind. I will the image of Peter, pale with worry, to fade from my consciousness. My task, meeting Aunt Darlene, necessitates a level head.

Brusque Darlene. Her arrow tattoo fills me with dread. When I took Olivia from the Nissan, my intent was to frighten Aunt Darlene, to teach her a lesson. *Loss brings out the best or the worst in people.* Mom's words. But what if I mistook Aunt Darlene? Learning that her sister died and discovering she's an aunt must have come as a shock. Has Aunt Darlene suffered enough from her loss? I bristle at her cavalier response to the gift of sweet Olivia, an unearned birthright. No. Aunt Darlene learned little.

I double-check Olivia's safety harness, and tighten the straps, satisfied that she is secure. I exit the car, kick the mud from the tires, grateful that the Jetta suffered no obvious damage from our off-road foray. I settle behind the wheel and remove the locket from the rearview mirror and slip it over my head. I turn the ignition key and drive. Keeping to the speed limit, I'll arrive early, before eight this morning, as Aunt Darlene demands in her letter.

Wrong Way.

The red-and-white sign is impossible to miss. Three nights ago I parked in this alley after following Aunt Darlene from Lakeview Hospital. Yet it feels like a lifetime since I took Olivia. *Wrong Way.* That alley sign had been trying to tell me something. I didn't heed the warning.

Bringing Olivia into The Rusty Sub Tavern is a test, an opportunity to observe Aunt Darlene. If I misjudged her and she proves trustworthy, and capable of caring for Olivia, I'll return her niece. I gather Olivia in my arms; she needs a fresh diaper. "Great timing," I tell her. I grab the plastic diaper bag. "Your auntie can learn to change your diaper."

With deliberate steps I approach the door.

Olivia's only living relative is recognizable through the mesh-screen door, her white button-down shirt tucked into khaki slacks. My mouth is parched and my pulse swishes in my ears. She invites me in, and the door springs shut. I'm inside a retro kitchen, the floor and walls tiled with clunky black-and-white squares.

I stand on a black square, Olivia clutched to my chest. The place smells not like greasy food, like I expected, but dish soap. A stainless-steel industrial dishwasher belches steam. The sink, a bone-colored basin, big enough to bathe a toddler, is wiped dry.

Aunt Darlene stands on a white tiled square, hands on her hips. Her gaze unflinching, but her expression isn't hostile or aggressive. Worse, she looks puzzled, like I'm a customer unschooled in restaurant etiquette, unable to decipher a menu or differentiate an appetizer from an entrée.

Understandable. I've changed. This is not Lakeview Hospital where we met. I'm no longer a scrubs-wearing nurse but road-weary and unshowered. The Rusty Sub Tavern is Aunt Darlene's domain. She says, "We can talk in the dining room."

I follow her from the kitchen into a hallway. The door on the left has a sign, *Head,* with a kangaroo logo signifying it's a bathroom equipped with an infant changing station. I make a mental note to visit that restroom and teach Aunt Darlene how to properly diaper Olivia. Hinges creak. Bar doors snap like window shutters, and I hurry after Aunt Darlene. The twin doors clap behind me.

The Rusty Sub Tavern is experiencing an identity crisis. The décor, sailor-shore-leave meets French café with a red laminate bar shaped like a giant oar. Hurricane lamps flicker with red, green, and white LED bulbs. A painted placard above the bar says *Ahoy*. I expect an aquarium, but the only fish is a giant Marlin, its eye a dull bead, with shellacked gills, mounted on the wall.

Aunt Darlene leads me to a table, the only one dressed in red linen. The restaurant tables are circular, tall, chic, with stools to accommodate two or three diners. Bistro seating. Not what I imagined from Aunt Darlene. She walks behind the bar. Glassware clinks. I sit on the edge of the stool with Olivia on my lap.

Olivia is fussy, due to her diaper, I pat her until she quiets. Aunt Darlene returns, wearing a white smock over her khakis, deposits a square cocktail napkin on the table and serves a glass with a lemon wedge on the rim. She says, "Perrier," her smile stiff. "On the house." Her shirtsleeves, rolled to her elbows, expose the cupid tattoo on her forearm that I'd noticed in the hospital.

I misinterpreted her tattoo. The spearhead is not an arrow but a red apple. Aunt Darlene produces a BIC lighter from her smock pocket. I'm about to object. Smoking indoors in front of Olivia? Out of the question. A wick sizzles. A votive candle flickers. Aunt Darlene arranges a centerpiece, a glass globe housing a candle, between us. Candlelight softens Aunt Darlene, her hair is the color of winter ale, her center parting less crooked. I notice the resemblance between her and Jamie. They share that same small nose, and thin, rosy lips.

Aunt Darlene says, "Turning up the house lights might give customers the impression that The Rusty Sub Tavern is open for service." Her tone is collegial, as if we are in cahoots, conspiring a surprise bachelorette party, hiding from the guest of honor, not discussing baby Olivia's fate.

The Perrier bubbles and the glass sweats. Clear drops seep into the red tablecloth. The lemon slice falls from the rim of the glass into the Perrier. Aunt Darlene produces a straw from her smock pocket and slides it beside the glass. "Compostable bamboo. I'm trialing sustainable, eco-friendly barware. Straws, stirrers, skewers. Still use paper order pads, but iPads are the future. Pricey. But in the long run, it's good business."

Aunt Darlene sounds like a savvy investor, not like the barfly I'd expected. I'm thirsty, but I don't drink the Perrier. Olivia stretches, I shift her to my shoulder. Aunt Darlene's focus is not on me but Olivia, the bald patch above her left ear.

Cubed ice settles in the glass.

Aunt Darlene says, "Why'd you do it?"

"She was crying." A partial truth. Admitting my love for Olivia leaves me vulnerable and off-balance. I feel Aunt Darlene gaining the upper hand. I pegged her wrong. Unless it's an act, Aunt Darlene is a resourceful businesswoman. She must be intelligent and capable of learning to care for her niece.

"That's what babies do. Cry."

Aunt Darlene produces a pen and a small order pad from her smock pocket. She rolls the pen between her palms. Not a ballpoint but a red Sharpie.

My spine is rigid. I tell her, "Leave Peter out of this. He has nothing—"

"I thought my special delivery would get your attention. Listen, Baby Nurse, I did both of us a favor, not sending the cops. I needed time to get my ducks in a row at the condo before Child Protective Services visits. I'm rebranding The Rusty Sub Tavern into The Tavern. Negative publicity is the last thing I want. In fact, I gave it some thought—a kid is a plus. Family friendly. The vibe I am going for."

Aunt Darlene uncaps the Sharpie, taps the order pad. Red dots spot the page like dribbled blood. "The social worker from Child Protective Services called. I made excuses the first time but she's visiting the condo today. An official wellness check. Your time with the baby is up. She's not yours."

Jamie's memory is a painful stab. I clutch Olivia with one arm and grasp the locket around my neck with my free hand.

Aunt Darlene leans across the table, aims the Sharpie point at my sternum. "I need the kid. Have your own baby. My sister's kid is spoken for."

The barb lodges behind my heart. I recoil.

I say to Aunt Darlene, "You never missed Olivia. Didn't care enough to stop me from taking her—" A thunderstorm of angry tears threaten to rain.

Aunt Darlene walks to the bar and returns with an iPad. She shows me the screen and says, "I parked where I could watch the kid on the security camera. I thought the baby would stay quiet in the car but my meeting with the liquor distributor took longer than usual. The kid woke up and cried."

I stare at the iPad. A figure takes shape on the screen.

Aunt Darlene says, "Turns out, I made a mistake leaving the kid in the car. I hadn't anticipated a baby-napper prowling the parking lot. I got you on tape, Baby Nurse."

The iPad frame tightens. Hazy, but the figure in Lakeview Hospital scrubs is recognizable. My back is to the Nissan. It's me, walking with Olivia, her car seat in the opposite arm.

Bile bubbles from my stomach and sours my mouth. I ask Aunt Darlene how she found our house. She gloats. "I looked you up, Baby Nurse. Your Facebook page needs updating but I found your wedding pictures, your honeymoon and that mini-mansion of yours."

"My husband's medical journal?"

"A stroke of luck. You think I don't care but I followed you for a few miles, lost track of you in the rain, and I assumed you returned her to the hospital. I drove around the hospital lot, didn't see your car but I found the clunky blue Subaru from your honeymoon post, parked in a snobby space reserved for important doctors. The doors were unlocked, and I helped myself to a magazine cover."

I want to scream, *You're wrong!* at Aunt Darlene, but my throat constricts and all I manage is a whisper. "You don't care about Olivia."

"You're self-righteous enough to believe no one is good enough to have Olivia. But how difficult can one baby be? I'll figure it out. I'll manage."

"That's not what I think." My face flushes hot with anger. Aunt Darlene has nerve. I know Olivia. We have a real bond. And Aunt Darlene has no idea what we have been through.

She sets the iPad on the table. She reaches for Olivia, grabs her and Aunt Darlene's icy fingers brush my arm. "Come to your aunt, baby."

Olivia shrieks.

Aunt Darlene says, "Child Protective Services are due at the condo this morning." A phone from behind the bar rings. Simultaneously, "Piano Man" at a noxious volume, plays from Aunt Darlene's smock pocket. "My cell phone. I need to answer. Quiet, baby."

I say, "Olivia's diaper. She hates being wet." I pull out the clean one I carried with me.

Olivia cries. She's relentless. Tears stream her cheeks. She gasps and purple splotches bloom across both cheeks and her forehead. Aunt Darlene jiggles Olivia, a nonrhythmic motion that Olivia hates.

Aunt Darlene fails to comfort Olivia. My decision solidifies. Besides not loving Olivia, Aunt Darlene views her as a business commodity, a prop to appeal to The Rusty Sub's clientele. Worst of all, Aunt Darlene lacks maternal instinct, the vital ingredient to mothering, one that I possess. I fight my urge to wrestle Olivia from her. My hands fist, nails dig my palms.

The phone behind the bar doesn't let up. Billy Joel croons from Aunt Darlene's smock.

Olivia sobs. Her watery blue eyes fixate on me.

Keep crying. Good girl.

Aunt Darlene yells, "How can I answer the phone? I need to answer. Make her stop."

"It's her diaper. Let me—"

Olivia is thrust into my chest. I clutch her. Olivia gasps. The reprieve is followed by more crying, although at a lower volume.

Aunt Darlene leads me to the restroom with the kangaroo logo. "I'm watching." She puts the cell phone to her ear. "Piano Man" abruptly ends. She says to the caller, "What's the problem? I'm in the middle—" The phone behind the bar abruptly ceases ringing.

I run into the bathroom. Intended for a single patron, the door has a lock. I turn the bolt.

Aunt Darlene hollers at whoever phoned, "You'll get your money. I told you. I need time. Now? What did you tell them?" There's a pause and Aunt Darlene's voice fades. I imagine she walked behind the bar.

Olivia's brow crinkles. "I'm worried too," I tell her. Aunt Darlene might be Olivia's family, but she's strapped for cash. Fostering Olivia comes with a monthly stipend, a guaranteed payday from the State. Aunt Darlene wants Olivia. But for the wrong reasons.

There's a window above the sink facing the alley where the Jetta is parked. There's no screen and unlatching the window is easy.

I hear footsteps outside the bathroom. Aunt Darlene hammers the door. "You done in there?"

I say, "Almost. Messy diaper."

Olivia resumes crying.

Aunt Darlene yells, "They're at the condo. I need the baby. Now. Clean and happy. You hear me?"

"Working on it."

I hop onto the vanity. And with Olivia under my left arm, I reach, hoisting us onto the sill. I can jump three feet and land without falling.

Aunt Darlene pounds the door.

The locket dangles from my neck and Olivia grasps it in her palm. I kiss her forehead and tell her, "I won't drop you."

The doorknob jiggles. "Give me—"

I shut my eyes. And jump.

CHAPTER THIRTEEN

My Converse thump. My right ankle rolls. I stumble, stabilize and open my eyes. Olivia is in my arms, wide-eyed and unhurt. I run, my right ankle pops. I reach the Jetta, peel Olivia's fingers from the locket. She willingly goes into her car seat, and I snap the harness. The Jetta starts, coughs, and I pump the gas pedal and nearly plow into the *Wrong Way* sign.

I imagine Aunt Darlene, livid when she breaks the lock and discovers the bathroom empty. I drive. It's early morning, after dawn but the sun is muted by cloud cover. There are too many whizzing cars to discern a blue Nissan in the rearview mirror from the blur of traffic. My heart clammers in my chest. At the first opportunity, I exit onto a side street. But the road is anything but smooth, the surface pocked, some holes patched with gravel, others open wounds. I swerve. My grip on the steering wheel is too tight. The Jetta jerks in response to my alternating pulses on the accelerator and taps on the brake. Like a nervous tick, I scan the rearview mirror. Except for a pickup truck, I'm the only driver.

In retrospect I wish my focus was on what lies ahead, not behind. The Jetta lurches and dives. Metal grinds. Vapor rises from the hood. I knock the steering wheel, hard. There's a knife-like stab between my eyes and my nose gushes warm, sticky goo. I scream, "Olivia!"

I have the sensation of being engulfed by a tidal wave. I blink but there's nothing to see under water. Suddenly, I break the surface. And I drink in brilliant white light. I wonder if I'm dead.

The bright light wobbles and dims.

A masculine voice tells me, "Hurry. Get out."

My lap belt releases. I climb from the Jetta and step from a ditch. It's quiet, except for a sinister hiss, air escaping the Jetta's punctured tires. The back seat is vacant. "Olivia," I cry.

The masculine voice tells me, "Look, behind you."

I hear Olivia sneeze. A few feet behind the Jetta, on the road, Olivia sits strapped in her car seat, illuminated by the headlamps of a parked pickup truck. I see the measuring spoons grasped between her hands.

I drove into a ditch. In addition to the flat tires, the Jetta suffers a dislocated front fender. I don't need to ask if the car is drivable, the Jetta kneels, in surrender, on deflated front tires. The fender remains lodged in the ditch. "What do I do now?"

The tall man adjusts his painter's cap. "Driving like you were, you hit the pothole with enough force to blow the front tires."

"Marcus?"

"Can't very well leave Genie's car like that. Stand clear."

Marcus hitches the Jetta to his pickup truck and tows it from the road. Eyes shut, head bowed, I bid the Jetta goodbye. Discarded in the woods, an undignified end to the loyal car Mom drove for a decade.

Marcus says, "This will do for now. It's out of the way. Truck's got space to spare. Ride with me."

From the wrecked Jetta, I hear Mom's gentle prompt. *Trust*

him. If Marcus was Mom's friend, it's time for him to become mine.

"Hurry," Marcus calls.

The truck is warm, but I can't stop shivering. Marcus has cleared the passenger seat for us, newspapers cover the floor mat. Olivia's car seat takes up the extra room in the front, forcing me to lean against the door.

My Converse toe a newspaper, days old. It's upside down, but I recognize Olivia's grainy picture on the bottom of the front page. The heading, *Lakeview Hospital NICU Baby Orphaned.* I was there when Jamie took the photo, Olivia, recognizable by the square patch of missing hair above her left ear. Jamie had made the picture her screen saver.

Marcus knows. Rather, he has known since the morning he brought me coffee in Mom's apartment. My nose throbs and my puffy lip make speaking difficult. Marcus reaches across Olivia's car seat, and hands me a folded cloth. "For your face," he says. I dab my nose.

The truck travels over the unpaved road, jostling gently. Olivia sleeps, head listing to the left, the position she'd preferred during her remaining days in the NICU. I take the blanket from the plastic diaper bag, fold it and prop her head. Marcus had the forethought to grab the bag from the Jetta. I say to Marcus, "Thank you."

I want to ask Marcus how he knew where to find me and why didn't he say something when he recognized Olivia as the Lakeview Hospital orphan. The unexpressed words roll into a hard marble that lodges in my throat. My questions for Marcus need to wait. He drives without offering an opening for conversation. For miles, Marcus remains quiet, but he steals quick glances at Olivia, at me, and returns his focus to the road.

The truck ambles along. The morning brightens, the sun emerges from the cloud cover and Marcus extinguishes the headlamps. Yet I squint like I'm peering through a kaleidoscope. My world has collapsed, reduced to Olivia, asleep at my side, and Marcus driving his truck. I clutch the locket, and my heart pounds in my chest, giving the locket its own pulse.

Marcus taps the steering wheel. His smile is broad and his white teeth flash. We're at an intersection. "Where do we go from here?"

"Mom's apartment? Can we—"

"No key. Even I can't get inside. The ficus, finicky thing, will need misting. The Super is showing the apartment. She'll rent it as is."

"But Mom's things." My eyes sting. I regret not taking better care of Mom's belongings. Her apartment will be occupied by a stranger.

"I fancy Genie knows what mattered most." He turns to look at me. "I don't know where you're running but seems to me, you're headed from trouble toward more trouble." The truck idles. "You ready to share them? It's the only way we can figure out where to go from here."

I've precious little time left. Child Protective Services must have paid Aunt Darlene a visit and discovered that she doesn't have Olivia.

My throat loosens and I swallow my doubt. I'm ready to trust Marcus. "We?"

"I've kept watch over you and Little One. Your mom, Genie, that's what she would want. She talked about you, her daughter, the baby nurse, and how big a heart you have."

"Mom said that. About me?"

"She worried that one day your heart would lead you to trouble. I've kept an eye on you since we met. I understand that Genie was right. She worried about you caring too much." Marcus gestures toward Olivia. "And Little One. I have a sense about things, and I could tell you were headed in the wrong direction. That's why I followed you. Been there more than once in my day."

"What would Mom say now? If she knew?"

"She'd warn—can't keep running like you are. Not with Little One. Not forever." Marcus releases the brake and the pickup eases onto the main road. "Where to?"

"Back roads," I feel Peter, calm and unflustered, answer for me. "We need to talk. Except I need to warn you. Knowing me. Helping me. Is risky."

Marcus laughs. "There you go again. Carrying the weight of the world. Slow down. Say what you need to say."

Marcus makes sharing my secrets easy. He nods. Mumbles, "I see. That is tough. You did what you needed to do." If he questions my judgement or my decisions, he keeps his doubts to himself. Focused on the road, painter's cap low on his brow, he drives. When I finish, I feel refreshed, like after a full night of sleep or dowsing my face with cold water.

Marcus pulls a cloth from his coveralls, wipes his mouth, and says, "That's some trouble you're in." A moment later he adds, "Lucky thing about trouble, it's never too late to reset your way. To turn what's wrong, right."

I bristle. "I have done what's right. All along. For baby Olivia." But not for Peter or Sheila. Certainly not for Marcus. Helping me could cost him his job.

"If you say so."

Olivia thrashes in her car seat and cries. Tears track her cheeks and her lower lip trembles.

"Need formula?" Marcus steers into a Wawa gas station store, parks at the periphery, hopefully outside the scope of the surveillance cameras.

Olivia is in my lap, mouth wide open.

Marcus looks pensive. "Tell me you aren't nursing another mama's child?"

My silence is answer enough.

Marcus exits the truck, taking the keys from the ignition and stowing them in the front pocket of his coveralls. He adjusts his cap lower on his brow, saunters across the lot and enters the convenience store.

The windows of the truck are sealed tight, and we're parked on the outskirts. But I imagine a bell dings when Marcus enters. I watch him tour the aisles, recognizable by his cap. He pauses at the self-serve coffee urns.

Olivia swallows noisily.

"Chocolate chip or blueberry?" A wax bag of muffins lands on the dashboard. Marcus plants two coffees in the cupholders, slams the driver side door, and fishes the keys from his coveralls. "We better go."

A black-and-white police van, lights spinning, pulls into the lot and idles in front of the store. For a moment I doubt Marcus. He won't meet my gaze, but he's likely embarrassed by my feeding Olivia. Has he betrayed me, notified the cashier that there's a kidnapped infant in the parking lot? I insert my pinky at the corner of Olivia's mouth and detach her from my nipple. She's all smiles and doesn't protest her car seat. She needs a diaper change, but it'll wait.

Marcus exits the Wawa lot. He drives, antsy, he checks the rearview mirror. The police van doesn't follow. "Amber Alert for Little One. I saw it on the store TV when I checked out." He dials on the radio, adjusts the volume. A reporter drones, "Three-month-old Caucasian female... with a bald spot above her left ear. Missing from her court-assigned guardian..."

My stomach drops. I shut the radio off. The truck rumbles. Olivia, lulled by the vrooming engine, sucks her lower lip and drifts to sleep, secure in her safety seat.

Marcus says, "Where to?"

"Just drive."

Encapsulated in the truck, I observe the world beyond the windshield. Familiar yet foreign, like I'm visiting for the first time. We've left the outskirts of Philadelphia and are deep in the Main Line suburbs. Merion, Bala Cynwood, Narberth, and Haverford. Stately mansions behind stone walls, tended gardens, a world shielded from heartache, with lawns perpetually tended green despite a dark, cold winter. A Tudor mansion captures my fancy and I imagine a scenario where Marcus parks in the circular drive. Peter opens the front door and invites us into the marble foyer, lit by a crystal chandelier. The house is a wonder: the library shelves leather-bound books, a dozen bedrooms furnished with plush beds dressed in hotel-quality linens, and a kitchen stocked with delicacies. Hungry, I devour the muffin and feel car-sick, and suddenly exhausted.

An hour later and Marcus asks, "Where we going?"

"And what would Mom tell me to do now?"

Marcus says, "No one has a perfect life. Tour the inside, and you'll discover their burdens. Invisible from the outside." Marcus tugs his cap. "From what you said earlier, you don't know much about Little One's aunt. She is, after all, the mama's sister."

My spine stiffens. "Aunt Darlene doesn't care—"

"But have you listened to her tell it? Offered to help?" Marcus breaks for a *Stop* sign.

"She abandoned Olivia in the car... I would never endanger —" Except I have. More than once. Olivia spent last night not in her crib, but my car. A car I wrecked. I jumped from a window with Olivia in my arms. A baby needs a predictable schedule, stability, and safety. Yet Olivia's life these past days with me is anything but. Driving at night, crashing into a ditch, squatting in a locked apartment, leaving the husband I love.

I was once Olivia's nurse, obligated to protect and heal her. But my heart bursts with an agonizing realization. Olivia is not safe. She is a wanted baby. Child Protective Services is searching for a former premature infant with a bald spot above her left ear. Law enforcement is searching for me. This is hardly the life Olivia deserves.

I kiss her forehead. She smells sour. Besides endangering her health, she needs a bath. Something I'm unable to provide in Marcus's truck. I gaze out of the windshield. Sunlight bounces from the glass. The effect is dazzling. I blink. Tears douse my cheeks and drip onto my lap.

I feel Marcus's glance. "You're sad. Mind me asking what about?"

"I'm a nurse. Trained to save people. But I keep losing the ones who mean the most to me. My baby. Mom. Dad. Olivia's parents." I can't bring myself to utter the excruciating truth, that I'll lose Olivia too.

"All that saving. A tall order. For you to fix what's wrong in the world."

"I want to fix it for Olivia."

"I was once like you, carrying other people's troubles, and all that heartache landed me in a hole."

I wait for Marcus to explain. We're on Lancaster Avenue, facing east, familiar territory. Minutes from Villanova University. Marcus breaks for a red light. Morning classes begin at Villanova University. Students in university sweatshirts, North Face fleeces, backpacks hooked on their shoulders, scurry the walkways. Marcus taps the steering wheel with his thumbs. "The best of intentions, even yours, comes with a price. My intentions, good or bad, were misunderstood and I paid with my youth."

A train whistles, signaling a predictable stop at the Villanova station in the rear campus. The morning riders; a mix of students, cooks, campus caretakers, and professors who live in Philadelphia and commute to the suburbs. A second whistle, and the train grinds the tracks. We're exactly where we need to be.

The chapel spire prods the sky. Clouds evaporate. I exhale. Marcus's tapping thumbs rest and we share a reverent hush. I point to the student commuter lot. "Here. Stop." Marcus steers the pickup into a vacant space in the commuter lot facing the St. Thomas chapel.

I hold the locket in my fingers and reaffirm my vow to Jamie. "If you're watching, you see me fail. Trust me one more time to do what's right for Olivia."

The prospect of continuing without Marcus has me feeling lonely even before I exit the truck. I force words through the tight spot in my throat. I thank Marcus. "Mom was lucky to have you. A true friend. When Mom taught, she never had time for a friend, her students took every minute." Or me. Mom rarely had time for me. I can't finish and succumb to raw emotion. Marcus pats my shoulder. "You were everything to Genie. Sure, she loved school. Students? They were part of the job. Her one regret was not being there for you when you came home from school."

"Mom said..."

Marcus squeezes my shoulder. "Genie said those very words. You're a lot like her. But only as much as you choose to be. Live your life. Not Genie's. Be your own woman, Baby Nurse." Marcus releases my shoulder. He rubs Olivia's cheek, and then hooks his thumbs in his coveralls. Before I can answer, the chapel chimes. Deep, mournful, the bells toll and reverberate.

Marcus asks, "You going in there? You want me with you?"

"This is something Olivia and I need to do. The two of us. Together." I unbuckle Olivia's safety harness, lift her, warm and heavy with sleep, and step from the truck. It's fitting that my final effort to protect Olivia brings me back to the school where

I learned to be a nurse. I'm ready to take these final steps on my own.

Marcus exits the driver's side, and we stand, shoulder to shoulder. A few cars pass but none stop and recognize me as a kidnapper. I leave the car seat but take the diaper bag, hoping to change Olivia in the bathroom. I ask, "What will you do?" Imagining Marcus returning to the Radcliff, sorting and recycling newspapers, is a stretch.

He tugs his cap and smiles. "Genie is gone. You and Little One are on your way. Time to move on. Try something new. Maybe I'll book that cruise." Marcus hops into the driver's seat but before shutting the door he says, "Genie left you with everything you need. All you got to do is slow down."

CHAPTER FOURTEEN

I step from the curb and cross Lancaster Avenue.

Directly ahead, St. Thomas of Villanova Church rises from the earth. Its spires reach like fingertips communing with the heavens. Feeling hopeful, I bounce on the balls of my scuffed Converse, climb the stone steps, inserting my feet into the smooth grooves slickened by over a century's worth of visitors. Individuals not unlike me, weighted with worry, burdened by debt, hardened by longing.

With each step, my angst lessens.

The church's face is unblemished despite enduring Pennsylvania's snowy winters, rainy springs, and humid summers. The immovable granite bricks preside over wedding vows, dignify the dead, and listen to lamenting students before final exams.

After my father's death, Mom and I had observed *shiva*, the ritual seven-day mourning period following a Jewish person's death. Tradition dictates an unlocked front door. Friends and synagogue members enter without knocking. Because Mom died during the pandemic, Peter and I couldn't observe *shiva* and grieved in private.

I approach the church's carved wooden entrance. I sense the doors are unlocked, the same way that a shiva house is open for condolence calls. Relying on faith, I grasp the iron door handle. I anticipate cold metal, but it's warm, as if recently held. I yank and the door parts a sliver, enough for me to slip through.

I stand in the foyer with Olivia in my arms, and I view the sanctuary. The center aisle is flanked by oak pews, all vacant. I've been here twice before, the first time with Mary, my lab partner and the second was for nursing school convocation, the official occasion when my classmates and I received white lab coats, though I now bear little resemblance to that nursing student, fingers trembling from nervousness, buttoning her brand-new lab coat, and reciting the Nightingale Pledge.

The starched white coats symbolized our dedication to learning. I kept the lab coat, but it's now stained with brown Betadine and missing a button. My heady desire to restore sick patients to health, naïve as it was, endures. But I've also since learned that healing is multifaceted. This is especially true in the NICU. Parents might take their baby home following months in the hospital only to obsess over every hiccup, and their parenting becomes a joyless chore, reduced to a series of stressful tasks. Their wish for a healthy baby must be mourned before parents can wholly embrace their new reality, loving a child with lifelong medical needs.

When a NICU baby dies, parents leave the hospital with arms empty. This is the line nurses straddle; despite our best efforts, not every patient can be healed, not every family can be made whole. I wrap Olivia in a hug. The hollow behind my heart contracts in anticipation of another inevitable loss.

Together we survey the white marble, polished to a gleam. Diffused light filters through blue stained glass. The church's silence is meditative rather than unnerving, and there's an inviting sweetness about the air. I let myself be drawn into the sanctuary. I came to find help for Olivia, to search for someone who works here; a priest, nun, or caretaker. Yet I can't resist sitting. I chose a pew, hoping it's the same one I sat in with Mary. "Quit trying so hard," she'd said and shushed me. There's no harm in resting for a moment, breathing the delicious aroma, gathering my thoughts. I wait. For what? Divine intervention to heal the relationships I damaged. A solution for Olivia. I fidget, toe the kneeler. I pick up a prayer book but replace it before Olivia can tear a page. How long must I wait for an answer, a solution to arrive? Mary didn't mention a timeline. I suppose God doesn't work on a schedule. Not like trains and buses. I close my eyes. And wait my turn to be helped.

Olivia is content on my lap, her head on my chest. One of us gets this "wait patiently game". Seconds, minutes, an hour of unaccounted time vaporizes, and slips past without me noticing. Sure enough, a rudimentary solution gathers shape. Imperfect but I mull the potential possibilities. "Yes," I say, "this plan might work. Olivia will be safe."

The church isn't unoccupied like I'd thought. I hear a woman's voice. I recognize the hum, tongue clucks, and mewing; a cappella warm-ups, intended to exercise the vocal cords in preparation for unleashing a singing voice. Similar to plucking cello strings before a concert to limber my fingers. Olivia yawns awake, alert and curious. There is singing. A soprano, impossible to locate, her effervescent voice resonates through the cathedral.

Olivia is content on my lap, for the moment, but still in need of a clean diaper and due to be fed. I wonder if St. Thomas has a nursing mothers' room. Except, Olivia is not my baby and I'm not her mother.

The church is suddenly silent. Olivia hoots, mimicking the singer's vocals. She is a remarkable, inquisitive baby. If I had my notebook, I'd record Olivia's latest milestone. Her lower lip trembles. Happiness morphs to angst. She cries. Magnified tenfold by the church dome, Olivia's lone cry echoes and I hear a choir of miserable infants. Rocking doesn't help. Wide-mouthed, Olivia protests her dirty diaper. I gather her, fists waving, legs pedaling. I've misplaced the plastic bag that contains a single, desperately needed diaper.

A voice says, "I thought I was alone." A woman walks from the front of the church, down the center aisle, her hair a black halo, dressed in jeans, distressed at the knees and a grey Villanova sweatshirt. Is this who I have been waiting for? The woman retrieves the diaper bag from the aisle, returns it to me. Her nails are manicured pink ovals. She waves her beautiful hand in front of her face. I can't tell if she is shooing me away or greeting me.

I ask the woman, "Do you work here?"

"Me? I come here to rehearse. But only when no one is around." The woman steps closer, her mouth a hard line. Not a scowl but not a smile either.

Hope dissipates. She doesn't seem like a willing helper. The opposite in fact. Disappointment saps my energy. "I'm sorry to disturb your privacy, to interrupt your vocal warm-ups. Your range is beautiful. Soprano, right?"

This time there is no mistaking the singer's smile. "I'm nothing special. I rehearse here while the space is vacant, but it won't be in an hour. There's a scheduled service." The woman's smile fades; she's close enough that the dim light reveals my shabby clothes, bruised lip. Another foot closer, she'll sniff Olivia's diaper.

I hear Marcus's parting advice to slow down. I sit with my back braced against the firm pew. Because I have nothing else to offer, I risk the truth. "Meet baby Olivia. She's the reason I'm here. Olivia is not my baby. We need sanctuary."

"Welcome to St. Thomas." The singer's lips soften, but her focus on me and Olivia is intense.

"Can we stay here and wait—"

"Not a good idea."

In the moment it takes me to regroup, and shimmy from the pew with Olivia, the woman is at the altar. She skirts a potted green fern, gestures for me to follow, and disappears behind a heavy drape. I hustle but needn't fear losing my way. I follow her voice. The song is one I recognize, Beyoncé, "The Best Thing I Never Had".

I tell Olivia, "I don't know where we're going, but I'll make it part of the plan." I part the thick ecru drape and duck backstage. The staging area during a concert is a hub of activity, a chaotic whirl. Musicians tune instruments, replace snapped strings, search for sheet music, adjust skinny-necked music stands. Meanwhile, the audience, or in the case of St. Thomas, the congregation, never experiences a disruption in the performance. For now, it is empty.

Olivia nuzzles my shirt as we walk.

"Just a little bit longer," I tell her.

"Be careful," our guide sing-songs.

The hallway is dark. I crouch to avoid hitting my head on the low ceiling.

The woman skips down a staircase. The steps are covered with a well-traveled runner. I feel less alone; how many women before me have sought sanctuary in this church? A door opens. The singer's voice is urgent. "In here. No one will disturb you."

Lights pop. I cross the threshold and face a frightening image. Me. Reflected in a mirrored wall. My hair looks like it has been caught in a wind turbine. My freckles are hidden under a smear of dried blood from my accident with the Jetta. I touch a discolored spot above my lip. It's sore but looks worse than it feels.

Amused, Olivia smiles and coos to the baby in the mirror.

Singing Woman says, "No one will dare enter the bridal suite." The door clicks shut.

We stand in front of the mirror. My fair complexion appears even paler in comparison to the singer's olive skin. We're about the same height. Our shoulders touch. I guess she is a few years younger than I am, but her pensive expression accentuates tiny lines at the corner of her eyes. I notice I've gained a few wrinkles of my own. "I'm Annabelle. I graduated from Villanova almost four years ago."

"Naomi. I'm a sophomore. Undecided about my major." Naomi tosses her thick black ringlets from her shoulders.

I sit in a chair in front of the bridal suite vanity. But I've seen enough of my reflection and angle away from the mirrors.

Naomi sits on a stool beside me, sets her phone on the vanity beneath the mirrors and holds out her palms. "I babysit between classes. I might study to be a teacher."

Olivia goes willingly. Naomi cuddles her and says, "I came to St. Thomas to sing, and I found you instead." Naomi takes a cosmetic case from the bridal vanity, removes a plastic comb, and runs it though Olivia's fine ginger hair. I shift, lean against the vanity, my hand inches from Naomi's phone. Vital for my plan. My phone was intentionally left at home to avoid involving Peter by answering his messages or calling when I feel desperate. Like now.

Naomi pauses, the comb poised over Olivia's left ear, the square patch of missing hair. Fear hardens her hazel eyes.

My stomach drops. "Sanctuary," I plead. My fingers close around the phone.

"How could you? Steal a helpless baby? I should call the police." She reaches for her phone, but I swipe it from the vanity. Naomi hugs Olivia, stands and steps away, putting several feet of distance between us. "I trusted you. Felt sorry for you. I took you for a domestic violence victim. But you are the worst kind of person, a kidnapper. And a thief. I am so stupid."

Humiliated, I slump in the chair. Naomi is right about me. I've become someone I don't recognize. Not a trustworthy NICU nurse but a person who takes what she wants.

I put Naomi's phone on the vanity. "Forgive me. It's a lot to ask after taking your phone. I need it to set things right. Please hear me out."

Naomi picks up her phone, fingers the screen. Olivia grasps Naomi's hair and yanks.

I can't help from smiling. "Olivia pulls my hair all the time. She must like you."

Naomi sits in the chair and wrestles her curls from Olivia's grip.

"You have no reason to trust me, in fact you have every reason not to. Give me one final chance. For Olivia."

Naomi's hazel eyes narrow.

"Olivia's parents died in a car accident three days ago. I took her, not only because I love her, but because I thought I was the only person who could protect her. Except I keep messing up. Everything I do to try to keep her safe falls short." Tears streak my cheeks.

Naomi softens. "I think I know how that feels."

"The irony is I'm used to making things right, restoring things that are broken. It's my job."

"Not everything can be fixed the way we want it," Naomi says softly. "Sometimes we can't control what happens. We have to take what life throws, even when it's unfair." After a pause, Naomi says, "Especially when it's unfair." She slides her phone across the vanity. "It looks like you need this. I'm a good babysitter, by the way. I can change Olivia." Naomi carries Olivia into the bridal suite powder room.

I take Naomi's phone, with permission this time. My final

plan hinges on one person, a woman I admire above everyone else. *Please, please, please answer.*

I text:

> It's me. Are you home or in the NICU?

My message delivers and seconds later is read. A conversation bubble wobbles. Robyn is typing. Naomi's phone buzzes with an answer.

> Home. Heard the news. Worried sick. Call Now.

Naomi emerges from the powder room with Olivia. Face washed, Olivia wears the clean onesie from the diaper bag, and she smells like a fresh diaper. Naomi rocks Olivia, singing a gentle but recognizable rendition of Lizzo's "Good as Hell".

Robyn answers her phone, her voice tinged with concern and anger. "Tell me you are ready to listen to reason. But first, are you all right?"

I falter, wasting precious seconds; what if Robyn gets in trouble for helping me? Or blames me for what I have done, the way Sheila did? I already lost my best friend; I can't lose Robyn too.

"Annabelle, are you all right?" Robyn asks again. Her strong, calm voice, as it always does, centers me. I plow forward. "Olivia and I need you."

"Where are you?"

I ask Robyn, "You still an emergency foster-care provider?" My entire plan depends on her answer.

"Since Robbie. Thom and I haven't stopped, even after Robbie's adoption."

"I need you to write this down."

I hear paper crinkle. I imagine Robyn flipping pages in her

sons' *Bob the Builder* coloring book and searching for a piece of broken crayon.

Robyn says, "Ready."

I tell her my idea. I hear a page turn. Robyn has suggestions, and I have the good sense to listen. When we agree on the details, I say, "Read what you wrote back to me."

Robyn does, her voice urgent but centered. We have a plan.

"I'm on the way," Robyn says. The call ends.

Olivia sucks her fist. She seems to say, *Discuss this later. Feed me now.*

I tell Naomi, "Olivia is hungry. This will seem strange, but I need to feed Olivia. One last time." Naomi stands, returns Olivia to me, and digs into the bag looking for a bottle. Instead, I lift my shirt, unhook my bra, and Olivia and I fuse.

Naomi's eyes widen. "You breastfeed? But the baby, how can—"

I explain. Too much to recount, so little time. But talking out loud to a stranger, voicing the truth, is strangely comforting. I sense Janice in her white lab coat nodding in a Zoom therapy session, along with Naomi.

Naomi is quiet for a while. "The baby you lost, is that why you did it, took Olivia, I mean?"

Is that why? "Grief. Disappointment has a way of sneaking up on us," I reply.

"That's why I sing. I feel different. Confident. When I sing, I feel I can let go, and when I do, I have the sense I am strong enough to conquer anything."

"Music is powerful. I used to be a musician once."

"What did you play?"

"The cello. It was my mother's favorite instrument. She loved that I was so invested in my high-school orchestra and private cello lessons, thought that I would take it to the next level, but that didn't happen..." I let the bittersweet memories flood back. Though it started with passion, my relationship with the cello shifted. Eager to master the instrument, perfect every stroke and pluck, I was controlled by what I thought the conductors wanted. The joy of creating music left, and I stopped the summer before nursing school. The shell of my cello case sits in one of the many empty rooms in our big house.

"I understand. But I can't just give up music. You and Olivia were the first audience I've had in months. I practice in private since I didn't make Villanova's select choir."

"But you'll audition again? I believe in you."

"Only if you play your cello again."

I've nothing left to lose. "I promise."

Olivia feeds with vigor, unaware that once again her fate is shifting. Olivia's fists release, one finger at a time, like flower petals blooming. I've listened to my colleagues relate their child's final time at breast. Sometimes the last feed is intentional, after achieving a milestone like baby's first birthday. For others the baby sprouted a sharp tooth or began eating solid foods. This is my final time with Olivia and the emotion is real. The bridal suite is well stocked with tissues. Boxes planted across the vanity. I quietly cry into a wadded tissue ball.

I fill Naomi in on the plan I made with Robyn. Naomi adds her idea, one that will shield Olivia from undue stress. Naomi scrolls her phone. "I know people." Her fingers work. *Ping, ping, ping.* The phone skitters and vibrates. "My friend is applying to law school. Here at Villanova. The Charles Widger School of Law?"

"I know it." The nursing school is behind the main campus, close to the law school. I passed the law library while walking from the Villanova train station to nursing school.

"I messaged her—she says—'sanctuary'—is a real thing. Law enforcement can enter a house of worship but prefer not to. That's good news. Right?"

Yes. Good news comes in small interments. I appreciate Naomi and her efforts on my behalf. We've just met but I feel her sincere concern, her genuine bond with Olivia. The bridal suite has a digital clock. Brides, after all, have a schedule to keep. I have less than thirty minutes remaining with Olivia. Part of my plan is to call Peter after Olivia is safe. Waiting and talking to him when this is over protects him. I know he would be at my side, but for his own good, it's best to wait and not involve him in the details.

Naomi works her phone. A moment later she says, "The Sirens. They agree to help Olivia. They were already scheduled to be here at the church for an event anyway."

I should have guessed from her perfect pitch; Naomi aspires to be a Siren. A singer with the Villanova women's exclusive a cappella choir. I swaddle Olivia into a compact bundle. Her lids flutter with sleep. I wonder if after we're separated, I'll appear in her dreams. I kiss her forehead. The tip of her nose. I inhale, filling my nostrils with her scent. I whisper close to her ear, "Don't be afraid. It's not that I don't want to keep you. I love you, and that's why we must be apart. You'll hear loud noises, commotion, but you'll be surrounded by generous women who will protect you."

I'm crying. Another wad of tissue. I stand.

Naomi looks fierce. Her hazel eyes flecked green. "They're here. We need to go. The church will get busy."

I want to ask about the event that intersects with ours, not that it matters.

Naomi exits the bridal suite. "Follow me."

We leave. I walk with Olivia cradled in my arms. I follow Naomi like a soldier deployed to battle. Knees stiff. Back straight. I hear voices. An angelic choir. "Listen," I whisper to Olivia. "Sirens. They're singing you to safety."

Naomi stops and says, "You sure you want to leave through the main entrance?"

"Yes," I say. I'm finished hiding. I'm ready to face the world, for better and for worse.

She hesitates and then wraps me in a brief embrace. Her hair smells like lavender and patchouli. She presses her cheek to mine and says the most beautiful thing, "You and Olivia? You're meant to be together. I can tell."

Naomi releases the hug. I want to thank her. But she's moving. Fast.

"Careful," Naomi calls to me over her shoulder.

Olivia and I are engulfed by a vocal tide. Naomi's soprano blends with a dozen women. The swell harmonizes. The wall of sound carries us to St. Thomas's grand entrance. Outside, sunlight severs the sky. I cup my hand above Olivia's forehead, shading her from the direct light. I blink but yellow-and-orange splotches swim. A camera flashes. The media is sparse, just one reporter and a pair of photographers from *The Inquirer*. The photogenic Sirens draw attention, seek the camera, strike poses, and shield Olivia. They sing a medley. The final one is poignant, Olivia still in my arms. James Taylor's "Sweet Baby James". I look for Robyn.

I hear her. And she's all business. Robyn commands a path through the crowd. "Coming through. Give me room." Her braids are drawn into a high ponytail. She scans the crowd, searching for me. Our eyes meet. Robyn inserts herself between the singers and holds out her arms.

Seconds. Only seconds to say goodbye. I tell Olivia, "I love you. I'm not giving up on you. I promise Robyn will take care of you. I will see you soon."

I'm Siren strong. There are no tears. I'm cried dry. I pass Olivia to the only woman I trust with my baby. Our hands touch and Robyn squeezes my fingers. And Olivia, briefly mine, is gone. Robyn and Olivia press through the crowd where Thom waits with a car. Olivia is safe.

My empty arms drop, hands fisted, anticipating the pair of cold cuffs. The singing ends abruptly. The pair of police cars parked in front of the church quiet their wail. Red-and-blue lights stop spinning.

A hearse rolls in front of the church. Attendants, attired in long black coats, off-load a casket. The event is a funeral. The police respectfully wait. The coffin makes its ascent and disappears into the church.

I stand at the bottom of the staircase, on the stone step. My heart still pumps. What amazes me is the sun. How it shines bright on this dark day.

ACT THREE

Let us never consider ourselves finished, nurses.
We must be learning all of our lives.

— Florence Nightingale 1820–1910

CHAPTER FIFTEEN

"I get to call someone, right?" I ask a second time in case the police officer can't hear me from the back seat, where I sit behind a plexiglass divider. My question goes unanswered. I worry he has forgotten about me. Maybe the officer, focused on navigating traffic, isn't interested in conversation. From the rearview mirror, I see the Sirens disperse from the church. And sunlight reflects from the roof of the hearse.

Several minutes pass, and I wonder in silence where we are going. A half-hour later and we've left the suburbs, the squad car merges into thick city traffic. Without remark, the officer parks, exits, opens the rear door, and motions for me to get out. I obey and he's patient, granting me additional moments to find my footing. Walking with my hands clasped behind my back requires balance.

The policeman leads me through the rear door of the Philadelphia detention center, where I'm passed to a woman in a khaki uniform. She's older than me, heavyset, and gives me a once-over with a bored expression. Maybe she wanted the day off, but at the last minute got called to work this shift and is stuck in jail, with me. Blue latex gloves snap, and though I'm wearing fitted leggings, her gloved palms pat my hips, thighs, my bra with methodical efficiency. She confiscates my Converse; I roll my filthy socks into the shoes. I'm barefoot on the linoleum floor, bits of gravel stuck between my toes.

The guard gives me black flip-flops. She drops my sneakers one at a time into a plastic bag. If she's disgusted by my damp, shredded Converse, or the fact that I need a shower, not a quiver of emotion registers on her face.

"The necklace." She slips the leather cord from my neck, examines the locket, and drops it into the bag.

"I need that." I watch the box containing Olivia's ginger strands rest at the bottom of the plastic bag.

"No jewelry." My wedding ring is removed from my finger.

Without it, I feel like I'm betraying Peter. There's no negotiating with the guard. She releases the cuffs from my wrists, not the silver bracelets I'd anticipated but plastic zip ties. The guard leads me to a phone in a hallway. She stands a foot away, arms folded across her broad chest.

I'm not even sure the phone has a chance to ring but Peter answers, "Belle."

"I'm sorry." Lame, but it's all I can manage.

Peter's voice is a steady stream, outlining a map to navigate my freedom. He pauses between, "attorney" and "bail." There's an unnatural quiet on the phone. No beeper, pagers, or alarms. I hear him breathe.

"Are you in the call room?" My throat burns and I wish I had a cold bottled water.

"Home." Peter's voice turns fuzzy. "Suspended. Indefinitely..."

The guard announces, "Time's up."

A second before the guard takes the phone, Peter intuits my unasked question, and answers, "Yes. Belle, I love you."

Footfalls travel the linoleum corridor. Buzzers sound. Electronic locks release, heavy doors thud. A toilet flushes. A faucet drips. Someone cries. Not a newborn baby but the low, pitiful drone of an adult woman. From the next cell, there's a hiss. "Hey. Baby-stealer. Why'd you do it?"

My cell smells like industrial laundry detergent, Arm and Hammer maybe. There's a pair of cots and I lie on my back, hoping that I don't get a roommate. "Cellmate" is the correct term. I plug my fingers into my ears. The hissing questions and the grown-up wail fades.

Somewhere, I hear Olivia's hungry cry. Warm milk flows from my breasts. Soaking my T-shirt, wetting the sheet. The wasted milk slows to a drip. My fingers search my neck for the cord, the locket's absence a phantom pain. My link to Jamie and Olivia severed.

I fear Olivia thinks I abandoned her. Abandonment, a damaging emotion for a baby. Babyhood sets the groundwork for a lifetime of healthy relationships. Trust versus mistrust, I learned in nursing school. If Olivia internalizes mistrust and expects abandonment rather than lasting love from the caregivers in her life, she'll have difficulty building friendships. I cover my face with my arm, cry into my elbow, muffling my sobs. Tears drip, pool in my ears.

Time arrests. There's little difference between day and night. Night is never dark, just less light than day. Meals punctuate the formless hours. Trays, with a hotdog or a taco or a patty on a starchy bun, accompanied by a mini milk carton slide through the slot in the cell door. The odor of boiled hotdog overtakes the laundry detergent smell, even after the tray is collected.

The milk reminds me of Olivia. Curled on my cot, hand at

my throat, I imagine Robyn coaxing Olivia to drink a bottle. Olivia has never had formula, only breast milk. Jamie's and mine. Does Olivia balk at the unfamiliar formula? Will hunger drive her to accept the foreign food? I remind myself that Robyn is both a seasoned nurse and an experienced mom.

Light shines in my face. "Safety check," the gruff voice shouts. Jarred, I sit on the edge of the cot. The light is gone, the footfalls pause, the gruff voice barks onto the neighboring cell.

My cell door rattles and opens. The guard is familiar; she'd taken the locket, my wedding ring, and my Converse when I'd arrived. I can't tell if she remembers me. She says, "Let's go."

"Me?" I stand, slide my feet into the black flip-flops. The plastic thong rubs the space between my big toes. The guard leads me from my cell into the corridor. The flip-flop soles stick to the puke-colored linoleum and snap when I walk. There's a divot in the floor, and I trip, stubbing my toe. Someone snickers.

Humiliated, my cheeks burn.

Three cells down, a toilet overflowed. The smell of urine is overpowering. My eyes tear. I mouth-breathe. A trick I learned from Peter, his preferred method of coping with noxious emergency-room odors like a fresh hemorrhage. I glance at the guard, but she's unbothered, her expression unreadable.

Someone hollers, "Baby-snatcher." A blob lands on the linoleum in front of my toe. The guard tightens her grip on my elbow, steering me around the yellow mucous.

The guard says, "Keep walking. Mind your business."

At the end of the corridor, the steel door opens, we walk through, and it clanks shut. In a nondescript room, furnished with a grey metal desk and chairs that look like they survived a fire sale, the guard hands me a plastic bag.

"Your belongings," she says.

I open the plastic bag, unleashing the embarrassing stink of decaying Converse. The locket Jamie gave me is in the bag. I loop the cord around my neck. The guard returns my wedding ring. The band slips on my finger with ease.

The guard says, "The flip-flops are yours to keep." She smiles. "Consider them a going home gift."

Peter drives the Subaru single-handed, the other clasping my hand. Our fingers lace. It's evening and I spent almost two days in jail. At the entrance of Woodline Manor, Peter flicks the high beams. The road dips, and my stomach lurches at the memory of wrecking Mom's Jetta.

I lean against the door, my forehead against the cold window glass. I want to ask about Olivia. Has Peter heard from Robyn? But words won't gel. All I can manage is to focus on a calming breath, one measured sip at a time. The Subaru lumbers up our driveway. The garage door grumbles and Peter parks in his usual spot, even though the Jetta's vacant spot is closer to the door.

Peter says, "The Jetta's totaled. Hauled to a junkyard. I got a message that it was scrapped."

Hand-in-hand we enter our house through the connecting garage door. Inside, something about the kitchen is different but I'm exhausted and can't figure out what's changed.

Peter says, "You can get that wet. Webster checked with Judge Kipper."

"A shower is what I need right now." I'm thankful for Peter's matter-of-fact tone. Like he's referring to a Tiffany bracelet, not the electronic surveillance device around my left ankle.

But I'm ashamed. Dr. Webster Cumberland, my husband's

powerful mentor, finagled my release from jail. My cheeks feel inflamed, red enough to match my strawberry-blonde hair.

Anxious to hide behind a veil of steam, I kick off the black flip-flops, leave them in the foyer, and climb barefoot, hitting the third step twice. The irritable step squeaks, protesting the weight of the hardware clamped around my left ankle.

My nightshirt is damp with sweat. I reach for my phone. It's charged and on the nightstand. Groggily, I open the infant monitor app. The screen, grey snow. But there is no mistaking the empty crib. Olivia is missing.

Then I remember.

I hear Peter talking downstairs.

I've slept for ten hours. I resist the urge to text Robyn and ask about Olivia. Robyn is probably busy. Olivia is a fifth child, the only girl in Robyn's household. Despite a big family, I trust Robyn to give Olivia the attention she deserves. Unlike Aunt Darlene who is probably under investigation from Child Protective Services and stripped of guardianship. I open a dresser drawer, search for something to wear. Sweatpants accommodate the ankle monitor and my phone fits in the deep pocket.

In the kitchen Peter is at the sink, dressed in a faded Tommy Bahama T-shirt and his blue hospital scrubs pants, tied low around his hips. His back is to me. He's on his phone, listening more than speaking. Steaming water flows from the faucet. Soap bubbles float above the sink and burst. I notice what's different about the kitchen—the red checkered curtain mounted over the window above the sink. Peter ends the conversation and sets his phone on the counter. He dries his hands hospital-style, using the dish towel to twist the faucet.

His face brightens. "You're awake."

"You're home."

The buzzer on the oven dings. Peter pours batter into a muffin tin. "Hungry?"

"Half starved."

Peter loads the muffin tin into the oven. "Banana chocolate chip." He programs the timer. "Twenty minutes." He sets a ceramic mug under the Keurig. "Coffee?"

"The curtain—"

"Keeping busy. I'm home with the time to really see our house. We have stuff. Lots of stuff. Closets with boxes." He points to the window. "I found curtains, color-coordinated towels, cannisters of Tide, and toilet paper...I stopped counting at fifty rolls."

I might have gone overboard ordering toilet tissue. "Anything else?"

Peter unlatches a cabinet. "Alphabetical pasta. A through Z."

The Keurig streams. Peter hands me a stoneware cream dispenser and a matching sugar bowl, wedding gifts that until this morning had never been put into service.

We sit at the counter on barstools that I vaguely recall ordering but had never assembled. I want to ask Peter when he'll return to his obstetrical duties at Lakeview Hospital. But I keep silent, stealing glances at him as he slides on oven mitts instead of sterile gloves and delivers half a dozen baked muffins instead of a newborn baby. Peter has changed. His hair has lost luster, his curls droop. Worry has chiseled hollows under his cheekbones.

I eat one muffin and then another. Peter tells me he missed me. But he doesn't mention Olivia or my arrest. His kiss tastes like chocolate, and he smells like banana. He sets a stack of envelopes, secured with a rubber band, on the counter. "These came while you were gone."

I recognize the mail. Forwarded Visa and Amazon credit-card bills from Mom's old apartment. My heart feels like it might burst with a mixture of love and empathy for Peter. With no warning he comes home to find his wife nursing a baby, she disappears, leaving him to discover a cache of unopened Amazon boxes, a mountain of unpaid bills, an Amber Alert and a phone call from the police station. Yet, instead of shunning me, Peter holds my hand and feeds me a homemade breakfast.

I open my mouth. Now is the right time to explain. But the words stick, and I can't pry a sentence loose.

Peter sorts an industrial-sized cardboard box of Keurig pods. French Vanilla in one pile, a row of Coconut Crème, a Starbucks Verona tower. He rolls a Green Mountain Hazelnut pod between his palms and says, "Our credit cards—I tried to post your bail—"

"Peter. I'm—"

"Every card. Declined."

"I can explain. The bills. I can fix..." I reach for his hand. The Verona tower topples. "Let me." I've made an epic disaster of our lives, but scattered coffee pods are a mess I can set right.

"No, Belle." Peter puts his hands on my shoulders. "The shock I've had—these last few days. I've been thinking. This isn't your fault, not by a long shot. I haven't paid attention, not the way a husband should. I'm preoccupied with earning a partnership in Cumberland's practice, I haven't been here when you needed me. And when I was home? I failed to recognize that you are hurting. Losing a baby, our baby, isn't an incision to be sutured, bandaged and forgotten." Peter's blue eyes mist. "Forgive me. And we'll find a way out together. The two of us."

We embrace but he releases our hug quickly, and tells me,

"You should get ready. Your attorney called; she'll be here in ten minutes. Strategy session."

"I have an attorney?" Two thoughts compete, neck-to-neck like racehorses. Lawyers are expensive. And I must be in a ton of trouble.

"Webster paid the retainer. He posted your bail too."

I tiptoe, barely touching the third step but it emits a pitchy whine. If Webster Cumberland hired an attorney, I need to make a good impression. I rummage through my cosmetics; I haven't had occasion to wear makeup in ages and I want to conceal the bruise above my lip, now faded from purple to yellow.

If it wasn't for Dr. Cumberland, I'd have one of those court-appointed public defenders—what if I got matched with a newbie? A rookie fresh from law school? I want to trust Dr. Cumberland's attorney. Yet I can't shake my doubt. I imagine the attorney Cumberland hired is like him and relating to an elderly silver-haired man with a bad back is a stretch.

Thinking about Cumberland makes the scar on my abdomen burn. Is Cumberland's guilt over what he did to me motivation for sending us an attorney? The liquid makeup is flakey. I blot it with a cotton ball. The bruise doesn't disappear, and my complexion looks jaundiced.

The doorbell never rings, meaning Peter met our guest on the porch. The front door closes. I hear Peter offer coffee. "Verona or hazelnut? Cream and sugar?"

I enter the kitchen. The visit would have occurred in our living room, except that we have no furniture. Peter waters the Keurig. He's changed from Tommy Bahama to an Oxford shirt tucked into his scrubs bottoms. There's a black Kate Spade messenger bag on the counter. A woman with bobbed copper hair, wearing a red pantsuit, perches on a barstool. She notices me and her debate with Peter over the merits of flavored coffee ends. I feel her examine me head to toe, her cinnamon-brown eyes absorb my banded left ankle, visible under my sweatpants cuff. She sets her coffee mug down, grips her messenger bag, and says, "I'm Vanessa. Your attorney."

I sit on a stool opposite Vanessa. She puts on tortoiseshell-rimmed glasses, removes her laptop from the black Kate Spade, and pecks the keyboard. "An outlet?"

Peter plugs the power cord into an outlet beneath the counter.

Vanessa's screen illuminates her prominent brow, jutting nose, and gullies under both cheekbones. A humorless face. Vanessa takes what she does very, very seriously.

Peter clears his throat. He rubs the birthmark at the nape of his neck.

I ask Vanessa if she knows how Olivia is faring.

She says, "I can share what I know if it puts your mind at ease. The infant is being fostered, with your colleague, a nurse, while the baby's aunt is being investigated. For future guardianship." Vanessa's brow furrows. "Your only concern should be with yourself. Your future."

I fish my phone from my sweatpants. No new messages. I think about Marcus and realize I don't have his cell-phone number. He has a phone, but the one time I saw him use it was when he took a picture of Olivia in Mom's apartment. I scroll for news. I find Naomi on Facebook. She posted pictures from the Villanova Sirens flash mob in front of the St. Thomas church. Olivia and I are in the middle of their troop, somewhere.

175

Vanessa shrieks, "What are you thinking?" My phone is gone, plucked from my palm by her boney hand. Vanessa pokes the phone with her polished blood-red fingernail. Powered off. My phone disappears, swallowed by the messenger bag. The Kate Spade hisses, zipped shut.

Peter rubs his neck.

I open my mouth.

Vanessa's palm silences me. "Hear me. Seriously. Ms. Kaplan, you are in trouble. Big trouble." Her index finger, a manicured red talon, is aimed at me.

My stool wobbles. I grip the counter, the granite glacier cold.

"Speak to no one. Travel nowhere. While I'm on the topic, you must surrender your passport." Vanessa's gaze darts to Peter.

Peter looks relieved to be tasked and scurries to retrieve my passport.

Vanessa snaps her laptop lid, reaches across the counter, and clasps my hands. I resist but her fingers are strong. She whispers, "Look at me."

I do. Her cinnamon eyes are intriguing, splotched with pinpoint green dots.

Vanessa is emphatic. "Like it or not, you need me. The State suspended your license."

"Driving?"

"Nursing. And in my professional opinion your privilege to work will be permanently revoked. Not to mention, your liberty is at stake."

My hands wilt, sandwiched between Vanessa's steel clamps. "I can't go back to the NICU—Ever?"

"No."

My shoulders sag. "It's not fair. I did the right thing. I gave

Olivia back." Speaking her name stings. *Olivia.* Her memory is a visceral pain.

"If you are charged with kidnapping, that's a federal crime, and if you are convicted, the sentence will include incarceration." Vanessa's voice is passionate. Like I'm her most important client.

"Prison? For how..."

"You're twenty-six. I can't let you lose your youth."

Decades in prison. Naively, I never thought about it. Isn't losing Olivia and my nursing career punishment enough? I blink at the sudden image of Vanessa as a fortune teller, her laptop a crystal ball. If her prediction proves correct, my future is bleak, a cosmic black hole. Even without the NICU, the world I'll inhabit will be cold and colorless. A joyless existence. My situation is dire, but a second revelation sends a chill down my spine. I say, "What about Peter?" He'll be here, in this house alone, wandering room to room, unable to tend to the patients he loves, punished because of my crimes. It's more than I can bear.

Vanessa squeezes my fingers. "You need to let me help you."

She's blurry, through my tears, which flow unchecked and dribble onto the counter. I blink and force myself to focus. I'm suddenly grateful to Dr. Webster Cumberland for sending Vanessa. With Vanessa on my side, I have an opportunity to repair the potholes I've dug. Peter and I owe Webster Cumberland. Peter will want to repay Cumberland, and that means working extra nights, weekends, and holidays. All because of what I've done. And that is bitter medicine for me to swallow.

Vanessa says, "Before we move forward with a hearing, you need a psychiatric evaluation."

"I have a therapist." And a string of missed appointments. I regret taking Janice's Zoom visits lightly. What if Janice thinks I'm crazy? What if I am?

"I'll set it up."

I might be crazy, but I love Olivia. I tell Vanessa, "All I wanted was for Olivia to be safe. I promised Jamie, her mother."

Vanessa releases my hands. "What did you say?"

I flex my fingers to restore circulation. "Jamie. Olivia's mother...I was Olivia's NICU nurse, and—I cared. Maybe too much."

"Start from the beginning." From behind Vanessa's laptop, keys are tapped rapid-fire, like pellets from a BB gun. Vanessa's chin remains bowed, and I see grey sprouts along her precisely parted hair. Vanessa's grey roots are reassuring. She's a seasoned lawyer who knows how to help.

Peter returns with my passport. He tries to put his arm around my shoulders, but I shake my head. With the locket, fragile as a dove's egg, cupped in my palms, I speak. Haltingly at first. But my voice gains traction. I tell Vanessa the truth.

She interjects an occasional question. "The notebook detailing infant care, you kept it?"

"Yes."

"Anyone willing to vouch for your nursing skills, particularly where Olivia Dutton is concerned? Can you name five character witnesses?"

I rattle off a list beginning with Robyn, and a trio of NICU nurses, and Dr. STAT. "I've had the same best friend forever..."

Except I hurt Sheila and she is angry with me. "Never mind." Marcus would help but asking him to vouch for me puts his job at Radcliff Apartments at risk, and he's done too much already.

Peter listens. He learns about Mom's apartment, the eviction for unpaid, overdue rent. And my compulsive Amazon habit. His jaw clenches, the muscles in his throat work but he says nothing. An hour later the birthmark behind his neck might be rubbed away.

The tap-tap-tap of Vanessa's keyboard ceases. She folds her laptop. "I have a game plan."

Peter shows her out, but they linger on the porch, speaking softly. Out of earshot.

I know they're discussing "strategy," code for my future, which is disappearing fast. I walk into the foyer, my gait unnatural. The house-arrest monitor hurts my ankle. I wonder how long I'll be under surveillance. But anything is better than years in federal prison. The possibility sinks into my bones. I lean against the banister, too weak to climb the stairs.

Peter closes the front door and holds an envelope. My debt radar pings. I sense Peter's internal debate whether to share the contents or keep it from me. He asks, "Got a minute?"

"Time? I've got plenty." I cover my ankle monitor with the cuff of my sweatpants.

"The news isn't good. Our mortgage is due. Overdue, technically."

I sit on the bottom step. "When can you go back to work?"

"Webster petitioned on my behalf. But until the Lakeview Hospital Board of Directors convenes and discusses my reinstatement, I'm suspended. Indefinitely." Peter sits on the step beside me. "Without pay." Our knees bump.

"We'll be homeless. Because of me." I hang my head. How do I apologize for ruining my husband's career? How do I say sorry without sounding trite after our home forecloses and strangers sleep in our bedroom? "You did nothing wrong. Weren't even involved. It's...unfair. You would be better off on your own. Without me."

"Don't, Belle. I know you can't mean that. If, I mean when, you're acquitted, the hospital board will reinstate my privileges." Peter points to the locket dangling from my neck. "What's that?"

I show him.

"Any chance Olivia's hair is a good-luck charm?"

"I'm certain of it."

"In that case, keep wearing it." We sit shoulder to shoulder staring at the front door.

CHAPTER SIXTEEN

The sun has set, the drapes drawn, the darkness scented with apple shampoo and Burt's Bees baby lotion. I make my way to the electrical socket in the corner to find the night-light bulb unscrewed. A subtle twist sends the cow leaping over the moon. The sunshine-yellow carpet is tracked by vacuum scars. On the changing table the portable tub is drained, the soap and diaper ointment stowed in the drawers. Towels in precisely-folded squares are stacked beneath the table.

There is something on the rocking chair. The pink onesie I'd stuffed in my scrubs pocket the night that Olivia was sent to the boarder nursery. I press the onesie to my cheek and inhale. Olivia's scent is gone, replaced by Tide detergent. I lay Olivia's onesie in her crib and activate the mobile. The shapes orbit. I sit in the rocking chair, my breasts heavy with knowing; Olivia is hungry. I untangle the pump tubing, connect bottles to flanges, dial the pump. The machine hums. White milk cascades. Time and distance haven't lessened my love for Olivia.

But loving Olivia led me to hurt the person I vowed to cherish. Marriage, I'm learning, doesn't just join two lives, but meshes them. Our fates are intertwined, braided by commitment. Taking Olivia from Aunt Darlene caused an irreparable wound in Peter's future.

Peter is innocent, yet his medical career is at risk, our credit exhausted, our house in danger of foreclosure. I feared Aunt Darlene's threat, but I shouldn't have. My impulsive actions, kidnapping Olivia not once but twice, damaged our livelihood far worse than anything Aunt Darlene might have done. Returning Olivia and arranging for Robyn's foster care hasn't solved our problems. Not the way I'd thought. Except I wasn't thinking rationally. Driven by wishes, and naïve wants, more child than grown woman, a collision with reality was inevitable.

Along the way I sullied nursing, the profession that I swore to uphold. I don't know if I'll earn the right to work again, and if not, I'll miss more than the salary. Lakeview Hospital's NICU was my job, but the NICU was also my home, the staff my family.

Is Robyn, my mentor, friend, and Olivia's foster mother, embarrassed by my actions? Are Coleen, Todd, and Dr. STAT gossiping at the scrub sink about me with Honor, the nurse practitioner? I imagine Nicki wearing a Disney pin appropriate for the occasion, Minnie Mouse dressed in black, ashamed of my downfall. If I'm not a nurse, a NICU nurse, then who am I? The locket rests over my sternum. Can there be enough luck inside this opaque box to undo the harm I've caused? I fear all the luck has bled away.

I long for Mom. Except Mom didn't have every answer. Teachers bestow knowledge but ultimately, it's up to the student to put the lessons into practice. I imagine Mom in her apartment, sitting on her loveseat, sipping coffee. I say, "Mom, it's Annabelle, your daughter. I'm sorry that I disappointed you."

Daughters. We're not porcelain dolls but imperfect beings. We cause the mothers who love us pain. When I was pregnant and working with Robyn in the NICU, my developing baby did gymnastics in my womb, and I agonized over every twinge. Robyn advised me to enjoy being pregnant. "NICU nurses waste their pregnancy worrying. Your baby will turn out fine."

My first labor contraction seized my torso in a ferocious grip during the night, and then vanished, leaving me to question if the pain was real or a practice Braxton Hicks contraction. I told Peter, "Labor can't hurt this much. No one would have a second baby."

Being an obstetrician, I'd expected Peter to take away my pain. Instead, he rubbed his neck and fumbled for his phone. "Webster. You awake? I'm bringing Annabelle in." Peter had been unnaturally panicked. "There's meconium."

The second contraction bit with razor-sharp fangs. Our baby wasn't due for another four weeks.

Turns out Robyn was wrong about my baby.

I stand and open the bottom dresser drawer. The box is where I'd left it when Peter brought me home from the hospital. Postpartum, post-hysterectomy, my dream contained in a box secured with pink ribbon. I sit in the rocking chair. The ribbon unleashes and I lift the lid.

Imprints in black ink. Paired feet. Hands to match. I study her finger-splay. "Yes." I tell my baby, "You have a musician's hands."

The rocking chair glides.

I've avoided exploring this crater behind my heart. But the time has come. I delve deeper. Feeling fugitive-like, trespassing in a private garden, stealing springtime's first daffodil. A measuring tape, marked with her length, eighteen inches tall, her weight, a mere five pounds. What I seek rests at the bottom. My memory is fickle, foggy from the hospital's narcotic infusion.

The baby I remember is incomplete. She has hair but is it the color of strawberry preserve or wisps pale as corn silk, or is her hair dark like a raven's feather? The proof is here, in this very box. A lock of hair. Clipped into a seashell barrette, a thick black curl. Our daughter, had she lived, would grow ebony curls. Like her father.

The crib card is blank. *Baby Girl—*

"Belle?"

"We're in the nursery."

Peter is framed in the doorway. Arms lax at his sides. There's enough light from the hallway to see his expression, a mixture of trepidation and resignation to find me in the nursery, yet again.

I say, "It's time. To do right by her. Our baby deserves a name."

His blue eyes cloud. He steps to my side. Together, we decide. I fill the crib card's blank space, in my finest calligraphy: *Leah Genie Kaplan.*

Our once quiet house is lived-in loud. Peter orchestrates the kitchen. A brusque rhapsody of pots clanging, knives chopping, dishes scraping and chiming glassware.

Each evening Peter calls to me. "Belle. Dinner."

Peter's inaugural meal began appropriately, with "*A*." He prepared angel-hair pasta.

He wears a *Kiss the Cook* apron over blue scrubs pants and a Ralph Lauren golf shirt. Peter doesn't apologize for that soggy first meal but conducts an autopsy. "Tomorrow, salt the water. To achieve al dente texture, set a timer." New to cooking, especially in our kitchen, Peter explores the unfamiliar terrain, opening and closing drawers, rearranging cutlery, folding dish towels. I doubt he'll become as comfortable in the kitchen as he is in the operating room, but Peter is a quick study.

I separate the pasta on my plate, loop a single strand, thread-thin like a premature infant's umbilical artery line. The remaining pasta clumps. The meal reminds me of the shifts I spent in the NICU. I miss my patients and my friends. I leave the table stifling tears.

The following night Peter prepares *bucatini*, thick, tubular pasta. The thing about Peter? He embraces challenge. He studies the art of preparing perfect pasta with the same passion that he brought to medicine. Peter's *Kiss the Cook* apron is stained with olive oil.

And the next day: "*Campanelle*," Peter says.

"They're lovely." Crinkled pasta petals, like gathered flowers, speckled with sea salt, pepper, and oregano.

"Italian. For little bells." Peter flushes. "For my Belle."

I kiss the cook.

Our once odorless house adopts restaurant aromas. Basil, yeasty bread, and garlic. Lots of garlic.

Peter washes dishes like he's sterilizing surgical instruments. The water isn't hot, it's scalding. He scrapes, soaks, and suds utensils, glassware, plates, and finally pots and pans. I work the drying station. Wiping the sanitized dishes.

I say to him, "We have a dishwasher. There're plenty of Cascade pods."

Silently, Peter dons pink rubber gloves. Submerges the salad tongs in a soap bath. "There's little else I can do. At least until I return to Lakeview." Peter passes the dripping tongs.

"I'm sorry." My apology is simple but genuine.

Peter asks, "Ready for a plate?"

"You bet."

I want my phone. But Vanessa won't budge, even when plied with dinner. *Ditalini,* cut pasta tubes drowning in butter sauce. I refill her wine goblet with Sauvignon Blanc. I say pleasantly, "Please. My phone. I want to text Sheila, my best friend."

Vanessa swallows and tells me, "I won't have you damaging your chance for acquittal. Anything you do, say, or post on social media, puts you at risk."

Peter excuses himself to retrieve a loaf of French bread from the oven. Vanessa says, "You're cleared. Your therapist deems you mentally stable, even remarked on your personal growth and insight. Congratulations."

"Janice said that?" I'm flattered. I haven't missed an appointment since returning home. And I have journal pages to prove it. The yellow floral journals are an Amazon purchase that I don't regret.

"There's an issue that I need to discuss. A sensitive topic and you have my condolences. The loss of your baby—"

I fold my hands in my lap.

"A miscarriage will evoke court sympathy. In your favor."

"Leah. She's a baby. Not a miscarriage." I tell Vanessa, "No."

"I'll do everything I can to keep the matter out of court. Leah, I mean—out of court."

Peter sets a baguette on a cutting board, brown and crusty. "So, what did I miss? You both look so serious."

Vanessa blinks like she has something in her eye. Staring at her plate she skewers a pasta tube, and says, "Court dates. I moved the hearing up. The Honorable Judge Steadman Kipper will be presiding."

Peter says, "Webster's buddy. Those two go way back. Attended Yale together. Webster delivered each of the judge's five children."

Vanessa smiles stiffly at Peter and then at me. I don't say

anything. A friend of Cumberland? Judge Kipper will decide my fate, much the same way that Dr. Cumberland had in a split-second, decreed me infertile. Or the judge might retire before ever considering my case. Which means Vanessa might never return my phone.

Dinner is *fusilli* with plum tomatoes and fresh basil. Peter grates a glacier-sized hunk of parmesan. He says, "Tell me when." His *Kiss the Cook* apron's latest stain is a green streak under *Kiss*. Peter tells me that Vanessa emailed him an update.

My fusilli twists are buried beneath a parmesan hill.

"Your hearing is tomorrow."

"When?"

"In the morning. Eat up. You'll need the energy."

Peter stops grating, taps the residual with a spoon. Parmesan sprinkles the rim of my plate. Extra cheese. A good thing.

Peter insists on washing and drying after dinner. He says, "Review Vanessa's strategy. Get ready for tomorrow. Put on your game face."

I don't argue and march upstairs. The third step squeaks, reminding me that I have a limited number of squeaks left in my future. I dial the shower as hot as Peter's dishwater. I remove the locket, hang it from the toothbrush holder, and step under the torrent, shampooing once but condition for an extra minute before rinsing.

The mirror fogs. I can't see my game face. I wonder if I'd recognize it. Do I have a game face? Have I fought for anything or anyone other than Olivia? Peter printed all fifty pages of Vanessa's notes but they're dense and I peruse the section pertaining to her. Olivia's prematurity, developmental needs, and her current condition.

> After her return, Olivia was examined by a neonatologist who proclaimed her in excellent health.
>
> The female infant, an ex-preemie, is interactive, and in fine condition. From my examination, I find that she suffered no ill effects since being discharged from Lakeview Hospital.

The doctor's signature is illegible. No surprise. I leave Vanessa's notes on my nightstand.

Our house has four bedrooms. I enter the one closest to the master bedroom and hear the humidifier purr, a precaution to preserve my cello while in storage. I lift the hard black case from where it rests against the wall and fold the metal chair, leaving the long-necked black music stand. For years, I toted my cumbersome instrument and the chair to lessons, rehearsals, and performances. Music required time and dedication, and I quit the summer before nursing school, telling myself college was more important. A viable excuse, and a partial truth. The reality is that I stopped playing because I wasn't perfect. A missed chord, tempo blunder, or minor mishap, for me was a catastrophe. Locking the cello in a closet silenced the music but also prevented a misplayed note.

Tonight, I'm not seeking perfection. I traipse the short hallway into the nursery. I close the door. Olivia's pink onesie is in her crib, where I left it. Leah's memory box is no longer stored in the bottom dresser drawer but on the bookcase shelf. I have a sense about Leah. If she'd lived, she would have loved books. A mother knows these things.

I unfold the metal chair, set it on the sunshine carpet. I

unbuckle the black cello case, liberating pent-up odors, furniture polish, and wood, a primal smell like an ancient forest. Despite the dim light, my cello is recognizable, the twirls in its maple-wood body as personal as a birthmark. I lift the neck and gently dust the body with a polishing cloth. The strings require tuning, a necessity after storage, and I manipulate the screws, listening to each string individually until the four strings ring in unison. Satisfied, I balance the cello on its endpoint. I'm centered, feet flat, knees bent, the cello leaning against my left shoulder. I grasp the bow in my right hand, at ninety degrees. Odd being a lefty, but that's how I learned.

I haven't played since Leah died, I even stopped casually taking the cello out for tuning. Her birth and death wrung me of song. Peter had encouraged me to spend time in a music studio instead of the nursery, even offered to be my audience. I couldn't bring myself to open the cello case, it reminded me of a black casket, and the instrument's curvy body was too much like my pregnant belly.

I address my cello, cautiously manipulate the four strings on the neck with my left fingers and glide the bow across its wide body.

The cello answers, a low octave.

I strike the bow across the strings. The cello groans. Its stately voice resonates in my chest. Liberated from hibernation, forgiving me the exiled months in a closed room, the cello sings. My cello and I perform without sheet music, executing scales, plucking strings, my fingers still nimble, though soft, my old calluses worn smooth. Memory warms muscle and wood. Like friends reunited after a long separation, the lapse in our conversation proves insignificant.

The door opens and Peter enters. He sits on the carpet, eyes closed, hands on his knees.

The cello finds melody, not a joyous noise but an eloquent

tale that protests the confines of the nursery's four walls. I let myself be led, trusting my cello. I close my eyes. Greater than the sum of clefts, keys, and rests, composition flows as paint splatters canvas. A mural with colors that defy the boundaries of natural law.

The cello cries for Leah, the daughter I lost. And Olivia? The cello strings fly unfettered toward a future not yet ripe. Finally, the cello breathes a last note and is still. Vibration travels my spine, reverberates in my chest, and thrums my heart. Bohemian color and raucous light recede. I open my eyes. There is only the memory of music.

I wipe the cello with a soft cloth. Return it to sleep. Set the bow, close and buckle the case. If I don't come home tomorrow, if I'm sentenced to jail, I'll enter incarceration having left the nursery in lasting song.

CHAPTER SEVENTEEN

Peter stands in front of the mirror, buttons his navy-blue suit jacket, and threads a tan leather belt through the loops of his trousers. "Nervous?" He's looking in the mirror, my reflection beside his, the question more like an admission.

I answer anyway. "Maybe. A little."

Peter is nervous enough for both of us. He's examined and rejected three neckties. I point to a blue tie. "The polka dots. Besides, it's a hearing, not an actual trial." I don't need to remind him. Peter combed Vanessa's notes with the same thoroughness he reads an ICU patient's pathology report. The notes explain that today's proceeding will establish whether I've committed a crime and if there's sufficient evidence against me to charge me with that crime.

Peter fights with his tie. "Scrubs are easier."

I couldn't agree more but I remain silent. In all likelihood, I might never wear NICU scrubs again and the realization sticks in my throat like a chip of slow-melting ice.

My wardrobe is limited because I'm not back to pre-pregnancy shape. I wear a brown skirt, like Vanessa recommended. I'd tuck my white shirt into the waistband, but it is still too snug. Vanessa instructed me not to apply makeup and to wear flat shoes. I check the mirror. I look presentable, except for the conspicuous ankle monitor.

Peter settles his collar. "We need to go." Peter is clean-shaven, his black curls trimmed above his shirt collar, and he smells brisk, like Old Spice.

"You went to the barber."

"Vanessa suggested a haircut."

I know how self-conscious Peter is, the birthmark on the back of his neck is his Achilles' heel. If—*when*—he returns to Lakeview, his neck and the red birthmark will be visible in collarless scrubs. I hug him. "Thank you."

Peter says, "Having you home tonight will be worth it. Hair grows back."

Vanessa explained the range of possibilities. I might be "remanded" to jail to await an actual trial, or the judge could let me come home with my ankle monitor. Vanessa warned that the attorney for the State is young, wants to make a name for himself, and might push the judge to charge me.

Vanessa meets us at the courthouse dressed in her signature red pantsuit, black heels, and ruby lipstick. Compared to Vanessa, I feel plain. Vanessa inspects me, her nod of approval means I've cleared the first hurdle.

The Philadelphia courthouse casts its dreary shadow over the stone steps. My ballet flats are thin and climbing the steps leaves my toes numb. The entrance looms, an inky cave carved into the unyielding mountain. My heart gallops. I want to scream, *I don't belong here.* Except I remember cashing Mom's pension check, a tiny infraction I've neglected to admit to Vanessa. My knees lock. I whisper to Vanessa, "I need to tell you—"

Vanessa tugs my elbow. "Later. No time now."

Peter presses his palm tight to mine.

THE BABY NURSE

I tell Peter, "I can't. Too scared." Life's compass is suddenly haywire, the needle points to a dead end. One minute I'm a nurse, a newlywed, half of a professional couple. But life swerved. Yet I understand that my actions nudged the compass needle to this inevitable place.

"You must." Vanessa pulls my elbow. She bullet-talks. "Eyes forward. Neutral facial expression. Not happy. Not sad. Not bored."

Peter interjects. "Belle. You can do this."

Together we arrive at the entrance. A uniformed courthouse security officer greets Vanessa. "Morning, Counselor."

Vanessa returns the greeting.

To Peter he says, "Cell phone." Peter produces his phone, and the officer snaps it into a case. The officer takes my phone-free condition for granted. He directs us through a metal detector. Vanessa goes first, waits for us to clear, and walks, her stride confident, black heels clicking against the marble floor.

The courthouse is a bewildering warren of hallways. The place smells like an office after the cleaning crew finishes their nightly chores; floor polish and copy paper. This is how patients must feel coming to the hospital for testing, surgery, to birth a baby, or visit a loved one. Overwhelmed by the buzzing activity, bubbling voices, uncertain who to trust. I vow that if I'm allowed to be a nurse again, I'll give visitors, lost in the hallway, not only directions but compassion.

Vanessa knows her way. She steers past attorneys, outfitted in blue or black, conferring in hushed tones, their heads bowed. A few greet her, "Morning, Counselor." Vanessa waves. I squeeze Peter's hand. Vanessa leads us through a heavy door into a room with a pair of long tables in the front, flanked by rows of dark wooden benches. I feel like I'm in middle school, the semester when Sheila's advanced chemistry lab met during lunch, leaving me in the cafeteria, friendless, uncertain where to sit.

Vanessa says, "Left." Her black Kate Spade messenger bag lands on the polished tabletop. I sit in a chair, the type I'd sat in behind the nurses' station at the hospital.

Peter says, "I'll be right behind you." He sits on a bench in the gallery.

I scan the rows. They are empty.

Vanessa snaps, "Straight ahead. Stay focused. No yawning. No daydreaming."

High walls meet a ceiling accentuated with crown molding. There's a window, the panes appear sealed and it's set too high to see outside. Cold air floats from a vent. I shiver and wish I'd brought a sweater. Peter would offer me his jacket, but I don't want to upset Vanessa by turning around and asking him.

Vanessa taps my shoulder. "I'll be right back." She strides several yards to a table identical to ours, and chats with a man dressed in a suit the color of charcoal bricks. He's fraternity-house handsome. Tall, thick-shouldered, clean-shaven, with close-cropped hair that looks sun-streaked. Fraternity Boy's face turns fuchsia. I hear a sound that I'd never associate with my attorney. A girlish giggle. Vanessa returns to our table, the corners of her ruby lips upturned in satisfaction.

A woman in a beige uniform and black, thick-soled shoes is planted in front of the room. She seems charged with protecting the platform and desk, partially enclosed by a railing behind her. I notice the gun harnessed across her chest, the black butt sticking from its holster. How frequently does she fire it? Her presence quiets an undercurrent of random chatter. She bellows, "Court is in session. The Honorable Judge Steadman Kipper presiding. All rise."

The only sound is the whispering vent. Vanessa nudges me with her elbow but I'm on my feet. The paneled wall at the front of the room splits, a black-robed man shuffles through the aperture. Bent with age, and, I assume, the burden of deciding the fates of people like me, he leans on a cane, tapping the floor as if clearing underbrush. The courtroom stands, holding a collective breath. The judge ascends a platform, his staff thumps each step. On the third thump he reaches his podium, settles into his chair, and faces the courtroom. He points the staff—at me.

I gasp.

But the bailiff seizes the cane by its pearly knob, stowing it against the back wall. Judge Kipper arranges his robes. His gavel lands, a decisive thunk. Vanessa sits. I do the same. Fingers to my throat, I feel for the leather cord, needing to find the reassuring locket. Instead, I feel my carotid pulse thrum. No leather cord. The locket is missing on the day I need it the most, left in the bathroom outside the shower. I whisper, "No." To my horror, loud enough to capture Judge Kipper's attention. He may be old, but his hearing is keen.

Judge Kipper addresses Vanessa. "Counselor. Your client is not well?"

Vanessa is on her feet. "My client is completely healthy. The court's concern is appreciated, Your Honor."

Vanessa squeezes my wrist. Behind me I hear Peter shift in his seat.

Judge Kipper leans forward, speaks into a microphone. "The purpose of this hearing is to determine if there is adequate evidence against Ms. Annabelle Kaplan to proceed with a trial." The woman seated at a desk adjacent to the judge's bench, dressed in Talbots tweed, types on a small machine.

Judge Kipper turns his attention to the table across the aisle. "I expect the State is ready?"

A chair scrapes the floor. Papers shuffle. The lawyer stands and speaks in a surprisingly alto voice. "Your Honor. Ms.

Kaplan, the defendant, willfully endangered the life of an innocent infant... knowingly removing the infant from her only living relative—without good—"

My hands fist. The fraternity boy—he might be a law school graduate—doesn't know what he's saying. Why doesn't Vanessa do something?

There's a soft mew in the courtroom. Like the undercurrent of a lawn mower or a fan whirling. Vanessa writes on a steno pad with a silver Cross pen, poised at an uncomfortable angle. Vanessa is a lefty. Like me.

The State attorney slides his hands into his trouser pockets. "Kidnapping. Reckless endangerment of a helpless minor. Without cause. Indeed, Ms. Kaplan has stated to the police that she didn't doubt the competency of Ms. Darlene Cobb's driving."

I feel Vanessa's stare. I had answered questions at the police station when I'd been arrested, but that was before I met Vanessa.

"The State will prove it has adequate evidence to charge Ms. Kaplan, a *nurse*," he emphasizes sarcastically, "with the crime of kidnapping and endangering a child."

"Witnesses?" Judge Kipper asks.

"The State plans to call the infant's maternal aunt, sole relative, after the tragic, unexpected deaths of the minor's parents, Ms. Darlene Cobbs. The hospital social worker provided appropriate papers certifying Ms. Cobb's legal guardianship." He waves a manila envelope at the judge. "If it pleases the court, I am in possession of the documents. I assure you, Your Honor, they are in order." Frat Boy presents his file to the bailiff, who delivers it to Judge Kipper. Frat Boy continues, "Ms. Cobbs will detail that her relationship with her niece suffered irreparable—"

Judge Kipper says, "Save the drama."

"Yes, Your Honor." The State's attorney smirks.

The bailiff guides a woman to the witness stand. I lean forward, not believing the woman in the ruffled blouse and pressed black trousers is Aunt Darlene. She verifies her name through lips accentuated by pink gloss. "Darlene Cobbs." She sits primly on the edge of the chair.

The State's attorney says, "Accept the court's condolences for the loss of your dear sister."

Aunt Darlene tugs her ruffled collar. "Thank you."

I stare at my fists on my lap.

The attorney walks to the witness stand and asks, "Tell us what you do for a living?"

"I own an eatery."

"An entrepreneur. Tell the court about the plans you have for raising your niece."

"She has her own room—nursery, I mean—in my condo. And I added a playroom in The Tavern, my restaurant."

"Your niece has not had the opportunity to enjoy these new accommodations, has she?"

Aunt Darlene shakes her head.

Judge Kipper says, "Yes or no?"

"No."

The attorney places his palms on the banister of the witness box. "Why hasn't your sweet niece spent even a single night in her newly appointed nursery?"

Aunt Darlene glances in my direction. I catch and hold her gaze until her eyes dart to Judge Kipper.

Blood pulsates behind my eardrums. I shut my eyes, count to ten.

Judge Kipper directs Aunt Darlene to respond.

"She was taken from me. The day I picked her up from the hospital. Before I could even bring her home."

The State attorney's voice booms, "Who robbed you of your right to provide loving care for your deceased sister's infant?"

"The baby nurse."

I open my eyes. Heat rises from my core, inflaming my face.

"Let the record show that Ms. Cobbs identifies Ms. Annabelle Kaplan. Did you attempt to re-establish guardianship, to reclaim your niece?"

"I did," Aunt Darlene says stiffly, "but that didn't work out either."

"Why not?"

"When The baby nurse brought her back, she wouldn't let me hold her and when I turned my back for a second—she took her."

Frat Boy gestures with both hands. "Took your niece not once but twice." The room is uncomfortably hushed. He asks, "And you did what's right, reported your niece missing?"

"I'm sorry for not calling the police the first time. I honestly thought, being a nurse, that she'd do the right thing, bring her back. But I was wrong. She grabbed her a second time."

The attorney tells the judge he is finished and meanders to his table.

"Redirect?" the judge asks Vanessa.

Vanessa stands. "Thank you, Your Honor. One question. Ms. Cobbs, your eatery has a bar?"

"It does."

"You serve alcohol. Tell the court what type?"

Aunt Darlene answers, "Beer. In cans, on tap. Wine. Red and white. Domestic but I'm expanding to a selection of French vintages. Scotch, bourbon, vodka."

"That is all. Thank you."

Aunt Darlene exits the witness box.

I breathe through my nose, afraid to disrupt the quiet. The particular details of my visit to The Rusty Sub, and conversation with Aunt Darlene remain secret. I vow never to tell a soul about what happened when I took Olivia that second time. Olivia could have fallen out of my arms when I jumped from the bathroom window. She could have suffered far worse, died even, when the Jetta crashed. I have no way of knowing because Marcus returned to haul the Jetta from the scene and had it crushed in the junkyard, destroying all evidence of my accident with Olivia.

Frat Boy calls another witness. Glenda-The-Terrible approaches the witness box, wearing her familiar white jacket; she swears to tell the truth. She appears physically smaller, encased in the witness box, but no friendlier. She puts on her glasses, and stares at Frat Boy, who stands directly in front of her.

He says, "In what capacity do you know Ms. Kaplan?"

"I'm nurse manager of the Lakewood Hospital Neonatal Intensive Care Unit. I supervise the nurses."

"As supervisor, you're acquainted with each nurse's work habits?"

"Intimately."

"Ms. Kaplan, has she required any disciplinary action?"

I sink in my chair.

"She has—a single event."

"Describe the incident."

"Overstepping caregiver boundaries. In other words, becoming over-involved with a patient. Nurses must care, but not too much. Or we risk losing our objective judgement."

"Yes." Frat Boy clasps the witness-box railing. "Detail how Nurse Kaplan violated her profession."

"She named a patient." Before being asked, Glenda-The-Terrible adds, "Baby Olivia Dutton."

"Let the court recognize the infant is the same Olivia that Nurse Annabelle kidnapped."

Vanessa is on her feet.

Judge Kipper motions for her to sit and tells Frat Boy, "Continue. But make your point."

"Your Honor, I have a final question for this witness. As Ms. Kaplan's manager, can you provide the court with some insight as to why she took such a liberty? Crossing the line, so to speak, and naming someone else's baby?"

"At the time the naming incident occurred, Ms. Kaplan had experienced a recent loss. The death of her baby. Stillborn."

Murmurs, shocked gasps sweep the courtroom. Behind me, Peter exhales, "Belle." Vanessa grips my shoulder. My greatest shame, the unsightly wound I keep bandaged, laid bare in open court. The baby I couldn't save, my own. My Leah.

Frat Boy says, "Enlightening information. Ms. Kaplan named the baby. And when circumstances were ripe, the infant's parents' untimely, or should I say in Nurse Kaplan's view, timely demise, she swooped in, stealing what she couldn't have naturally. A baby of her own."

The courtroom erupts.

I'm grateful for the raucous noise, it muffles my sobs. Vanessa stands, her hand on my shoulder. "Objection."

Judge Kipper's gavel thunders. "I'll have order."

The noise dissipates. Except for a faint mewing. Glenda-The-Terrible exits. Behind me, Peter whispers, "Belle. Be brave."

Judge Kipper addresses Vanessa, "Counsel. For Ms. Kaplan."

Vanessa clasps a folder, tucks her chair behind the table and says, "Your Honor, in the interest of brevity I will provide the court with sworn statements from Ms. Kaplan's colleagues."

The bailiff comes forward, takes the manila folder from Vanessa, carries it to Judge Kipper. He puts on round, wire-rimmed spectacles. "Continue. Senior citizens can read and listen at the same time."

"Naturally, Your Honor." Vanessa's voice is friendly, conversational, unflustered, like the proceedings are unfolding as she expects.

Vanessa strolls to the front of the room. "The fact is, Ms. Kaplan, a trained professional nurse, acted as a Good Samaritan. A nurse bound not only by professional obligation to protect and heal, but Ms. Kaplan shares an additional sacred bond with baby Olivia. Nurse Kaplan promised the infant's mother, now deceased, that she'd protect the baby. While unusual, bonding between a parent and a nurse does happen during long hospitalizations. And the infant's mother welcomed Nurse Kaplan's suggestion to name her infant. Ms. Kaplan's actions are not only based on professional nursing standards but on a sacred trust. The infant, Olivia Dutton, is known intimately to my client. Ms. Kaplan was versed in the infant's feeding schedule, temperament, and emotional needs. In fact, she kept detailed records of the daily care she provided to baby Olivia."

I sit tall and exhale.

"A Good Samaritan. A practiced nurse. A loyal friend. A young wife," Vanessa says with passion, "all describe my client." Vanessa nods at me and tells Judge Kipper, "These attributes explain Nurse Kaplan's action, removing Olivia Dutton from an unsafe parked car where the baby was left behind, unattended, by the witness, Darlene Cobbs. In the hours and days that followed, my client continued to act as the baby's nurse, meticulously recording the care she administered." Vanessa displays my yellow floral notebook.

Judge Kipper says, "I'll have a closer look."

The bailiff retrieves the notebook from Vanessa and delivers it to the judge. He flips the pages. "Certainly, retrieving the infant from a parked car can be explained. But the second incident?"

Vanessa says, "Nurse Annabelle removed the infant from her aunt's establishment, which the State's attorney neglected to report, is a bar, Your Honor. Not a suitable environment for a baby."

Frat Boy stands. "Objection."

Vanessa says coyly, "Retracted."

The State's attorney sits.

Vanessa says, "My first witness is an expert who will speak on the condition of the baby."

The bailiff escorts a tall woman wearing a white lab coat to the witness stand. The witness quickly mounts the steps. It's Dr. STAT.

Judge Kipper asks her to state her name and occupation.

"Eunice Fine, attending neonatologist, Lakeview Hospital."

Dr. STAT's name. Eunice? I swallow my shock. Dr. STAT, I mean Eunice, raises her right hand. Lines wrinkle her palm. She swears to tell the truth.

Vanessa thanks Dr. STAT. "No doubt you're busy."

An understatement.

"Your credentials and professional affiliations have been verified and are provided to the court." The bailiff presents what I assume is Dr. STAT—Fine's—resumé to Judge Kipper. Vanessa says, "I'll get right to the point. You examined Olivia Dutton after Ms. Kaplan rescued—"

Fraternity Boy is on his feet. "Objection. Leading—"

Judge Kipper glances at Vanessa. "Counselor. Don't make me warn you again."

"Withdrawn. My apologies." Vanessa smiles. She doesn't look the least bit sorry. "Doctor. You examined Olivia Dutton immediately following her return to social services. Describe the baby's condition."

My palms are damp.

Dr. STAT says, "Olivia Dutton is in excellent health. Her vital signs were normal. She was well hydrated, with above adequate weight gain since hospital discharge."

Olivia grew. My breast milk did that.

"Did Olivia suffer any distress while in Ms. Kaplan's care?"

"On the contrary. Developmentally she progressed, exhibiting a social smile and vocalizing appropriately."

"One more question. You have worked with Ms. Kaplan in the NICU. Do you trust her nursing judgement?"

My heart stammers.

"Implicitly." Dr. STAT looks at me. The corners of her mouth upturn. Vanessa and Judge Kipper thank her. She steps from the witness box. Dr. STAT exits the courtroom.

I thought that Dr. STAT had been too busy to notice me in the NICU, much less care about my life. But I was wrong.

The mewing, like the cry of a fragile newborn, resumes. I wonder if Vanessa hears it. But Vanessa is focused, not distracted by random noises. She says to Judge Kipper, "My next witnesses will attest to Ms. Kaplan's skill as a nurse."

Judge Kipper closes the manila folder. "In the interest of time, if the State agrees, and I expect that you will." Judge Kipper's glasses slip, and he peers over the wire rim at the young attorney.

Frat Boy stands. "Yes, Your Honor."

"Again, in the interest of time, the witnesses on behalf of Ms. Kaplan will rise from their seats in the gallery. Nurses, stand where you are."

Feet shuffle. There's murmuring. Laughter.

Judge Kipper says, "Bailiff, if you will administer the oath."

Because Vanessa told me to keep my gaze forward, I can't see what causes the commotion. Behind me, I hear Peter's surprised inhale.

Vanessa walks to my side and says, "You should turn around."

I pivot. NICU nurses, some wearing hospital scrubs, others dressed for professional business, pack the gallery. I wonder, with so many nurses in court, who is left to care for the NICU patients?

Lakeview Hospital's NICU nurses raise their right hands. Twenty voices vow to tell the truth. I see Nicki, the good luck Minnie Mouse with a four-leaf clover, pinned to her scrubs. I fixate on Robyn. She wears a pink wrap dress, her braids in a ponytail. I assume she left Olivia with Thom. Robyn gazes at the bailiff, not at me.

Judge Kipper addresses the nurses. "Do you attest that your statements which I have printed before me, are true?"

In unison, the nurses respond, "Yes."

"Nurses, you may sit."

Vanessa paces and addresses the courtroom. "A baby cries alone in a car. Annabelle Kaplan, a professional nurse, a Good Samaritan, is unable to ignore the distressed infant. But Ms. Kaplan was more than a professional nurse, that day. More than a concerned citizen. Ms. Kaplan was driven by maternal instinct. Arguably the most powerful of all innate impulses, women have accomplished remarkable feats, possessed superhuman strength, for the sake of protecting their young. Olivia was in need. And Ms. Kaplan, as mothers have done since the beginning of time, ushered baby Olivia to safety. Showered with Ms. Kaplan's loving care, baby Olivia thrives today. Ms. Kaplan is a nurse, a Good Samaritan, but she is also a mother, a grieving mother, with courage enough to intervene. And grace enough to comfort a baby in distress. I ask the court a simple question. Put yourself in Ms. Kaplan's place. You discover a baby trapped in a car. What would you do?"

THE BABY NURSE

Vanessa's hands fold across her heart. She bows to the gallery, returns to our table, and sits at my side.

I want to throw my arms around Vanessa. I want to thank her a thousand times. But Vanessa doesn't meet my gaze. She's hyperalert, as if by osmosis assessing the courtroom's temperature, Judge Kipper's mood, anticipating the State's response. Vanessa tips her head in my direction, and I remain still. The corners of Vanessa's lips upturn.

The room is oddly quiet. The stenographer's fingers rest on the typewriter keys, the State's attorney stares at his notepad, and behind me Peter inhales sharply. I wait for his exhale. Before I hear Peter breathe, the bailiff commands me to stand. My knees quiver. Vanessa and I stand as a single unit, her hand on my shoulder.

Judge Kipper lifts his gavel.

A woman shouts, "I have something to say."

The bailiff, hand on the butt of her pistol, scans the gallery for the voice. Noise erupts. Bodies shift. Shocked gasps.

The woman insists, "Listen to me."

I know that voice.

Judge Kipper sets the gavel on the podium. "I'll have quiet. Bailiff, bring the individual forward."

Vanessa says, "Your Honor, this is highly irregular."

I glance at the other attorney, and he looks bewildered.

Judge Kipper says, "I agree. But I'll permit it. Be seated."

The stenographer types.

The bailiff escorts Sheila, dressed not in her Kitty Haven coveralls but an ankle-length denim skirt, Birkenstock sandals, and an LL Bean corduroy coat with deep pockets, to the witness stand. Sheila sits.

The bailiff says, "State your name and vocation."

"Sheila Murphy. I own Kitty Haven." She takes her right hand from her pocket, raises her palm, and promises to tell the truth. She doesn't look at me. I'm all nerves. I sit on my hands to stay their trembling. What does Sheila need to tell the judge about me?

Sheila is dwarfed in the witness stand. "Does this work?" She taps the microphone. Static erupts from the speakers. "Can you hear me?"

Judge Kipper is surprisingly kind. "The court hears you. What is your relation to Ms. Kaplan?"

Sheila leans forward, lips kissing the microphone. "Annabelle is my best friend."

The courtroom, me included, have stopped breathing.

Vanessa grips her pen, her knuckles pallid knobs.

Sheila looks at Judge Kipper. She says, "Judge. Sir. Do you have a best friend?"

I hear Peter cough. Vanessa is frozen, otherwise I'm certain she would notate her steno pad. The State's lawyer is gleeful, like a fraternity-sponsored April Fools' prank is in play.

Judge Kipper rearranges his robes. "My dear, it's been some time since anyone has asked me a question. I've been on the bench for eons and I appreciate a fresh perspective now and then. I'm happy to answer. Yes. I'm blessed with two best friends. I'm married to one."

A tide of nervous laughter washes over the room.

Judge Kipper adjusts his glasses. No longer looking at Sheila but across the room. "My other best friend stood at my side when I married. He stewarded my sons into the world. I dare say our days are numbered, he and I have exhausted life's marrow—"

A door clicks. Unable to resist, I twist in my seat, and see a man, the back of his head covered in shaggy grey curls; unmistakably Webster Cumberland. He exits the room.

Sheila says, "Then you understand, sir. Annabelle is my best friend. I want to tell you the type of friend she is and how trustworthy she is. I've known Annabelle the longest of anyone in this room, since we were girls. I lived with my dad, but he wasn't around much. He'd disappear for days at a time. Other kids, if they knew, would think I was lucky, getting to do what I wanted, without a parent enforcing rules and curfews. Except when Dad was home, he drank. Vodka, straight from the bottle. And drinking made him mean. He cursed me. Hit me too. He threatened to give me away. Drop me off at an orphanage if I told anyone. So, I kept my mouth shut, even lied to the school nurse about the bruises. But Annabelle knew. She was there one night. He didn't see her and started yelling, called me horrible names. Before he knew what was happening, Annabelle demanded he stop and replayed the recording she made on her phone. Dad went into his bedroom and shut his door. From then on, anytime I was scared, I called Annabelle. She came over or I went to her house. Without Annabelle, I don't know if I would have survived my childhood."

Frat Boy stands.

He's met with Judge Kipper's steely gaze. Frat Boy sits.

Judge Kipper says to Sheila, "You are fortunate indeed to have a friend to share your unconscionable situation."

Sheila digs in her jacket pocket and places a grey ball onto the witness stand. The ball expands into a kitten. It stretches, finds the microphone and meows. The mewing I heard before, amplifies, precipitating shocked giggles across the room. The kitten's ash-colored tail undulates. I recognize the kitten's grey fur, and although it has grown since I'd fed it infant formula from a nurser nipple, it is no bigger than a collectable Beanie Baby.

Judge Kipper says, "A delightful exhibit."

The kitten leaps from the witness stand onto the judge's podium.

I dare exhale. Judge Kipper likes cats?

Sheila says, "Annabelle is trustworthy. So much so that I am allowing her to adopt this kitten without filing an application. Can the court witness the adoption?"

My mouth falls open, as does Vanessa's, and I assume everyone else's behind me. Vanessa recovers immediately with a wide grin as whispers spread out over the room. Judge Kipper is exuberant. "Excellent. Bailiff? You'll get a copy of this kitten's official rehoming. Ms. Kaplan? Approach." The kitten curls in the judge's palms, kneads the sleeve of his robe.

Vanessa stands. I do the same. We walk to the bench.

Judge Kipper says, "Ms. Kaplan, do you agree to take Ms. Murphy's kitten into your home, name it, provide it with food, shelter, appropriate pet care?"

I answer, "I promise." I hold Sheila's gaze. What passes between us needs no words. Our shared history is enough.

Sheila smiles and says, "A name?"

The kitten's coat is elegant. "Cashmere."

Judge Kipper says, "Let the court mark this happy occasion. Cashmere has a forever home. Mrs. Kipper will be thrilled when I tell her about these proceedings." Cashmere the kitten is passed from Judge Kipper to the bailiff, who smiles, wishes me luck, and delivers the kitten, cupped in her hands, to me. The kitten weighs less than a premature infant.

Sheila is guided to her seat where she is enveloped by NICU nurses. Applause explodes. Nurses love to see a baby find its way home.

Peter stands, leans across the railing and I pass Cashmere into his open hands.

The gavel pounds. Once, twice, a third thump. Judge Kipper says, "Attorneys."

Vanessa leaps to her feet. At the next table, the opposing lawyer rises.

The judge says, "My chambers. The both of you. We'll hash

this out." He removes his spectacles, stowing them in his robes and stands.

The bailiff barks, "All rise."

Chairs scrape, feet shuffle, voices mutter.

The bailiff retrieves the cane, hands it to Judge Kipper and the judge descends the platform, the tapping cane reverberates, a definitive thump signifying that he reached common ground. The bailiff opens the door and Judge Kipper's black robes sway, the hem lifted by a breeze as he disappears.

Conversation buzzes the gallery.

"Quiet. Be seated," the bailiff says. "Attorneys, the judge will have you visit his chambers."

I ask Vanessa, "What's happening?"

"Don't move. I'll be back." Vanessa marches from the table.

"But what's happening?" I ask again. "This is bad, right?"

The frat-boy attorney joins Vanessa. He says something to her, and she shakes her head in response. The bailiff ushers the pair through the door. I lean on the table, hoping to spy into the secret chamber but the bailiff blocks my view and seals it shut. I slump, deflated.

I imagine Judge Kipper in the sanctity of his private chamber mulling over my actions. But the judge is not what I expected. He treated Sheila gently. Listened with an open mind and allowed her to gift me Cashmere. Will Judge Kipper's kind heart remain open, or clamp closed as he considers what I've done? I stare at the judge's door. Enough time passes that I anticipate a worst-case scenario. Judge Kipper emerges, scolds me publicly, and Vanessa, who I've come to admire, shuns me. I'll be left friendless, lawyer-less, sentenced to a dingy cell until I'm an old lady. Sheila will have no choice but to rescind Cashmere's adoption.

Thirty minutes later and the bailiff signals the judge's return. "All rise."

Behind me, Peter shifts. I'm afraid to disobey Vanessa by straying from my chair but I do it anyway. I turn and tell Peter, "I love you."

Peter, Cashmere in hand, whispers, "Me too. No matter what."

I stand. Vanessa race-walks to my side. I could be mistaken but there's a slight crease at the corners of her mouth suggesting a smile.

Judge Kipper, suddenly spry, ascends to his podium, the gavel sounds with a righteous clobber. "I've reached my decision. Ms. Kaplan and her attorney will remain standing."

Vanessa and I stand together, the surveillance monitor on my ankle a restrictive, and I fear, permanent weight. Frigid air blasts from the vent. Behind me, I hear Cashmere's steady purr.

Judge Kipper adjusts his robes, steeples his fingers, and gazes at me.

Straightening my shoulders, I force myself to meet the judge's stare.

He says, "A most unusual morning. Ms. Kaplan, you have the support of your colleagues. A loyal friend. An attentive spouse behind you. You are wealthy beyond measure. But your actions are puzzling. Responding to a distressed infant, comforting her, removing the infant from danger are understandable. What troubles me? Your failure to relinquish the infant to social services in a reasonable time frame. Say, within the hour you discovered her in the car. Choosing instead to harbor the baby for three days—both unnecessary and reckless."

I tremble. Vanessa puts her hand on my shoulder.

Judge Kipper says, "In my judgement, your duty as a Good Samaritan, a trained nurse, expired after removing the baby from the car. A reasonable expectation would be to return the infant to the hospital immediately, not covet the baby for so many days. You are a fine citizen, invested in your community, with no criminal record. For this reason, and not because of the splendid creature that graced our courtroom..." The judge pauses, scans the spectators for Sheila, I assume.

His attention returns to me. "Ms. Kaplan, I see no reason to pursue criminal proceedings. I recommend that you be released and complete community service. And in regard to your nursing license, I'll forward the case to the State Board of Professional Nursing. They will decide what should be done about your professional license."

Vanessa says, "Thank you, Your Honor."

The cheers are loud. As I said, NICU nurses love happy endings. I fall into Peter's arms. Over his shoulder I scan the crowd for Robyn. But she's gone.

CHAPTER EIGHTEEN

"You're free to go." The guard removes my ankle monitor.

Peter kisses my cheek, drapes his jacket over my shoulders and leaves to retrieve the car. Vanessa hooks my elbow, guides me from the courtroom through the maze of corridors, past the clustered lawyers advising clients in hushed voices. A correctional officer opens the courthouse doors.

The air outside is damp and earthy. Cashmere sleeps, secure in my arms, protected from the drizzle by Peter's jacket. Rain mists my eyelashes, dews my lips; free water from heaven. I vow never to take the gift for granted.

A Pennsylvania Correctional Facility van with barred windows lurches from the curb. Not everyone was lucky today. I say to Vanessa, "Thank you. For everything." It's not nearly enough.

"We're not done yet. I'll be in touch about the hearing with the State Board of Nursing."

Peter's Subaru eases into the spot vacated by the correctional van. Vanessa's goodbye hug is stiff. She waves to Peter and walks back into the courthouse; her messenger bag swings as if weightless from her shoulder.

Peter drives. I settle into the passenger seat with Cashmere in my lap. The wipers swish. The rain percusses the roof like a team of galloping hooves. Peter navigates Woodline Manor's recently paved entrance. The newly laid asphalt is slick and unmarred. I hold Peter's hand. He's wearing new, unpilled wool gloves. He says, "Found this pair in the closet. There's an entire box. All in my size."

The Subaru bounces from paved to unpaved road.

Peter says, "Almost home."

Almost. I close my eyes and fight the urge to tell Peter, *Let's move.* We might be forced out anyway. But I hear a no-nonsense baritone telling me, *Can't run from trouble.*

Peter says, "Welcome home."

I open my eyes. The garage grumbles. Peter unlocks the connecting door and the three of us walk inside. Peter holds my hand, I carry Cashmere, who meows.

The locket is in the bathroom, suspended from the toothbrush holder. I slip it on, thankful for the luck that protected me from afar. I imagine Jamie doing the same for Olivia, invisibly shielding her daughter from life's harm.

Without the ankle monitor, I pull on a pair of black leggings.

Peter has a medium-sized Amazon box tucked under his arm. "An impromptu house for Cashmere." Peter puts the box on the bed. He has the kitten in his palm, his finger over Cashmere's heart, peers under the kitten's whip of a tail. "Do cats come with an instruction manual?" Peter has performed hundreds of prenatal ultrasounds, identifying fetal gender, sharing the information with parents who value planning above surprise. In the delivery room, Peter's announced, "It's a girl" or "It's a boy." But Cashmere? Peter says, "Your guess is as good as mine."

Peter gently sets the kitten in the box. We stand, admiring Cashmere, a grey ball, nested in colorful wool gloves. The kitten blinks. Cashmere kneads a red glove, yawns, and burrows beneath a green glove. A contented purr rises from the box. I tell Peter, "I'll call Sheila later and ask for that instruction manual."

Peter walks to the mirror, reknots his tie, and dusts kitten fur from the front of his jacket.

I stand behind him and wrap my arms around his waist. The jacket smells like his Subaru; leather, and old periodicals with a whiff of kitten. "You look handsome."

"I'm going to the hospital."

"The Board of Directors?"

"Webster is convening a meeting. I could be back to work this evening."

"You got this."

We smile at each other. The couple in the mirror smiles back, but their happy expression is tempered by wisdom. Faint lines corner their lips and crinkle the edges of their eyes. The people in the mirror are no longer naïve enough to believe that love cures life's every ill.

A truck labors and I part the nursery curtain. The familiar green pickup with the dented fender rattles as it ascends our driveway. I launch down the stairs, skip the third step, fling the front door wide and wait on the porch. The truck parks in front of the garage, coughing sulfurous breath. I wave and call out, "Marcus. Come inside."

The driver steps from the truck, adjusts his beret, and returns my greeting with a cheerful thumbs up. It's not Marcus. I shiver from disappointment. The man is close to my age, way younger than Marcus. Instead of a painter's cap, he wears a black beret. His work pants are unstained and his Doc Martins unscuffed. *Miko* is embroidered on the front of his Radcliff Apartment-issue fleece jacket.

Miko removes his beret. Amber curls tumble over his forehead. "You must be Annabelle. Uncle Marcus told me about you. I'm Miko."

I'm drawn to this youthful version of Marcus. I know so little about the details of Marcus's life, yet without him I wouldn't have been able to spend those days and nights with Olivia. Marcus has a nephew. "Miko, any chance you drink coffee?"

"Cream and sugar." Miko follows me into the foyer. He pauses, absorbing his surroundings. "Big place you have. Compared to the apartment."

An echo boomerangs from the unfurnished living room. Miko follows me into the kitchen and sits on a barstool. "Uncle Marcus wants you to have this." An envelope slides across the counter, plain, letter-sized, and unsealed.

My pulse canters. Has Miko read the note inside? What if the information details an incriminating secret? I sit on the barstool across from Miko and open the envelope. Miko's light-brown eyes are watchful. A single photograph slips onto the counter. I turn it over, there's no written message on the back, no caption under the image. I understand the cliché about pictures: *Worth a thousand words.*

Miko doesn't seem surprised by my tears. "Uncle Marcus warned me his gift would have an effect. He told me this is the sole copy. He deleted the original from his phone."

The picture is of Olivia, on my lap, in Mom's apartment, the only picture of her that I have. "Thank you. I'd like to thank Marcus—"

"Uncle Marcus is gone."

I press Olivia's picture to my heart. "He can't be."

"Retired from Radcliff. His ship set sail from Miami this morning. Cruising to Jamaica."

Happy news. Marcus. On his way to the island of his dreams. I close my eyes and imagine Marcus leaning against the ship railing, his cap shielding him from the hot sun.

Miko finishes his coffee and I program the Keurig to refill his mug. Miko says, "Better get going. The Radcliff superintendent is a stickler, doesn't trust me to fill Uncle Marcus's shoes. Can't say that I blame her."

I smile. "Your uncle is a special person."

"Before I go, Uncle Marcus left me delivery directions. Where should I unload your stuff?"

"My what?"

"From the apartment. Uncle Marcus told me you'd want the lamp, chair, the loveseat—"

"Lamp?" I find my jail-issue flip-flops and help Miko.

Miko lifts the green tarp from the pickup's cargo bay. Gone are the gas can, newspapers and Marcus's red toolbox. Miko unloads the first item onto a dolly. "Uncle told me you're a nurse—good thing. This plant needs medical attention."

I recognize the clay urn and the braided tree trunk. But Mom's ficus looks like it suffers from depression. The leaves droop, in need of misting. I cart it inside. Ficus likes light, and I feel Mom direct me to set her plant in front of the window. I talk to the plant, like Mom used to do. "Don't give up. Better times are ahead. You'll like it here."

Miko and I make four trips with the dolly until only a single box remains in the pickup truck. Miko says, "My uncle packed this box."

"What's inside?"

"Uncle's lady-friend—" Miko pauses, pink-faced.

"I know that Mom and your uncle were friends."

Considering Miko's reaction, I can't help wondering if there was more to Mom's relationship with Marcus.

"A book. Uncle told me that she loved to cook."

I whisper, "Thank you, Marcus."

I hear Marcus laughing into a headwind. He tells me, *No trouble. None at all.*

I ask Miko to stay for dinner. "We're having pasta. *Gemelli.*"

Miko takes his beret from his jacket pocket, puts it on and explains that he loves pasta, but that he has class tonight. He's working at Radcliff Apartments to save money for tuition. In the meantime, he attends community college and is getting prerequisites out of the way. "I nearly forgot—one more item."

I stand on the porch. Miko opens the truck's passenger door and carries Olivia's car seat by the handle. He passes it to me and says, "Uncle Marcus told me you'll need these too." Miko points to the plastic measuring spoons from Mom's kitchen in the seat. "For Little One."

I thank Miko. He promises to come for dinner over semester break. I tell him by then we'll likely serve *ziti*. I stand on the porch while the truck bounces down the driveway. At the bottom, Miko honks the horn and I wave until the pickup is out of sight. I remain outside in my flip-flops, listening to the truck's tailpipe rattle. Not until the sound fades and finally vanishes do I go inside.

Cashmere laps cream from a saucer, pink tongue darting and whiskers quivering. My phone, finally returned to me, recovers its charge after confinement in Vanessa's messenger bag. I take a picture and make Cashmere my screen saver. I text Sheila with questions, reminding her that I'm without a car and can't shop at a pet store or visit a vet. My phone zings with incoming texts.

Sheila has a care package for Cashmere. I respond on Cashmere's behalf:

> meow

Peter's emojis: a hospital, a syringe, a checkmark. Positive news from the board meeting. I'm happy. Peter was born to be a doctor; I can't imagine him being satisfied doing anything else. I respond with a beating heart, congratulations, and a balloon release.

Fingertips tingling, I text Robyn:

> Miss you. How are you and Olivia?

Send.

My message delivers. I watch. Three minutes elapse but my message remains unread. Maybe Robyn is busy. Juggling five kids can't be easy.

Cashmere is one of four and must miss their litter mates. I search my phone's lullaby app, find a maternal heartbeat loop, push play, and set the phone in Cashmere's box. Cashmere's triangle ears alert. Cashmere sleeps, consoled by swishing heart tones. I get to work.

Mom's lamp stands on a sturdy foundation, the neck arcs, its head a linen drum. Plug mates socket, and the bulb's iridescent glow transforms the living-room walls from bland oatmeal to vanilla-wafer delicious. I maneuver the loveseat kitty-corner, the upholstered chair with mint-green piping across from the coffee table and Windex the table glass. Mom's taste was eclectic. There's an Art Deco frame that suits Olivia's photo, and I prop it on the coffee table.

Finally, I unroll the carpet, stomping the creases flat. I hear the Subaru, followed by a second vehicle. Car doors slam. Peter and Sheila arrive, stand side by side in the foyer, and view the living room. Peter absorbs the addition of furniture with clinical curiosity. "A lamp, a chair, a sofa, excellent."

Peter kisses my cheek, whispers that everything with the Lakeview Medical Board went as he hoped. I'll get the details later. Peter walks to the kitchen. Water strums the sink, his pre-dinner scrub. The fan above the stove whirls. Cabinets unlatch, pots clang. Peter announces, "Dinner in thirty minutes."

Sheila scoops Cashmere from the glove box and instructs me in the specifics of kitten-care. She then shovels clay pellets onto a tray. "Clean the litter daily or Cashmere will find an alternate spot to evacuate."

Sheila lectures without pause. I jot notes about calorie requirements, growth, and sleep. Sheila is serious about developmental play. "Pouncing, stalking, climbing, scratching are innate feline behaviors." Sheila demonstrates stalking behavior by tossing and chasing a toy mouse. Cashmere watches, unblinking. Diapers are my forte. Litter boxes? Not so much. I'd be lost without Sheila's coaching.

Cashmere crouches, tentatively paws the fake mouse. Sheila offers effusive praise, "Good job, Cashmere." I can't help but feel proud.

Sheila passes me the mouse along with a spare. "Hide it. In case the original becomes lost."

I relate, having counseled new mothers that storing a spare of their baby's favorite items prevents a midnight trip to the Target store to replace a lost pacifier or security blanket. But keeping Cashmere healthy is not all play. Sheila explains the vaccination schedule and recommends a vet. Again, I take notes.

There's a lull. Both of us sit in silence. I take a breath and tell Sheila, "Thank you. For trusting me with Cashmere and for testifying at my hearing. You and Cashmere made all the difference. I'm sorry for involving you with Olivia and I apologize for not telling the truth upfront. I made a mess of things, and I had no business risking Kitty Haven." Just so there's no doubt in Sheila's mind, I add, "What I said to you—was wrong."

Sheila takes my hand. "I am sorry too. Best friends should be there for each other, and I wasn't. I should have visited you more after what happened with your baby. But after I saw how sad you were in the hospital, I didn't know what to say. Staying away was wrong."

"Talking about stuff was easier when we were younger."

"Growing up. It's harder than I thought."

The aromas of Asiago, olive oil, garlic, and basil waft from the kitchen. Peter asks, "Hungry?"

"Yes," Sheila and I answer in unison. We take our seats at the kitchen counter, Cashmere on Sheila's knee, humming with contentment.

After dinner, Sheila leaves. My phone is buried in Cashmere's box under a red glove, or I'd have seen Robyn's text earlier. Her message is chilling.

> I don't have the baby.

Peter calls me, "Belle? You should see this. This is no ordinary cookbook."

I try to answer but words won't come. A desperate exhale escapes, a sound like ice cracking.

I text and then answer Robyn's call on the first ring. She launches into a one-sided conversation. "They took Olivia. The case worker came. Family court mumbo-jumbo—"

"When?" My voice is shrill.

"Two days ago." Robyn sounds sad. "I kissed her for you—little Robbie won't come out of his room—says he misses 'Ollie.' That's what he calls her."

I can't explain my anger. Except that I'm not thinking clearly. "How could you? I trusted—"

Robyn sounds exhausted. "Fernanda had a court order. I had no choice but to give—" Children cry in the background. "The boys. Robbie. He needs—"

I'm ashamed for lashing out. Robyn's sons are traumatized, and she must feel overwhelmed. I ask, "Where's Olivia?"

"Annabelle, you need to come to your senses. Where else would she be? She's with her aunt." Robyn ends the call.

Helpless to do anything else, I cry.

CHAPTER NINETEEN

We spend the next morning looking for Cashmere. Peter sifts the glove box. Yellow, green, and red gloves. He reaches the bottom, overturns the box as proof. "No Cashmere." Peter wears hospital scrubs, rubs his bare neck.

I hand him a mug of hot coffee. "Hazelnut. For your commute."

He drinks deeply. "Let's find Cashmere. I'll worry the entire way."

I call the kitten. There's a trail of kitty litter in the foyer where Sheila put the litter tray. I sweep the stray pellets into a dustpan. Peter and I inspect the kitchen. A muted thump sends us jogging to the living room.

Pawprints smudge the glass coffee table. I right the toppled Art Deco frame. A band tightens around my heart. Olivia's picture. She's on my lap, her eyes bright blue. I imagine Aunt Darlene pacing The Rusty Sub Tavern, jostling Olivia in a discombobulating rhythm. They are strangers, tossed together without benefit of a bond. How is Aunt Darlene managing Olivia's endless schedule? Naps, play, meals, diapers, and baths?

Peter says, "There you are." Cashmere nestles, asleep on the loveseat, in Mom's indented cushion.

"Sheila warned me," I say. "Kittens become cats fast."

Peter hugs me. I wish him luck on his first full shift back at the hospital. He says, "I tried to tell you last night—your mom's cookbook? It's more than recipes. Check it out."

Peter hesitates in the foyer. I sense he's worried about leaving me alone in the house. I say to him, "Cashmere will be company."

Hand on the doorknob, Peter lingers for a kiss. His stethoscope, draped around his neck, bumps my sternum. I hold the circular diaphragm, a giant disc compared to my dime-sized neonatal stethoscope. I want to change into scrubs pants, grab my stethoscope, and report for work in the NICU. Not long ago, Peter and I travelled as a team to Lakeview Hospital when our schedules matched. We'd parked, strode the hospital lobby, waited together for an elevator.

Not wanting to spoil Peter's return, I say, "I have plenty to do. I'll check out Mom's cookbook."

Still, he stands at the threshold, blue eyes pensive. "You're not—I mean, going to do—"

"No. I promise... you have my word." Neither of us say her name. Or discuss how Aunt Darlene won the trust of social services and has custody.

Peter leaves. The Subaru reverses from the garage, Peter waves, buoyant behind the wheel.

Inside, the house is silent. I hear my pulse throb. Cashmere sleeps, not interested in pouncing on Sheila's toy mouse. On the coffee table Olivia appears forlorn, a still life framed in Art Deco. I flop on the loveseat, ponder how best to gain information about Olivia. Without a car, I can't go to The Rusty Sub Tavern for the lunch special, order a drink at the bar, procrastinate before paying, hoping for a glimpse of Olivia.

I rub my forehead, erasing the crazy fantasy. The scenario won't work. Peter would be devasted if I chased after Aunt Darlene and Olivia, jeopardizing my freedom. I imagine Vanessa, her tall forehead wrinkled in displeasure. I tell myself, "No." Olivia is with Aunt Darlene. I love Olivia, but she is not my baby. For better or worse I'm no longer her nurse. The responsibility to rescue her no longer rests on my shoulders. Still, thinking of her stings.

I reach for the recipe book on the coffee table. Mom cooked from memory, but on occasion, she'd had the book splayed open on the kitchen counter to confirm an ingredient, search for a substitution, or add a recipe card.

Growing up I had other concerns besides meal preparation. My adolescent preoccupations involved sleepovers with Sheila, cello lessons, memorizing my Torah portion for my Bat Mitzvah, studying for the SAT. I'd never asked Mom how she learned to cook, but assumed it was 'mother' knowledge. A skillset mysteriously bestowed upon women Mom's age. I never considered that Mom vetted recipes, tasted food combinations, or adjusted spices to suit Dad's palate. I rarely offered to help in the kitchen, instead I anticipated a spread, appropriate to the occasion, and it would appear, like magic. Thanksgiving stuffing. Birthday cupcakes.

Except there had been no magician's wand. Mom worked after work. Teaching didn't end when the school bell rang, but Mom still managed to prepare my meals. The book, I'm about to learn, is proof that I mattered to her even more than I realized. I sit on the loveseat beside Cashmere, the book on my lap. The cover is scrapbook style with screws in the spine for the addition of pages. I read the title, *Gold Family Recipes*. A lump rises in my throat. I open the cover. Flipping the pages feels intimate. Like peeking into her diary, which in a sense I am.

The cardstock pages tell Mom's story.

THE BABY NURSE

I turn to the section titled *Annabelle*. A snapshot of a woman with black plastic-framed glasses, her red hair bobbed, holding a swaddled newborn. The notation reads, *Home from the hospital. Dinner: brisket and peas.* I gasp in horror. Mom had cooked after giving birth? She hadn't. The meal was a gift from the PTA.

A photo, me in a highchair, being fed mush from a spoon. Directions for homemade applesauce. Granny Smith and Macoun apples, peeled, cored, boiled, puréed. No added sugar, a pinch of cinnamon. The recipes, interspersed with pictures; a series of birthday parties, sixth-grade graduation, with comments in the margin, notated when Mom became health conscious. *Use olive oil, not butter.* Her trick for getting me to eat cauliflower, a vegetable I dislike to this day. I laugh and remember I never suspected cauliflower hidden in the baked noodles. *Annabelle ate a second helping.* Mom's calligraphy is lovely. I read out loud and hear her voice.

The holidays include Mom's Rosh Hashanah kugel, sweetened with brown sugar and honey to usher in the Jewish New Year. I'm surprised to learn the recipe was her mother's, my grandmother, who died when Mom was a teenager. Passover matzo balls; Mom's secret, add vegetable stock, not water, to the matzo meal.

The first meal Mom cooked after she returned to the kitchen following Dad's death: barley soup. I remember Mom washing, peeling, dicing bright-orange carrots, trimming green beans, barley pearls simmering, the lid bouncing from the pot as steam escaped. Hours later Mom ladled the aromatic soup into white bowls, and I understood that despite Dad's passing we'd continue to relish meals. In other words, live.

The following page is a picture I'd never seen before. Black and white, yellow at the edges, an infant in a knitted swaddle wearing a bonnet. The handwriting is unfamiliar and the message beneath the photo penned on thin, fragile paper:

Yeder mentsh hot zikh zayn pekl.

Yiddish. Mom had preserved the picture and the message, but without explanation. Who is the baby and what does the Yiddish mean? Mom on occasion had dropped a Yiddish word, a fusion of German, Hebrew, and Eastern European languages. But when I'd ask Mom to translate, she'd wave her hand, shooing my question, saying, "An idiom, it doesn't exist in English."

I reread the Yiddish. The words roll over my tongue, rhythmic and comforting. Familiar. I grasp but fail to glean their meaning. "Thanks, Mom." I close the cover. I'll research the Yiddish. But I receive the gift of what is left unwritten, none of Mom's students' names are etched on the pages. As envious as I was of the kids in Mom's class, I need not have been. Mom was dedicated to her students but devoted to her daughter, me. I set the book on the coffee table with Olivia's photograph.

The letter from Lakeview Hospital arrives by certified mail later that afternoon. I sign the receipt and take the envelope into the living room. I unseal the envelope and read. My termination is effective immediately. My nursing license is sure to be revoked next. I break the news to Cashmere. "It's official, I'm unemployed." I sink into the loveseat, clutch Jamie's locket, and ask, "What am I going to do?"

The furniture from Mom's apartment absorbs my question. There's no echo. But I hear a whisper. *"Find a job."*

A few weeks later, I'm carrying my cello out through the door. I've gotten a job as a cello teacher in an after-school music program in Philadelphia. The music director had been one of my private instructors, and he agreed to interview me despite what happened with Olivia since there were no pending criminal charges. I fall into a routine rehearsing cello music in the afternoon with Cashmere as an audience and work three evenings a week at the high school. Occasionally I go early, pack my dinner to save money, and assist in the school band room with afternoon music rehearsals. The students are rowdy, unnecessarily robust on percussion, but they're fun and several show promise.

My first paycheck is a fraction of my nurse salary. Vanessa helps me iron out the details of a debt consolidation plan, including reimbursing the check I'd cashed from Mom's pension. A step in the right direction, I no longer dread the mailbox. Collectors never leave voicemail. The hole behind my heart can't be filled by household goods, even with guaranteed same-day shipping. And my Amazon Prime account is cancelled, so I'm never tempted by *Top Picks for Annabelle*. Janice, my Zoom therapist, who I continued to meet after the hospital and court-mandated sessions, suggests that I write in my journal when I feel the need to scroll-shop.

More weeks pass. Peter works full time at Lakeview Hospital but pulls fewer overnight shifts because he's studying for boards. I suspect that Webster Cumberland had a hand in Peter's schedule. Dr. Cumberland has done a lot for us. But gratitude and Dr. Cumberland mix about as well as extra-virgin olive oil and salad vinegar. Bitterness still tempers the good feelings I have towards him. Despite these doubts we invite Dr. and Mrs. Cumberland to dinner one evening. Peter reviews mock board questions while waiting for water to boil. We're having *vermicelli* with red sauce.

Peter's button-down is as blue as his eyes. Instead of scrubs pants, his khakis have a crisp crease. He's dressed not for a casual dinner but an interview. I get it and change from yoga pants into a cream-colored sweater dress and comb my strawberry-blonde hair into submission.

Dr. Cumberland's gunmetal-grey Mercedes tackles the driveway with barely a whisper. Peter stands at the front door. I search my closet for appropriate footwear, find black flats, and run downstairs, striking the third step as the Cumberlands enter the foyer. A breath of the outdoors swirls around the couple, hinting of tilled soil and sprouting daffodils. Dr. Cumberland clasps Peter's hands and exclaims, "Son, this is a solid house. Indeed, it takes years for a foundation to settle." Dr. Cumberland introduces his wife, Edith. Tall and broad-shouldered like her husband, the couple crowd the foyer.

Webster and Edith Cumberland resemble one another the way that long-married couples trade individualism for unity. Their outfits coordinate. Corduroy slacks and a knitted vest over a long-sleeved business shirt for the doctor; Mrs. Cumberland in a pink sweater set, the same corduroy slacks and matching brown leather loafers. They're silver-haired but Mrs. Cumberland's curls are lacquered, tinged blue, and frame her powdered face.

Perhaps that's what will happen to us. Without realizing, Peter and I will morph into one another. Webster gifts Peter a wine tote. Webster's voice rings through the foyer, "Stag's Leap. Private reserve from Napa. Give the wine time to chill and show me this bucolic property."

Mrs. Cumberland grips her patent leather clutch by its gold clasp. "A tour. Now? Too dark to appreciate the sights, don't you agree?"

Obviously, Mrs. Cumberland has no desire to traipse through the property at dusk. I say, "Perhaps Mrs. Cumberland would prefer to remain inside, where it's brightly lit?" There's satisfaction in flicking the lamp, illuminating a furnished living room.

Webster says, "Splendid." He claps Peter's back. "A men's tour it is, my boy."

Peter's smile, directed at me, is a private *thank you*.

Peter and Webster clomp from foyer to porch, voices rising with laughter at a shared joke, fading as they stray from the house to the survey marker at the woods' edge. The light from Peter's phone bounces in time with their synchronous, springy stride. Peter's black hair absorbs the night, but Webster's silver curls shine as if reflecting starlight. I watch from the window, two figures, one dense-boned, tall, slightly bent, the second lean and wiry. The older man puts a hand on his younger companion's shoulder.

"Would you like a tour inside the house instead?" I ask.

I take Mrs. Cumberland through our kitchen, and our newly furnished living room. Then she points to the closed door between the kitchen and the foyer. A room we've not used since we moved. "The dining room," I say.

Mrs. Cumberland enters the room with a gasp. We walk the expansive oak floor, stopping to admire the stone hearth stacked with birch logs on a black grate. French doors lead to the rear terrace. A chandelier hangs from the recessed ceiling. I swivel the dimmer switch. Bulbs glow, glass balls extend from silver arms like an iridescent snowflake. Underneath the chandelier, the room is bare.

Mrs. Cumberland says, "You'll have a lovely dinner party here."

I say, "But first we need a mile-long table. For now, Peter and I eat our meals on the kitchen counter."

When we return to the living room, Cashmere is perched

on the loveseat. Mrs. Cumberland gasps, "A kitten. What a darling creature."

"Cat lover?"

Tears moisten Mrs. Cumberland's pale-blue eyes. "I had a cat this same shade. Smokey was his name."

"Would you like to hold Cashmere?"

Mrs. Cumberland puts her purse on the coffee table, the gold clasp clinks the glass. She sinks into the loveseat, crosses her thick ankles. Cashmere cooperates, nesting on Mrs. Cumberland's knee.

I sit in the chair. The same one Marcus occupied the night I brought Olivia to Mom's apartment. I rub the worn seam, the mint-green piping that Marcus had picked loose. Olivia's picture is angled in my direction. A tingle deep in my breast reminds me that my milk isn't gone yet. Mothering hormones, reluctant to quit.

Mrs. Cumberland strokes Cashmere's fur. "Where did you find such an adorable creature?"

I tell Mrs. Cumberland about Kitty Haven.

"Adopt? A wonderful notion. I never considered it. A cat makes a house home. Don't you agree, dear? And call me Edith. 'Mrs. Cumberland' makes me sound ancient."

I tell Edith that I agree, a kitten transforms a space. "My friend Sheila would love to meet you. She always has kittens up for adoption."

Edith says, "You have the most unusual taste in furniture. The lamp? To die for. Palm-frond print on this loveseat? Unique."

Peter and Webster return, accompanied by a damp gust. Four shoes stomp the foyer tiles. A cork pops. Stemware clinks. Edith leaves Cashmere on the indented loveseat cushion. We go into the kitchen. Peter pours. I distribute the goblets to our guests.

Webster offers a toast. "To Dr. Kaplan, I have no doubt you'll ace the obstetrical boards..." Webster hesitates, sadness veiling his blue eyes as he maintains watch over Peter, glass raised. The toast hangs, an emotional fragment, a spent shell casing, leaving Peter and I to imagine what's insinuated. Does Webster intend to invite Peter to share his practice? A career with benefits, loan repayment, profit sharing, and health insurance.

Peter flushes and says, "I'll drink to that."

Webster twirls the stem of his goblet, agitating the wine. The glass is chilled, the wine the color of melted butter. The first sip tastes like caramel apples. I catch Peter's gaze. He stifles a full smile, but I see it in his eyes. He's thrilled to host Webster and Edith in our home.

I say, "Thank you, Webster. The vintage is excellent."

Cumberland raises his glass in my direction.

Delicate *vermicelli* strands tangle between fork tines. There are no leftovers. I rinse the plates of marinara sauce and load the dishwasher. Peter and Webster move from the kitchen counter into the living room, quizzing each other with mock obstetrical board questions. Obstetrical terms; *gravity, gram-positive cocci, eclampsia, gestational diabetes* volley across the coffee table. Edith retrieves Cashmere from the sofa and the kitten purrs in the crook of her elbow. With her free hand she passes me the flatware and says, "It's heartwarming. Seeing him happy."

"Cashmere loves you. You do have a way with cats."

"No, dear. I mean Webster. It's been years. But I believe your husband helps him move on."

I pop a Cascade pod in the dishwasher.

"Move to where—"

"From losing WJ. Our son. WJ died in high school... such a sweet, gentle boy. Webster's never been the same. But your husband brings out Webster's paternal instinct. Your husband resembles our son. Same black curls, blue eyes."

Edith's admission shocks me. Her pale eyes glisten like wet sea glass. I imagine her as a violet-eyed young woman, before decades of tribulations and an ocean of saltwater tears depleted her irises of their brilliant color. The glaring light surrounding the doctor subdues, softening Dr. Cumberland. I misjudged Webster. He knows our pain because he lives with it himself. For decades, despite his grief, he ushers newborns into their mothers' arms. And when a woman's life, mine, is in limbo, he acts. Bearing such weight is bound to round the doctor's shoulders, chisel his hands and grey his hair. I too have done what a patient needs and borne the consequences of the decisions.

I remember the Yiddish words in Mom's cookbook that I've since researched. Roughly translated, *Every person has their own burden.*

I tell Edith, "I'm sorry. I understand."

"Of course, you do, dear."

My phone vibrates just as the Cumberlands' car glides from our driveway. Caller ID flashes *Vanessa.*

"Hello?"

Vanessa asks for Peter too. "I've news. For you both."

Has Judge Kipper had a change of heart? Reversed my release, sentencing me to life in solitary? Peter and I huddle, the phone between us.

Vanessa asks if we can hear and repeats, "This development impacts both of you."

We answer in unison, "We hear you."

"Olivia Dutton's aunt, Darlene Cobb has contacted Child Protective Services with the intent to relinquish guardianship."

I exhale a hiss of breath.

Vanessa says, "There's more. Darlene Cobb, as Olivia's only living relative, requests that Olivia be placed in your care."

My tears splash the phone screen.

Peter shouts, "Yes" without hesitation.

"You'll need a car seat," Vanessa says after telling us where to meet her tomorrow. I detect a brimming wide smile in her voice. Peter and I stand on the porch; the night is cold, and we embrace to warm each other. Stars prod the ebony sky, their pulsations, not random blinks, or the final flicker of an extinguished world but intentional Morse code.

CHAPTER TWENTY

Vanessa tells us that the case worker is forty-five minutes behind schedule. "Not to worry," Vanessa says, "the paperwork will take that long, if not longer." Peter and I are escorted to a bland room at the Office of Children and Families in Philadelphia that reminds me of the police station. We sit on grey folding chairs around a rectangular table and complete a health form, list our immunizations, verify our identity, our permanent address, and current employment. I feel inadequate. No longer a nurse, I work as a part-time cello teacher. But Vanessa tells me not to worry, "Prior credit-card debt and suspension from your nursing career won't prevent you from fostering."

I dutifully complete my stack of paper and pass the clipboard. Peter signs the forms requiring joint signatures. I ask Vanessa, "Where's Olivia?" Even though I know.

"With her aunt. They're due anytime." Vanessa reminds me that Aunt Darlene's relinquishment is voluntary, not court mandated. Social services determined there was no neglect or mistreatment while Olivia was with Aunt Darlene.

"But why?" I hold the locket between my fingers. I have a million unanswered questions.

Vanessa taps her laptop. "We'll find out. In good time."

"She'll change her mind." Giving Olivia back is unfathomable.

A social worker, not Fernanda, retrieves the clipboard, returns our drivers' licenses, sets an iPad on the table, and tells us to watch a foster care training video. She sounds apologetic but I welcome the distraction. Twenty minutes later, the screen fades, smiling moms, dads, babies, and school-age children wave. I swipe my sleeve across my cheeks. I'm emotional, the way I was when pregnant and a commercial for breakfast cereal had induced melancholic tears.

Peter loosens his shirt collar. He took the morning off but is due at Lakeview Hospital in the afternoon. He folds his hands in his lap. His lips are pale, pursed, and I can tell he's worried. I ponder a worry of my own. What if Olivia and I don't connect, after two months, our bond lost and irretrievable? Will she smell like Aunt Darlene or like fried clams, The Rusty Sub Tavern dinner special? Does Olivia blame me for giving her to Robyn, only to be uprooted from Robyn's kid-friendly house?

Still another worry prods. One I refuse to mull. Can Peter and I recover from the disappointment if we leave this dreary room without Olivia? I want to assure Peter that whatever happens today, I'll be all right. But I don't get the chance. The door bursts open. In walks Fernanda, carrying Olivia.

An anxious buzz infects the room. The sequence of events is unnatural. Fernanda acts like we've never met, and hones to Vanessa. Olivia, puffy-eyed, sucks her thumb, obviously in need of a nap. Lock-kneed, I stand, arms outstretched, but Fernanda passes Olivia not to me, but to Vanessa.

Behind Fernanda, is Aunt Darlene; hair parted like a curtain across her blotchy face, she stands in the doorway. Her bloodshot, sleep-deprived eyes tell me plenty, but I want to ask her. *Why?*

Olivia shrieks. The room erupts. Vanessa struggles to contain Olivia's wiggling arms and kicking legs. The volume of Fernanda's conversation with Vanessa increases, overtaking Olivia's wails. Peter paces, attempts to offer to console Olivia and is rebuffed.

Peter approaches Aunt Darlene. She gives him a thermal bag with a *Rusty Sub To Go* sticker. Aunt Darlene pulls an envelope from her apron and says to me, "I need to leave—new tables for The Tavern are being delivered any minute." She presses the envelope into my palm. "Read this. You'll understand." She steps from the doorway into the hall. "I'd kiss the baby goodbye, but she won't miss me."

I follow Aunt Darlene into the hall and tell her, "Peter and I will take good care of Olivia."

Aunt Darlene's lips turn into a smile but her eyes stay sullen. "We never hit it off. I thought my sister's kid would cooperate, but it didn't work that way." Aunt Darlene's phone sings from her apron pocket. 'Piano Man.' She digs out the phone, shouts into the receiver, "The table is how long?"

She rushes to the exit, stops, and over her shoulder says to me, "That kid never sleeps. Never naps. Not ever."

I bid Aunt Darlene goodbye.

I re-enter the room and Vanessa struggles to wrangle a hysterical Olivia. Vanessa sees me and asks, "Ready to take over?"

I accept. Olivia grasps my hair in her fist and yanks. I laugh tears, hug Olivia and inhale. Olivia doesn't smell as I'd feared, not like beer or fried food or reconstituted infant formula. Olivia's hair smells like dish soap. She stops crying, her flails cease. But her heart beats against mine, quick as a kitten's.

Peter detaches Olivia's car seat from its base with a loud snap. I tell him, "You're a pro."

He blushes and totes the seat by the handle, gently setting it in the living room without waking Olivia. Peter goes upstairs to change into scrubs. He returns and says, "Text me a list of what Olivia needs. I'll stop at the store on the way home tomorrow morning, in time to meet the social worker for our home study."

We have Olivia. We don't need a thing. I know I'll figure out the details later. Cashmere leaps from the glove box, meows, slinks around Olivia's car seat, the circumference complete, surrenders, a purring sphinx at Olivia's feet. Even Cashmere agrees. Olivia is where she belongs. I don't need to hide her. She's home.

Peter lingers, plants a kiss on Olivia's hand. "I don't want to be an absent parent, missing every milestone. I want to hear Olivia's first word. Be there when she crawls. Watch her eat ice cream for the first time."

"I promise to text you a picture when Olivia wakes up." We hug. I tell Peter, "You're going to be a great dad." I mean it.

Turns out the wait is long. Olivia sleeps and sleeps. I lift her from her car seat, carry her to her crib and I notice her outfit, a faded blue sailor suit and white tights. I wonder what Aunt Darlene fed Olivia. I regret not asking her while I had the opportunity. I unzip the thermal bag, and hold one of the plastic bottles. The bottles contain creamy white milk, frozen solid.

A shiver travels along my spine. "Impossible," I say. Yet there's a sense of familiarity. I flip the bottle. The label, donor number 565, is me. I'd methodically pumped breast milk to the fill mark, delivering these very bottles to Edwin. He'd graciously accepted. Why Edwin hadn't pooled all my donated milk and how he funneled it to Robyn and Aunt Darlene is a mystery.

I select a bottle to thaw and add the remaining bottles to my supply in the freezer. Olivia stirs. Excited, I lower the side rail, but it's a false alarm and she returns to sleep. I stroke her forehead, her skin warm, not hot, pink, not flushed. Her breath steady. Olivia sighs. A satisfied sound. I say to Olivia, "There will be plenty of opportunities to play, read, and eat. Rest now."

I raise the crib rail. It engages with a reassuring click. Olivia is on her back, limbs splayed like a butterfly emerging from its chrysalis, sunning its wings. I catalog her changes. Her darkened eyelashes, the patch of thin hair above her left ear now filled, her nails, half-moons extending from each fingertip. Still too young for nail clippers, which can damage or nick an infant's cuticle; I'll use an emery board before she scratches her face.

I cue *Adagio for Strings* on my phone, the piece I'm coaching my students to play. Complex for seasoned orchestral musicians, it's one of my favorite compositions. Incredibly, Samuel Barber was my age when he conceived it. The students embrace my challenge to learn difficult, rather than diluted music. The violin, cello and bass sections have met for rehearsals before school and during their lunch period.

Adagio's violin introduction pierces the nursery, and I sit in the rocking chair, succumbing to the tide of violas. A breath of cello, dignified, restrained, and reassuring. I unseal Aunt Darlene's envelope. A folded paper menu slides onto my lap. On the flip side of beer on tap and fried clam appetizers is Aunt Darlene's red Sharpie printing. The locket is a warm weight over my heart.

Adagio shifts and bursts, an unsettling lament.

DEAR BABY NURSE: I DON'T CARE THAT YOU DON'T LIKE ME. NOBODY WHO KNEW JAMIE DOES. JAMIE WAS PRETTY, AND POPULAR. OUR MOTHER'S FAVORITE. I SETTLED FOR LEFTOVERS, EVEN THOUGH I WAS FIVE YEARS OLDER. I GOT JAMIE'S CAST-OFF CLOTHES, WORN

THE BABY NURSE

TENNIS SHOES, THE SMALLER BEDROOM. MY SISTER WAS PEGGED FOR SUCCESS, WHILE I OFTEN GOT INTO TROUBLE. WHAT I DIDN'T KNOW WAS THAT SHE WAS DEPRESSED. WE WEREN'T CLOSE BUT IF I'D KNOWN SHE WAS HURTING, I WOULD HAVE DELIVERED HER A MEAL.

I THOUGHT I COULD MAKE IT WORK WITH HER BABY. TRUTH WAS I WAS SCARED, BUT I TRIED. BUT HER KID WAS MISERABLE. SHE NEVER SLEPT AND CONSTANTLY CRIED. DAYCARE WAS FULL, I SIGNED UP, BUT A SPOT NEVER OPENED, AND NANNIES ARE TOO EXPENSIVE. WORKING IS IMPOSSIBLE WITH A CRYING KID.

THEN JAMIE TOLD ME WHAT SHE WANTED DONE WITH HER BABY. A BAG OF JAMIE'S PERSONAL ITEMS TIPPED OVER: A STUFFED BEAR, A HAND-KNITTED KID'S CAP, POLAROID PICTURES. THE JOURNAL MY SISTER KEPT HIT MY TOE AND OPENED TO THE PAGE SHE'D WRITTEN ABOUT HER DAUGHTER'S EARLY BIRTH. SHE AND DON COULDN'T AGREE ON A NAME. SHE WROTE ABOUT A RED-HAIRED NURSE WITH THE GUTS TO END THE DEBATE BY NAMING THE BABY, OLIVIA. PERFECT. JAMIE WROTE, SHE WANTED OLIVIA TO GROW UP AND BECOME STRONG AND COMPASSIONATE, LIKE NURSE ANNABELLE.

BEFORE YOU GET A BIGGER HEAD, LET ME TELL YOU, BABY NURSE, YOU AREN'T PERFECT. YOU'RE A TERRIBLE JUDGE OF CHARACTER, BUT I KNOW YOU MEAN WELL. I DIDN'T WANT TO INVOLVE THE POLICE AND LAWYERS IN THE FIRST PLACE, AND I'M ACTUALLY GLAD THE HEARING TURNED OUT LIKE IT DID. SOMETIMES, THE LAW DOESN'T KNOW WHAT'S BEST FOR US. I'LL BE AT THE ADOPTION HEARING AND TESTIFY THAT OLIVIA BELONGS WITH YOU AND YOUR DOCTOR HUSBAND.

P.S. IF YOU'RE AS NICE AS JAMIE SAYS, BRING HER

> KID TO THE TAVERN SOMETIME (BAR'S REOPENING WITH A NEW NAME). I'M ADDING A KIDDIE MENU.
>
> SIGNED, DARLENE COBBS

I pegged Aunt Darlene wrong. Grief's lenses morphed her struggles with Olivia into something sinister; in reality, Aunt Darlene did the best she could. Like the rest of us. I fold the letter, slip it into the envelope, and put it on the bookcase near Leah's memory box. Humble tears blur my vision, but the future is clear. Peter and I are parents.

From her crib, Olivia coos. She's awake, sees me, and smiles. I capture a picture. "For your daddy," I tell her. Olivia's smile is pink gums, but there's a nub, a faint suggestion of a future tooth. Olivia won't be a baby forever, but a toddler, a little girl, a teen, and someday a woman. I'll relish every moment.

Peter responds, a trio of red hearts.

Olivia's smile fades, confused by my tears. I tell her, "Not all tears are sad." But there's time for Olivia to learn about complex emotions. I lift Olivia from her crib. She grabs the locket in her fist. I tell her, "You are a lucky baby. Your mommy, Jamie, wanted the best for you." I sit in the rocking chair, feed Olivia, and tell her all about Jamie, her incredible mom.

EPILOGUE
THREE MONTHS LATER

The Pennsylvania Board of Nursing, based in Harrisburg, convenes to make an official ruling on my license. Vanessa arranged a Zoom hearing. The options, Vanessa explained, are license suspension, complete revocation, or censorship. The most favorable outcome, censorship, would permit me to recover my license and work as a nurse in the future.

I'm nervous. What will these official, professional nurses think about me and what I've done? Vanessa leads me to an immaculate conference room that smells like expensive air freshener. The oblong table is dark, polished wood, a pitcher of ice water and glasses in the middle. Vanessa directs me to the swivel chairs parked near a flat screen at the head of the table.

Peter enters, toting Olivia, asleep in her car seat. He says, "Diaper change. Still getting the hang of it."

Vanessa's face brightens. "You brought the baby." She bends her knees for a closer view. "Her outfit is adorable. I love the yellow daisies on her sweater."

The screen on the table transitions from black to grey. An office comes into focus. I'd imagined Judge Kipper's courtroom with my old NICU manager, Glenda-The-Terrible presiding. But two women sit behind a table. One looks matronly, like a librarian. The other wears a white lab coat like my nursing-school professor.

Neither of them smiles, but stare stoically into the Zoom screen.

Vanessa asks if they can hear us. They can.

The matronly nurse calls the hearing to order. She says, "Our purpose is to review and pass ruling on the status of Ms. Annabelle Kaplan's nursing license."

When my name is read, I tremble and clench my hands in my lap. I glance at Peter.

He's out of camera range, holding Olivia. He winks at me. I inhale but the breath catches in my chest.

The librarian nurse reads a written statement from Lakeview Hospital detailing my official work record beginning with the reprimand in my record for naming Olivia and ending with my suspension.

Vanessa sits at my side, spine straight, her expression unreadable.

The nurse in the white lab coat reads a synopsis of events involving Olivia. She ends with "No formal legal charges were pursued."

Vanessa says, "Ms. Kaplan has a prepared statement. I believe when you hear her words, you'll agree that she acted from nursing values, caring for and protecting an infant, the most vulnerable of patients."

I stand and face the screen. My legs shake, the paper with my statement crinkles. I place it on the table, but the words blur. Black type on stark paper.

One of the women says, "Ms. Kaplan? These next five minutes are yours."

Vanessa touches my hand. I look at Olivia, her thin, heart-shaped lips, the subtle dimple, her ginger hair. The digital clock on the wall reminds me of the operating room, seconds separate life from death, a positive outcome from a negative. I flip the paper over, stand tall, and address the Pennsylvania Board of Nursing from my heart.

"Not long ago, I was a student. Learning to be a nurse is more than reading a pharmacology textbook, memorizing medications and their zillion potential side effects. There wasn't room enough in my brain for every treatment algorithm: strokes, heart attacks, septic shock and labor and delivery complications. Different specialties, different patients, different physical processes. With one commonality: nurses care. It's why we wake up at five in the morning for a shift that begins before breakfast and ends after dinner. It's why we work weekends, midnights, holidays and celebrate our birthdays in the breakroom. It's what enabled me and my coworkers to enter the hospital without hesitation, during the early Covid pandemic, protected by a paper mask that we rewore for a week. The rest of the world stays home, but nurses, we confront what others avoid."

I look to Peter. He's focused on me, Olivia content in his arms.

"An apology sounds trite, but I genuinely regret crossing boundaries, making assumptions, hurting my coworkers. I apologize for bringing shame upon the profession that I love. But caring is the cornerstone of nursing, and if I'm stripped of my license, in my heart I'll remain a nurse. Because I'll never stop caring."

I sit. The room is silent. The nurses on the screen are motionless at their table.

There's a five-minute recess. Vanessa checks emails. Peter

passes Olivia across the table. She sits in my lap, content with the plastic measuring spoons. Ice settles in the pitcher at the center of the table.

The screen returns to life. Peter takes charge of Olivia.

A microphone screeches. The librarian nurse reads a statement. "Ms. Kaplan, the Pennsylvania Board of Nursing has reached a decision. We have considered your words, and the support of your coworkers at Lakeview Hospital, along with Dr. Edna Hayes, your Drexel University advisor.

Vanessa and I stand. My heart thrums like an out-of-tune guitar.

"Nursing is a profession of privilege. Those engaged are charged with innumerable responsibilities. This board agrees that you grasp the gravity of that responsibility. Yet you acted impulsively. Good intensions considered; you were no longer the infant's nurse but a private citizen. It is the directive of this board that your license to practice nursing be suspended for three years. After that time, if you meet the stipulations, your license will be reviewed for reinstatement."

Vanessa asks for details. The stipulations are straightforward; abiding the law, no additional legal issues. Additionally, the professorial woman says, "Continued enrichment. Dr. Edna Hayes is our respected colleague, a member of this board, and she recommends that you pursue your studies. We couldn't agree more. We recommend that you channel your passion into tangible results."

The hearing adjourns. I'm still a nurse. Not without hope, just without a license to practice. My phone vibrates. It's Edna Hayes from Drexel University. The old me would have let it ring, go to voicemail, but I answer. "Dr. Hayes. Thank you."

We schedule a phone conference for the following week. My future is filled with Olivia and Peter, and my music students. And I'm in graduate school, no longer resentful but appreciative of Dr. Edna Hayes, a research expert. I anticipate the future and immersing myself in a meaningful thesis topic.

It's a lot to absorb. I pick up Olivia. She smiles as if privy to a secret.

Gravel crunches on the driveway but Peter's shift doesn't end for several hours. From the nursery window the car on the driveway is familiar, a blue Nissan. The driver leaves the engine to idle, the passenger door parts, and a woman with a cardboard Amazon box travels the walkway with purpose. I race down the stairs, skip the third step, and open the front door.

Aunt Darlene stands with the box. "I brought you something. Planned to leave it on the porch." She tucks a strand of hair behind her ear. The redness is gone from Aunt Darlene's eyes. She's not looking at me but at the foyer behind me.

"She's upstairs."

"You should have this. It's too valuable to trust the postal service with shipping." Aunt Darlene thrusts the box in my arms. She jogs from the porch onto the driveway.

The box isn't heavy. An item shifts, bumping the side. I put the box in the foyer and run outside to catch Aunt Darlene, already in her Nissan. Clear plastic garbage bags with crushed Coors, Bud Light, and Pabst Blue Ribbon cans fill the back seat, obscuring the rear windshield. I tap the window, wave frantically. The window lowers, a whiff of stale beer escapes. Aunt Darlene says, "In case you're wondering? Recycling. I take The Tavern's used cans to the transfer station once a month."

Recycled cans. My cheeks burn with shame. "Come inside. Please."

Aunt Darlene doesn't answer. She stares through the windshield, palms on the wheel, the Nissan idles roughly.

I say, "I'll show you around. That way you'll know where your niece lives."

The car engine rests. Aunt Darlene exits, slams the door. "I can't stay long."

Aunt Darlene treads upstairs, peeks in the nursery, disbelieving that Olivia naps. I show her the living room. Cashmere meows. I say, "Don't worry. Olivia and the kitten have an understanding."

"Wait till the baby crawls."

Cashmere hisses. We laugh. In the kitchen Aunt Darlene studies our appliances, nods her approval. I tell her Peter is the chef in the family. She asks, "What's behind the door?"

I open the door to the vacant dining room.

Aunt Darlene crosses the threshold, paces the planked floor methodically, counting her steps out loud, stopping in front of the fireplace. "According to my measurement, it'll fit."

"What will?"

"The farm table I ordered. The furniture warehouse shipped the wrong piece. Too much of a hassle to send back. But it'll fit here—I mean if—"

"Yes. Peter and I would love a dining-room table. How much—"

"Free. Got a friend with a truck?"

"Actually—"

Olivia cries. No need for the nursery app, Olivia makes herself heard. I retrieve Olivia from her crib, change her diaper, tell her, "You have a visitor." I carry Olivia, dressed in pink leggings, a white cotton sweater, and pink socks. The kitchen is vacant. The front door is open, the blue Nissan and Aunt Darlene, gone.

The single item in the box that Aunt Darlene delivered is indeed too precious to mail.

I recognize Jamie's scrapbook. The one she'd proudly

showed to me on that March evening in the NICU, when she gave me the locket. The cover displays a preemie encased in an isolette, a photograph of newborn Olivia. I sit on the loveseat, the book in my lap, with Olivia, her head on my shoulder. Reverently, I turn pages and read, listening to Jamie's voice.

Page Seven:

Sometimes I worry that I caused my baby to come too soon. The night before my C-section, I told Don I was tired of being pregnant. I had a headache, the doctor said it was high blood pressure. What kind of a mother says such an awful thing? I feel guilty. If only I'd kept her inside a bit longer.

I hold the locket, tell Jamie it's not her fault.

Page Ten

It's not that I want to die, but if I do... Sorry, I think about it. I'm in the hospital every afternoon visiting my baby, and I see sick people in the hallway, and in the elevator. Today I saw a man with no legs. Half a person in a parked wheelchair. I wanted to run into the bathroom and vomit. I wish I was kind like Nurse Annabelle. She will make a wonderful mom.

I flip the pages to the final section, written before Olivia's planned discharge from the NICU. The ink is smeared, and the paper pocked with what must be dried tears.

Olivia is big enough to come home. I'm as ready as I'll ever be except there is no family to welcome her. I have a sister but we're night-and-day different and we never get along. It's stupid but when we were younger, we fought over clothes and whose turn it was to borrow the car. I got the new clothes and Darlene took the car keys. But I'm a mom now, and the fights with Darlene seem small and silly.

I want Darlene to meet Olivia. There's no need to dig through past hurts. Why not start fresh? I'll invite Darlene for coffee, and she can hold Olivia. 'Aunt Darlene' has a nice ring to it!

Jamie never made her phone call. But I will take up where she left off. I set the journal on the coffee table beside Mom's recipe book.

Imperfect women, that's what mothers are. Fresh tears stream my face. I tell Olivia, "You will grow up surrounded by a family of strong women who love you, each in their own way." It's a promise I know I can keep.

Olivia's gymnastics cause the scale to wiggle. She stretches, grabs her feet, and kicks the tray. The scale recalibrates and digital numbers flash. Over fifteen pounds. About seven kilograms. I lift Olivia from the scale and put her on the examination table. The white paper sheet crinkles. "Great job, Olivia, you're growing. You're ready for the next-size diapers."

My heart melts. No matter how big Olivia gets, my arms never tire of holding her.

I'd scheduled Olivia's NICU follow-up appointment specifically with Dr. STAT. She tests Olivia's reflexes, coaxes her to roll over. Dr. STAT asks about stranger anxiety. I tell her that Olivia is a friendly baby. "Not that I leave her much, and only with a trusted babysitter, her name is Naomi."

"Introducing solid food?"

"Applesauce is her favorite. Homemade. A family recipe."

"Excellent. Olivia is on track, considering her chronological age is nearly eight months but her adjusted age, accounting for prematurity, is about five months."

Peter and I are officially Olivia's foster parents, but we intend to adopt. Vanessa, along with Fernanda, guided us through the adoption process. I give Dr. STAT a form from Child Protective Services. Dr. STAT fills in Olivia's weight, signs, and returns it.

I ask, "You'll be there, right? In the NICU. It starts in a few minutes."

"Wouldn't miss it. You can dress Olivia."

I diaper Olivia and put her in the outfit I selected for the celebration. A pink floral dress and yellow socks. Olivia pulls the socks off and I collect them. It's warm enough that her feet won't get cold. I snap a barrette into her hair.

"This is your day," I tell her.

I take a moment to tuck my blouse into my high-waisted jeans. It feels odd, coming to the hospital wearing regular clothes instead of blue scrubs, but I am adapting to all the changes in my life. The locket remains at home, too fragile for wear. My strawberry-blonde curls dust my shoulders, sun-streaked from our afternoon walks.

I carry Olivia, stopping a few feet from the visitor's window. The woman ahead of us, wrapped in a hospital robe and nubby socks, enters the NICU. The doors part briefly, she shuffles through, and the doors reconfigure.

I don't recognize the unit clerk. She checks my visitor's badge. "Can I help you?"

"I'm here for a visit. Approved by the nurse manager."

The doors swing wide open. Monitors buzz, an IV pump rings, a ventilator alarm squawks. I stand, holding Olivia in the hallway between the Acute Care NICU with pods of plastic-walled isolettes and the Special Care Nursery with rows of cribs. From the hallway I hear water drum the scrub sink.

Robyn sees us. Her white lab coat is buttoned and smartly pressed, her long braids drawn into a bun. She smiles. "I'm looking forward to this."

I tell her, "Leadership agrees with you. Robyn is the new NICU nurse manager. Glenda retired. (In hindsight, she was not-so-terrible, just doing her job.)

Then the event that Robyn and I planned is underway. Static crackles from the overhead speaker. The unit clerk announces, "Staff, come greet baby Olivia at the double doors. It's her official NICU send-off."

Face masks are no longer required, and we are surrounded by smiles. Nurses admire Olivia's floral dress and comment on how big she is. Olivia smiles, unfazed by the attention.

Honor studies the spot above Olivia's left ear. "Her hair is long enough for bows."

Coleen traded her Danskos for a new pair of neon-green Crocs, which are blazingly bright next to my white Vans. Dr. STAT arrives. I scan the group; Edwin was invited but he is missing. Because of Edwin, Olivia is exclusively breastfed, the way Jamie had intended. I ask Robyn and she says, "Edwin sends his congratulations from Bangor. He moved to Maine."

There's another overhead announcement, "Congratulations, baby Olivia."

Cheers and applause. We pose for a group photo. I send a picture to Peter with a heart emoji. He responds with a pizza emoji. I tell Olivia, "We're meeting Daddy in the café for lunch."

The double doors open. I walk through, Olivia in my arms. At last, Olivia leaves the NICU the way she deserves. The doors shut behind us. I carry Olivia, retrieve her stroller from the hallway, and we board the elevator. The doors clap and the elevator descends.

I realize that I hadn't looked back. The NICU is the past. And I am leaning into the future. In the ensuing years, there will be time, plenty of time to reminisce about the NICU. I'll explain all of it to Olivia. How we met, nurse and patient, but became mother and daughter.

THE END

BOOK CLUB QUESTIONS

1. What expectations are women expected to fulfill to be considered perfect mothers? Is the expectation to exclusively breast feed unrealistic?
2. Olivia's natural mother, Jamie Dutton, experiences postpartum depression. How might estrangement from her sister, Darlene, have contributed to Jamie's postpartum depression?
3. After a brief encounter in the hospital nursery, Annabelle deems Aunt Darlene an unsuitable caregiver for Olivia. What factors lead Annabelle to reach her conclusion? Do you agree with Annabelle's assessment?
4. What makes Annabelle vulnerable to compulsive shopping? Are items more tempting when viewed online compared to shopping in person?
5. Annabelle and Peter are a young couple, but how well do they know each other? Should Peter have been aware of Annabelle's unresolved grief for their stillborn infant? Does he bear responsibility for Annabelle's actions?

BOOK CLUB QUESTIONS

6. How does Annabelle's love for classical music impact her grief process?
7. Annabelle was reprimanded at work for overstepping a patient-caregiver boundary by naming Olivia in the NICU. Is it possible for a nurse to care for a patient without developing a genuine emotional bond?
8. Annabelle and Sheila were childhood friends, but they grew apart. How does becoming an adult complicate a relationship? Is it possible to sustain a lifelong friendship?
9. Annabelle remarks that she did not know her mother, Genie, as well as she had thought. What assumptions does Annabelle have about her mother? Is it possible for children to truly know their parents as people?
10. What would you do if you discovered an infant alone and crying in a parked car? How would you intervene if making a phone call was not an option?
11. Does Annabelle receive a punishment that fits her crime? Does she recognize her mistakes and make amends?
12. What do you think the future holds for Annabelle, Peter, and Olivia?

ACKNOWLEDGMENTS

I am grateful to the dedicated team at Bloodhound Books for making this book possible. A special thanks to co-founder and publisher Betsy Reavley, editorial and production manager Tara Lyons, and Ian Skewis, for your skillful copy edits. Thank you, Jeannie De Vita at Book Genie, for believing in this book. Your advice, editing, and compassion means the world to me. Thank you, Michael Lee at Book Genie, for creating a beautiful author website. I am grateful for Kimberley Lim's masterful manuscript guidance. Thank you to Marcia Bradley, whose early advice set Annabelle on her path. I am grateful to Beth Richards for being present when I needed teaching guidance, coffee, and writerly feedback (not necessarily in that order). Thank you to my students at Goodwin University, the University of Hartford, and New England Jewish Academy: reading and writing together has been a privilege. I am grateful to Seton Hill University's MFA Writing Community. A special thanks to my mentors, Albert Wendland, for holding me to high standards and Heidi Ruby Miller, whose counsel continues to influence my writing. Thank you to my critique partner Lisa Page and writers David von Schlichten, and Dana Jackson.

I am grateful for the support of my loving family: my husband Timothy J. Holsbeke, our children Miriam and Max, and my sisters Jennifer Cronin, and Liz Facenda. I am fortunate to be a member of a second family, one that never sleeps, the NICU team at Connecticut Children's Medical Center in Hartford, Connecticut.

ABOUT THE AUTHOR

Stacey H. Rubin graduated from Villanova University and began her career as a United States Army Nurse Corp officer. After military service, Stacey earned a Master of Nursing degree from The University of Florida and is a nurse practitioner in a neonatal intensive care unit in Hartford, Connecticut.

Desiring to pursue her love for writing, Stacey earned an MFA in Writing Popular Fiction from Seton Hill University. She has taught literature and writing to high school and college students. She is the author of the nonfiction *The ABCs of Breastfeeding: Everything a Mom Needs to Know for a Happy Nursing Experience* published by AMACOM (2008). *The Baby Nurse,* published by Bloodhound Books is her debut novel. Stacey lives in Connecticut with her husband, and they are parents of two grown children.

For more information visit staceyhrubinauthor.com.

A NOTE FROM THE PUBLISHER

Thank you for reading this book. If you enjoyed it please do consider leaving a review on Amazon to help others find it too.

We hate typos. All of our books have been rigorously edited and proofread, but sometimes mistakes do slip through. If you have spotted a typo, please do let us know and we can get it amended within hours.

info@bloodhoundbooks.com